Time Meddlers

ALSO AVAILABLE FROM THIS AUTHOR:

Time Meddlers Undercover

Time Meddlers on the Nile

TIME
MEDDLERS

DEBORAH JACKSON

Time Meddlers
First Edition © Deborah Jackson 2006
Second Edition © Deborah Jackson 2012

Published by Deborah Jackson

Cover Design and Typesetting by Matthew Birtch
Illustrations by Jessica Jackson

First published in the United States by LBF Books

This book is a work of fiction. Any references to historical events, real people, or real locales are used fictitiously. Other names, characters, places and incidents are products of the author's imagination, and any resemblance to actual events or locales or persons, living or dead, is entirely coincidental.

For Jessica and Liam:
treasured characters who inspire
lively and compassionate characters.

CONTENTS

1

The Walking Corpse

"I DON'T WANT TO GO TO SCHOOL HERE," SARAH YELLED AT HER FATHER. "You dragged me away from all my friends and plunked me down in this *wilderness.*"

Sarah's dad, Donald Sachs, tried his best not to smile. "Ottawa isn't a wilderness, darling. It's a rather large city."

Sarah scowled and tossed back a tangle of curls. "You call this a city. We're out in the sticks. Look around. There's only trees and mounds of snow."

"Most kids like trees." Her dad swept his hand through his raven-black hair and peered out the window of their new two story house. Sarah followed his gaze.

They were on the last row of a new construction of the suburb, and their backyard opened up on a field. Corn stubble, laced with frost, extended between pockets of wooded land. The landscape shimmered like nothing ever did in slushy metropolitan Toronto.

Sarah blinked as the light seared her eyes. She still preferred the slush.

"Well, I don't," she said. "I hate it here." She stamped so hard on the solid tiles in the foyer that pain jolted up her leg.

Tears crowded the corners of her eyes.

"Like it or not, dear, we're here for good."

"I want to live with Mom."

"Mom doesn't . . ." He gritted his teeth. "Your mom is too busy right now, darling. I know it's hard to move in the middle of the year, but we'll just have to make a go of it, okay? You'll make new friends and eventually you might come to like this place."

Sarah swiped at her eyes. "Yeah, sure," she said.

"Now you know you have to go to school."

Sarah wanted to protest again, but it wouldn't make any difference. She pulled on her snow pants, wrenched on her coat, zipped it over her chin, jammed on a hat, laced up some oversized boots, and yanked on her mittens. "I feel like a polar bear," she growled.

"You look like one, too," he said.

She slammed out the door.

"Watch for cars," her father called after her.

Sarah trudged through the deep snow, anger heavy as a bear on her shoulders. Her eyelashes were soon dusted with feathery flakes. The frigid blast of winter numbed her face in an instant. *What a place to live.* As she rubbed her mitts together to try to restore circulation to her hands, other kids emerged from the houses in the sprawling subdivision. They dashed past her, tossing snowballs at each other and rolling in the snow. If only she were back home, with her friends—Keith and Jamie, the basketball stars. Even the bully Bob would be a welcome sight compared to these strangers. How could they be having fun in this

Arctic wilderness? She clutched her coat around her like a shield from the laughter that filled the air.

She could have tolerated this—the cold, the strangers—if only Mom had come with them. If only Mom hadn't insisted on staying within the shadow of the monstrous highrise where she worked, and Dad hadn't walked out on her. Sarah could have endured living in a cabin in the backwoods of Northern Ontario if they were all still together—a family.

It hadn't worked out that way, though. Dad, as a politician, had to travel back and forth to Ottawa, and spend most of his time in this city. Mom, who was a successful fashion designer, wasn't willing to sacrifice her own career for Dad's *convenience*. She'd heard the arguments over and over. No one had asked Sarah what *she* wanted to do. Or where *she* wanted to live. So here she was, walking through a blizzard to get to a school in the middle of nowhere.

As Sarah walked, stewing over her miserable life, a flicker of movement across the street caught her eye. A boy was walking parallel to her with hunched shoulders and a twisted grimace on his face. He was kicking snow and punching shadows. He seemed oblivious to the frolicking kids, or to her. His eyes focused on the snow like it was an enemy.

Sarah looked away from him, but every now and then she'd look up and find they were keeping pace with each other. The boy seemed typical of kids from this northern town—bulky parka, Maple Leaf toque and a cold-flushed face under the snowflakes—yet he was different. He was distant from the others—an outsider, like her. She couldn't stop watching him.

Finally they reached an intersection and he turned in her direction.

It looked like he was about to cross the street. Yet he didn't look up, didn't pay attention to the traffic lights, didn't even glance down the street; he just kept walking.

Sarah saw the red Explorer racing down the icy street. She cried, "Hey, kid. Look out!" Her stomach clenched and dropped as if weighted by heavy ball bearings. The SUV jammed its brakes, skidded from side to side on the slick asphalt and went *right through the kid*. The boy kept walking, untouched.

Sarah stood there in shock, immobile. The boy walked past her, meeting her eyes for a split second.

"Wh-who-what are you?" she asked.

He shrugged, smiled and kept walking.

Sarah sank down in the snow bank and watched him continue up the street and into the yard of the red brick school. She shook her head. Had she really seen what she had just seen? The Explorer slammed to a stop, twisted halfway across the road, and the driver jumped out of the car. He looked back at the intersection, one hand poised in midair and the other scratching his head.

"He should be dead," he muttered. "Thank goodness, thank goodness."

Sarah blinked. Snowflakes whipped into her face and pasted to her eyelashes.

"I must have missed him, hadn't I?" he called over to her.

She nodded, but as she turned away from the driver she whispered, "You hit him dead on."

2

Conversation with the Corpse

SARAH WALKED THE HALF-BLOCK TO MARSHLAND ELEMENTARY
School in a daze. She headed across the playground and in through
the double doors at the back, the images of the car and the boy still
flickering through her head. It only took her a few minutes to find
her classroom at the end of the hall, since she'd been there last week
for a meeting with her homeroom teacher that had included her
father—the new divorcée. But she hadn't met the students yet. It was
a moment she dreaded.

So when she shuffled into the Grade Six classroom, where the
desks were arranged in parallel lines like the bars of a prison cell, she
was shocked again by the appearance of the boy. He'd shed his blue
parka and toque and was leaning back in his desk, fingers laced behind
his head, in a "nothing ever happens to me" attitude. Sarah was even
more ruffled to find her desk was right in front of his.

She sank into it. "Hi," she said.

He nodded, eyeing her from beneath hooded lids. He had tawny hair that drooped over his face and sleepy green eyes that made him look like a snoozing cat. Sarah wasn't surprised when he yawned.

"Um," she said, struggling for something to say.

"Name?" He saved her the trouble.

"Excuse me?"

"Do you have a name?" He flipped back a wisp of hair.

"Yeah. Sarah."

"Good."

"What?"

"Not a good name. Good that you have one. I'd hate to sit behind a 'what's her name.'"

Sarah frowned. "Smart aleck."

"That's me." He smiled and it lit up his eyes.

"What's your name?" she asked.

"Matt."

"Good," she said. "I'd hate to call you 'that walking corpse.'"

Matt grinned. "Not bad." He leaned forward, his pale face centimetres from her own. "Wait until you see my next trick."

Sarah leaned back. "Can't wait."

They stared at each other as the rest of the class shuffled in. Sarah didn't break eye contact with Matt until a tall boy with thick chestnut hair and a lopsided grin brushed past her.

"'Scuse me," he said.

Sarah shrugged. "No skin off my nose."

"Wouldn't hurt none, though," he chuckled.

Sarah's hand flew to her nose. The hawkish protrusion was a sore point with her and it would figure that the first boy she met—well, second, considering the amazing Matt behind her—would make a nasty comment about its size. She looked around. Some students within earshot were smirking. She wondered how long it would be before they roasted her for the toasted tint of her skin or her coffee-coloured eyes. When she looked a little closer, though, she discovered that, just as in Toronto, the classroom was a mosaic of different cultures.

Matt startled her as he leaned forward again, even closer this time, and whispered, "Beaks add character. Do you see that scrawny thing across from us with the button nose? Boring. Nothing to tweak."

Sarah nearly gaped at the boy. She didn't know what to make of him. He was insulting, but somehow she thought the comment was supposed to make her feel better. She didn't have time to ponder this, though, as Madame Leblanc entered the room.

First the teacher's gaze swept over the students. Her eyes were twin olive beads set deep in her face between hilly cheeks, like the buttons of seat cushions. They settled on Matt, contracted, then flew past to land on her, and relaxed. The tension eased from Sarah's shoulders. The teacher brushed her with a smile, squeezed past a student the same height as her and ambled to the front on squeaky loafers. A puff of dust shot into the air as she leaned against the front of her desk.

"*Les amis,*" she began. "We have a new student. Welcome, Sarah Sachs."

The class murmured, "*Bonjour.*" A few people snickered at her name. Matt continued to stare at the back of her head as she faced the front of the class. She could feel the pressure like a drill.

"Don't mind him," whispered the button-nosed girl opposite her. "He's weird."

"You're telling me," Sarah whispered back. She looked up to see

Madame Leblanc's smile wither and turn frosty.

"No talking, Sarah," said the teacher.

"*Ou-Oui, Madame.*" Some students giggled in the back of the room. Normally she was quite fluent in French. She'd been taking French Immersion since kindergarten. Why did she have to stumble over her words now?

"Ah," said Madame. "We will not make fun of her language. After all, she is from Toronto."

More people snickered. Even a chortle erupted behind her. Sarah was instantly offended. "Toronto is the hub of Canada."

"And Ottawa is her wheels, *cherie.*"

Sarah's face flushed. "Toronto is the centre of—of—"

"The universe," Matt finished for her. Everyone laughed.

Sarah's eyes ached. "It's a wonderful city."

"With wonderful people," said Matt. "If they weren't all snobs."

Now her head was pounding. "You are a *walking corpse*," she rasped at him.

"That's quite enough," said Madame, which was a little strange since she'd started mocking Toronto in the first place. By the way she glared at Matt, though, Sarah could tell there was something more to it.

"Matthew Barnes, your father should hear about your behaviour."

"Yes, he should." Matt held up a slim black cell phone. "Why don't you call him?"

The class erupted in giggles.

Madame Leblanc's rosy cheeks blanched. Her face scrunched up into an angry mask and she spat out, "You're heading for a detention, Monsieur Barnes."

"I'll dial the number for you," Matt continued as if he hadn't heard her. "But I'll bet he's on safari or something again and can't be reached."

"I'll see you after school, Monsieur Barnes, and you'll give me that phone now."

She walked over to him with her hand outstretched. Sarah watched in astonishment as Matt defied her, sneering. Madame Leblanc grabbed the phone. For a second Sarah thought Matt was going to hold on to it, but he finally let go.

"Your father would not be proud," she said.

Matt rolled his eyes. "He doesn't care."

Madame Leblanc marched back to the front of the class. She didn't hear him whisper at her back. Nobody seemed to hear except Sarah. "He never cared."

At recess, Sarah talked to a few students. Even fewer talked back to her. She stood in a corner of the yard, which was basically an island of ice and slush in an ocean of snow. Only a narrow strip of asphalt peered from the drifts, a half-buried basketball court where the nets slapped against their poles in the wind. Sarah scuffed her boots idly on the ice. What a typical winter playground this was; nothing to do but stand and watch. One boy drew her gaze more than any of the others.

Matthew Barnes gleefully tossed snowballs over a fort onto some younger kids' heads. He went on to smooth the snow on an icy patch and watched while people slipped and fell. Then he ambled over to a tree and shook the snow off the branches to bury the kids underneath. No one joined him in his antics; he was a loner.

"Why are you watching him?" asked Chelsea, the button-nosed girl from her class. "He's a jerk."

"Who is he, really?" asked Sarah, shifting her gaze to Chelsea. The girl had an autumn blaze of red hair and a sprinkling of freckles all over her face. Her neck was long and slender, like a giraffe's, and her green eyes sparkled with flecks of gold. She could have been pretty if she didn't look down her tiny nose all the time.

"Nathan Barnes's son," said Chelsea. "Never know it, would you?"

"Nathan Barnes," said Sarah. "*The* Nathan Barnes?"

"The one and only," said Chelsea. "Explorer, scientist, archaeologist *extraordinaire*. And he's cute, too. Ever seen his picture in *Science Digest?*"

"*Science Digest? You* read *Science Digest?*"

"Doesn't everybody?"

"Not exactly," said Sarah. "But I read other things. I've definitely heard of Nathan Barnes, but I never knew he had a son."

"He probably doesn't want to admit it. Look at how messed up his kid is."

Sarah pondered Chelsea's words as she watched Matt, a cross between class clown and class criminal. It didn't seem possible that he was the son of such a brilliant man. "I see your point. But maybe there's more to him than what we're looking at right now. After all, Dr. Barnes has made some amazing discoveries."

"Yes, he has," said Chelsea. "New tombs in Egypt, undiscovered First Nations villages. Even some new evidence of Atlantis."

Sarah turned back to Chelsea. "Have you ever met him?"

Chelsea shook her head. "He's not around here much. His assistant looks after Matt. Sort of like a godmother, I guess. He hates her, too. I think he hates just about everyone and everything."

"Chip on his shoulder," said Sarah. "I can relate."

"I wouldn't bother relating," said Chelsea. "It's not worth it."

Sarah took a deep breath. Should she pursue the subject of the incredible death-defying boy with a girl she'd just met? She'd probably look like an idiot, but curiosity was clawing at her, and besides, she didn't really like this girl. She had to know. "Have you ever heard of anything weird about him?"

"What do you mean?" asked Chelsea. "The guy is totally weird."

Sarah looked off over the grounds, avoiding Chelsea's gaze. "I don't know. Just different, unexplainable stuff."

"Like what?"

"Oh, nothing," said Sarah quickly. How could she explain the impossible? "I wonder if he'd introduce me to his dad."

"Don't bother," said Chelsea. "He'd rather toss you in a snow bank than do something nice."

"How do you know? Have you ever asked?"

Chelsea snorted. "Like I would even *talk* to the toad."

"Then you don't know," said Sarah. She turned her back on Chelsea and marched in the direction of the Barnes boy.

"Don't hold your breath," Chelsea called after her.

As Sarah approached Matt, her courage seemed to fail. Her boots plodded through the thick snow; her breathing quickened until she was panting. She was almost ready to turn around and walk the other way when he looked up and saw her.

"Well, if it isn't the new girl."

"Sarah," she said.

"That's right. You have a name." He winked and let a slight smirk escape.

At least he contained a glimmer of warmth. Maybe if she brought up his father, he would open up to her. "I heard your dad is Dr. Nathan Barnes, the explorer."

Matt's half-grin became a sneer. "Yeah, what of it?"

"That's cool," said Sarah. "Really cool . . ." She ran out of words.

"How would you know?" he asked

"I wouldn't, really. But I would if I met him."

Matt's pale face flushed and darkened. Maybe she was being too pushy.

"Are you trying to get an invite? To see the great Houdini?"

Sarah frowned. "I don't understand."

"No, you wouldn't."

"Well, I just wondered . . . I've read so much about his adventures. Maybe you could tell me some stories."

Matt's eyes crimped and his lips pinched together. "Stories. I could tell stories all right."

She smiled encouragingly, trying her best to ignore the spitting-cobra look. "I'd love to hear them. Maybe I could come over sometime. I moved into the new subdivision down Cattail Street."

"I know where you live," said Matt.

"How do you know?"

"Because I saw the moving truck. I saw them build your house. I live at the other end of your street."

She beamed. "Wow, that's great. We're neighbours. Maybe we could hang out sometime."

"Forget it." Matt scowled. "I don't *want* to hang out. I don't *want* to be friends. And you're not going to meet the great Dr. Barnes. So, *get lost.*"

Sarah felt as if he'd slapped her. Her hands curled into fists. "Chelsea's right," she said. "You are a jerk."

Matt looked skyward and waved his hand as if to dismiss her just as the discordant clang of the school bell jolted through the yard. Sarah glanced at the cluster of kids lining up at the door to get in.

She knew she had to go, but her feet were locked. She looked Matt up and down. "Who would want to be friends with you?" she said.

He shrugged. "Should I care?"

"Yeah. You should."

Sarah spun around and stormed off towards the school. Matt lingered, then eventually sauntered in the door behind her. She turned around once to scowl at him, but she stopped halfway between a grimace and a snarl. His body was suddenly hazy and blurred. An aura surrounded him like an explosion of northern lights. *What was going on here?*

3

Truce

SARAH PLOPPED BACK IN HER CHAIR, SHOCKED, CONFUSED AND A LITTLE frightened. What lingered the most, though, was a cloud of anger. Nor was she the only one with bitter feelings towards Matt. Several class-mates aimed vicious stares at him after his pranks in the schoolyard.

Sarah hated having him seated right behind her. She dropped her pencil a few times just to cast a glance backward and ensure he wasn't tying knots in her hair or snapping elastics at her back, or disappearing for that matter. The last time she dropped the HB, he snatched it up before she could and poked her in the back with it.

"Butterfingers," he whispered.

"Corpse," she snarled.

He actually grinned. "I like that one."

"Good, 'cause from now on that's all you are to me."

"What was I before?"

She arched her eyebrows.

"Before you learned about my *famous* father?"

"Nothing," she sneered. "Nothing before and nothing after."

"A corpse is more than nothing. A dead man walking. A zombie without a brain."

"You to a T. Especially the lack of brains."

"Really?" He smirked.

Snap. She hadn't seen the teacher sneak up on them. She hadn't thought their whispers would carry to the front. The ruler on her desk woke her up in a hurry, and Madame Leblanc's flushed face left her no doubt—she was in for it.

"You have work to do, have you not?" said Madame.

"*Oui, Madame.*" She kept her eyes downcast and tried to sound sufficiently humble, though Matt was still grinning—the creep.

"Since you don't know how to be quiet, you will have to join Mr. Barnes in detention."

Oh no. Not the first day. Dad's going to kill me. "But, but—" She was about to say Matt had started it, but that was being a tattle-tale and she wasn't about to be labelled. She clamped her mouth shut. Why was Madame Leblanc so angry all the time, anyway? She'd seemed so kind at the interview. Was it because of Matt's *attitude?*

She glanced sideways and spied the woman nervously picking at her sleeve. Despite the detention, a seed of pity for Madame sprouted inside her. Sarah had only experienced one day of Matt and already she was fuming.

At that moment the bell rang. Sarah stood and glared at Matt, but he only grinned. He actually seemed quite pleased. She couldn't stand it.

Their next class was history. Now that they were in Grade Six, two of their classes were taught in English, and this was one of them. The teacher—Mr. Fletcher—entered the room with a broad smile. He seemed the typical history teacher. He had sculpted grey hair—not a strand out of place—and the lines on his face suggested the ancient world. When he began to speak he sounded like a jet engine in mid-flight.

"I am Mr. Fletcher," he introduced himself to Sarah. "And today we'll be talking about Champlain."

Sarah glanced behind her and saw Matt roll his eyes.

"Champlain was the first and greatest explorer," continued Mr. Fletcher. With her knowledge of history, this statement disturbed Sarah. She put up her hand.

"Yes, Sarah?"

"I thought Cartier was the first French explorer to reach Canada. And the first ones, I think, were the Vikings. If you're talking about the Americas, there was Christopher Columbus—"

Mr. Fletcher sighed. "I've only begun to explain, Sarah."

"I'm sorry," she said. "I only wanted to point out—"

"That you're wrong," said Matt.

Mr. Fletcher's eyebrows drew together in a deep frown. He licked his lips and began again. "I was going to say, the first and greatest explorer to reach the Ottawa region."

"Weren't the aboriginal people here first?" asked Matt.

Mr. Fletcher puffed loudly through his nose. "Yes, the First Nations were here before Champlain; but Champlain discovered this region."

"How could he discover it if there were people already here?"

"He discovered it for France," Mr. Fletcher said through clenched teeth. "Now, Mr. Barnes, Miss Sachs, if you would let me continue . . ."

"Go right ahead," said Matt.

"You're bad," whispered Sarah, trying her best not to snicker.

"Champlain sent one man, Étienne Brûlé, up the Ottawa River and on to Lake Huron with the Wendat people, also called the Hurons. The exchange of a European for a Wendat was a trick perpetrated by Iroquet, an Algonquin chief. He originally promised to exchange the young Frenchman for an Algonquin—the Algonquin lived in this region—but the Algonquin had no intention of letting the French have access to their land, so they offered Champlain a Wendat so he could learn their ways instead."

"Champlain wasn't very smart, was he?" said Matt.

Mr. Fletcher scowled. "Smart enough, Mr. Barnes, to exchange pots and kettles for valuable furs and knowledge of the land."

"That doesn't seem fair," said Sarah.

Matt looked at her curiously. "No, it wasn't," he muttered in an irritated tone. This seemed odd to Sarah for a boy who didn't seem to care about anything or anyone.

"All's fair in love and war, my dear," said Mr. Fletcher. "Remember, the French were at odds with the British and every parcel of land, every advantage they could gain, would help them defeat the British."

"Didn't they lose?" asked Matt.

Mr. Fletcher slapped his head with his hand. "That doesn't matter at this point. Now I suggest, Mr. Barnes, that you just listen from now on and refrain from making any more comments. You might learn something."

"Okay," said Matt, "but I'm warning you, if I can't take part I sometimes . . . you know, nod off." He yawned loudly, cracking his jaws.

Sarah scrunched up her face and watched him crookedly from her seat. He had the most outrageous gall she'd ever seen in anyone. Yet, despite the teacher's obvious frustration, he got away with it. Why was that? Were the teachers afraid of him, or did he hold something over their heads?

Mr. Fletcher turned and wrote some names on the board. Of course Champlain was at the top, then Étienne Brûlé, Iroquet—the Algonquin chief—and a date—1610. Sarah immediately started jotting everything down. But it wasn't long before a desk-rattling snort broke her concentration. She glanced back at Matt in disbelief, but there was no mistake. His head was resting on his arms and his eyelids were fluttering.

Sarah shook her head and continued to copy down the facts. The Algonquin were at war with the Iroquois, her teacher explained, the Five Nations people who lived on the other side of the St. Lawrence River and Lake Ontario. The similarity of the names confused Sarah at first. "Iroquois—Five Nations people," she wrote in her notebook. "Iroquet—Algonquin chief—Iroquois enemy."

Mr. Fletcher continued his lesson until the bell rang. Sarah sighed. Finally. The last class of the day. At the sound of the bell, Matt jerked awake and stuffed his empty notebook back into his desk. He stood up, stretched and sauntered out the door. Sarah just caught his smirk when he looked her way. She lifted her full notebook off the desk, intent on throwing it in his face, but he just ducked and laughed as he walked into the hall.

The last class was Phys Ed—time for the jocks to judge everyone else's fitness and skill, particularly the new kid, and jeer if they weren't athletic stars. As Sarah entered the gym they all turned and stared. Whispers hissed among her peers. Matt looked up from where he was dribbling a basketball by the foul line. His eyes contracted as he followed her movements.

"Hey Sachs," he yelled.

Sarah glared at him. She felt like flipping him a rude hand sign.

"Heads up!" The basketball came careening over the floor towards her head. Sarah snatched it out of midair and whipped it back at him with a snap of her wrist. Matt ducked, the ball shaving his head and bounding off the wall behind him. He looked at her, his face flushed, his mouth hanging open. It was the first time she'd seen him lose his intractable cool.

For the rest of the period it was *her turn* to smirk, show off, and even sneer, a little. She was in her element now, having spent long hours on the basketball court with her best friends in Toronto, Keith and Jamie. She remembered Keith's jaw drop open the first time he'd seen her, lobbing a ball from the middle of the court right into the net. She'd never looked back—they'd made an instant connection. Too bad she couldn't make any connections here.

She dribbled over the court, weaving in and out like a Harlem Globetrotter. Despite the solid body of Matt in her face, she managed to sidestep him with ease and come in for a sensational lay-up that sent the ball sailing through the mesh. She loved seeing the stunned expression on Matt's face. It was now a contest between them. The rest of the players ceased to exist for them. They continued to square off until Matt was called for a third foul on her and the final bell rang. They each headed off to their respective dressing rooms, glaring at each other until they passed the archway.

Sarah dreaded spending the next hour in detention together. She had had just about enough of Matt for today. She trudged down the hall towards her homeroom, where Madame Leblanc was tapping her toes. She nodded at Sarah, then tore off some pages of French literature for her to copy on the board.

"You must complete it all," she said.

Sarah sighed and picked up the piece of chalk. She'd just begun to scratch out the first words when Matt sauntered in.

"You're late," snapped Madame Leblanc.

"I'm here," said Matt, as if that in itself was better than she could hope for.

"Humph." She handed him the papers.

Matt squinted as he examined the words. "You really don't expect me to write that *I'm a sorry idiot in a world of prodigies.*"

Sarah stopped writing and looked over his shoulder.

"If the shoe fits, Monsieur Barnes," said Madame.

"I think the shoe's on the wrong foot," he replied. Much to Sarah's surprise he did shuffle up beside her. He studied the chalk as if it were a worm, then jotted down the lines in enormous block letters that took up half the board.

"We are not amused," said the teacher.

"We rarely are," he quipped.

Sarah tensed as she caught Madame's movement out of the corner of her eye. She'd raised her hand menacingly behind Matt, as if she wanted to swat him like a fly.

"Lawsuit," he said calmly.

"You are a disgrace!" she screamed. "I'm calling your father."

"Wait," said Matt. He snatched the cell phone from her desk. "Here it is." He smiled.

Sarah bit her lip. The altercation between the two felt like a twister at her back, swirling with angry force. In exasperation she turned to Matt and said, "Can't you suck it in just this once?"

He looked at her curiously. "I suppose," he said and turned back to the board. He began scratching obediently, in normal size this time. Sarah felt the winds die down, and sighed with relief.

As they continued their assignment in silence, Madame Leblanc watched every movement. A parade of goose bumps along with the odd prickling sensation travelled all over Sarah's back. She wouldn't be surprised if she looked sideways and saw a swarm of insects chewing on Matt. But he kept scribbling away with his chalk, oblivious. After a dreary, excruciating hour, they finished copying their five-page documents and the teacher released them.

They didn't speak to each other as they dressed in their winter coats and boots. They pushed the double doors open together. They headed in the same direction. Sarah couldn't stand the silence any longer.

"What is your problem, anyway?"

Matt looked her up and down, his cold gaze unnerving. "No problem. Life's a circus, most of us are in the sideshow, and then . . . we die."

Sarah shook her head in frustration, sending snowflakes careening off her hat in all directions. "You're unbelievable."

Matt wiped the fluff off his face without a crack in his calm, unruffled expression.

"I get it," she said. "You're miserable, so you want everyone else to be, too." She stared at him until he looked away. "Am I right?"

Matt shrugged.

"So join the sorry miserable club. That doesn't mean you have to make my life any worse than it already is."

"Oh, your life is bad, is it?" said Matt, eyeing her expensive parka.

Sarah winced. She hadn't failed to notice the cheap coat he wore, or the fraying fabric of his jeans. "Money doesn't make everything peachy, believe me."

"Really?" said Matt. "I suppose your dad beats you."

"Are you telling me yours does?"

"The world famous Dr. Barnes? Oh, come on now. How could he ever do anything wrong?"

Sarah stopped walking and grabbed Matt by the arm, turning him towards her. "What are you saying, Matt? Are you abused? What?"

Matt chuckled. "You wouldn't understand."

"Try me."

"You'd have to see it for yourself."

"Just tell me."

"Look," he snapped, wrenching his arm from her grasp. "You can't help me, all right? Not you, with your nice little family, the minivan, and the politician dad."

"I don't have a minivan," she said. "And how did you know my dad was a politician?"

"He's got the look," said Matt.

Sarah's face flushed. She bared her teeth. "Have you been spying on me?"

"Why would I do that? It's not like you're *interesting* or anything."

"Gosh! You really are a piece of work. I'm trying to help you and you push me away." She began walking, stamping deep impressions in the snow. Honestly, he wasn't worth the trouble.

Matt hung back. "I'm sorry," he finally called after her. He raced to catch up. "I guess I am a sorry idiot."

"Madame Leblanc had you nailed," she said.

"But don't tell me there were any prodigies in *that* room." Matt pointed back to the classroom. Madame Leblanc's large frame was visible through the multiple panes of the window as she dusted off their laborious scribbling with her chalk brush.

Sarah raised her eyebrows. "What about Chelsea?" she asked.

"Ch-Chelsea!" Matt choked and sputtered.

Sarah let out a rip-roaring laugh. "Got ya," she said.

"Sure did," said Matt, heaving a tremendous sigh and then laughing along with her.

"So what do you say we have a truce?" suggested Sarah, holding out her hand.

He looked at the proffered hand, pausing. With a slow nod, as if he'd come to a difficult decision, he clasped it firmly and shook. "Agreed."

"So?" she said.

"So what?"

"Are you going to invite me over?"

Matt's eyes bulged in astonishment. "You really are a sucker for punishment."

"That bad, eh?"

"I'll let you judge for yourself."

"Great," she said, rubbing her mitts together. "And you'll introduce me to your dad?"

"I knew there was a catch."

"There always is," said Sarah. "If you want a friend, you'll have to let me in on all your secrets."

"A friend?"

"That's what I said. Does it sound that crazy to you?"

"It just never crossed my mind," said Matt.

"Well, it hadn't crossed my mind either, until just now. But it looks like we could both use one."

Matt wrinkled his forehead as he considered her offer. "Okay," he finally said. "We'll give it a shot. Are you ready?"

"Ready for what?"

"To meet the infamous Dr. Barnes."

"Don't you mean famous?"

"Not for a second," said Matt.

4

The Infamous Dr. Barnes

SARAH SQUINTED AT THE EXTERIOR OF MATT'S HOUSE. IT DWARFED the other houses on the street, rising out of the snow like a breaching whale. She looked from Matt's ragged parka to the mansion, all the while rubbing her forehead. As she drew nearer, though, she could see chips and gouges in the grey brick, and strips of black paint peeling from the multiple garage doors. One of the shutters—a New England touch splashed onto an Upper Canada construction—was hanging off one hinge, and some of the shingles had blown off the roof. Matt keyed in a code for the garage door opener and they went inside.

"No one home yet?" asked Sarah.

"Nadine doesn't get in from the office until six."

"Is that your mother?" Sarah pretended ignorance.

"My mom died when I was born," said Matt, avoiding her gaze as he shut the door. "There's just Nadine and, well . . . my father."

"Oh," said Sarah. "I'm sorry."

"Don't be. I never knew my mom."

"Who's Nadine then?"

"She's my dad's assistant. I live with her when Dad's away." He slid his backpack from his shoulder and stashed it in the front hall closet. He wriggled out of his parka like a moth from a cocoon and left it to molder in a pile of slush on the floor. Sarah twisted her lips, biting back a neat-freak comment as she hung her coat on a hanger in the closet.

"I thought your dad was home. You said I could meet him."

"You can," said Matt. "Come on. I'll show you."

He loped up the stairs, which rose in a lighthouse spiral from the front hall into the upper reaches of the house. Sarah followed, listening for some sound of human life. There was nothing other than the swish of their feet on the hardwood. They emerged in a long hall that extended the length of the dilapidated mansion. Every other step they took evoked an eerie squeak from the floorboards that ricocheted off the walls and ceiling of the vast arched hallway. At the end of the hall Matt stopped. "This is my room," he said, pointing to a mauve door, a bruise in the stark white corridor. He pushed it open.

"Your dad sleeps in your room?" asked Sarah, raising her eyebrows.

"No. Well, sort of. Come on in. I'll show you."

Sarah stepped into the room, and sucked in her breath as she gazed at a cyclone-swept trail of debris. Clothes and sports equipment, empty Coke cans and candy wrappers littered the floor, choking out any sight of the carpet. Grimy bed covers were thrown in a heap at the bottom of the bed. Holes and tatters grappled with every item, as if they'd been attacked by ravenous rats. Sarah wouldn't have been surprised if he'd told her a bomb had been detonated in the centre of his room.

"If your dad's here, we'll never find him," she said.

"Very funny." Matt threw some clothes off the swivel chair in front of his desk. He pulled up another chair from the corner and swept the magazines off it for Sarah. "Take a seat. There's something I have to show you."

Sarah wiped the seat with her hand and sat down as Matt logged onto his computer. As she swung her foot around she kicked over a stack of music and video game discs on the floor, along with a rather thick book. Normally, she wouldn't have given it a second thought, but the book looked strange. It had a cracked cover and thick paper yellowed with age. The title seemed totally weird for a boy who slept through history class—*The Decline of the First Nations*.

"What's this?" she asked, picking it up.

Matt's eyes widened. He snatched the book from her hand.

"Nothing," he said, setting it on the other side of the desk.

"I thought you didn't like history."

"I don't."

"Then why the book? It even looks well-read."

"It's just an old book I found in the house. I read a couple of pages. So what?" He gave her a stern, drop-it look.

"So nothing," said Sarah, taking the hint. "What do you have to show me?"

"This." He activated the memory on the computer and brought up old messages, the most recent dated Sunday, February 10—yesterday. "I'll introduce you to my dad."

The video sprang to life and there stood Professor Barnes, beside a stepped pyramid of pristine whitewashed limestone surrounded by lush green palms and ferns.

"Hi Matt. I hope you're doing well. As you can see I'm surrounded by the mysteries of the Maya. We found a new city in Guatemala. I can't tell you the exact location." He raised his hand to his mouth, leaned in to the camera and whispered: "Top secret. But I can tell you there'll be revelations here that will shock the world. People in ancient societies were much more intelligent than we gave them credit for. Anyway, thought I'd drop you a line. Take care. End transmission."

The screen froze. There was a moment of heavy silence before Matt finally spoke. "There you have him. You've met my dad."

"Is this some kind of joke?" asked Sarah.

"No joke," said Matt. "You've seen as much as I have."

"Excuse me. You've lost me somewhere. That was just a video feed from Guatemala, from a Mayan pyramid."

"Exactly. That's all I've ever seen of him. My dad is a computer-generated image. Get it?"

"He's not real?"

"I don't know."

"What do you mean, you don't know? Of course you know. He's around here sometimes, isn't he? You're putting me on."

Matt leaned back in his chair and linked his hands behind his head. "I wish I were."

"You mean he's never home?"

"Never."

"Even when you were a baby?"

Matt shook his head.

"But that can't be. No dad would—" She stopped. Her eyes watered as she looked at Matt, his face as calm as a windless sea. Yet she could see a slight tremor in his lips. "Then who looks after you?"

"Nadine."

"Is she nice?" asked Sarah.

Matt pursed his lips, as if he needed to mull over his words. "She's… busy. Issuing news releases for the press. Logging all of Dad's amazing discoveries. She carries him along in her briefcase."

"What does that mean?"

"It's her uplink, or whatever you want to call it. All her contact with him seems to come from his old computer in the lab. She carries the laptop with her whenever she's not there, which I guess is connected to it. She never lets me see it. Yells at me when I catch her with her hand in the cookie jar."

Sarah frowned. "I don't get it."

"When she's into the case, I have to stay away. Top secret, you know. What I think, is that he's dead, and she's just playing this game for all it's worth." He riffled his hair and looked away.

Sarah bit her lip, her heart swelling. "I'm sorry."

Matt shrugged. "I don't know him, really. Except for these." He pointed at the frozen screen, the image of a tall, disheveled genius. His eyes were mossy-green like Matt's, his sandy hair tousled. But when she looked beyond the man, the image was blurry, and something else bothered her, too.

"Matt," she said. "That pyramid doesn't look very old."

Matt glanced back at the screen. "I know."

"The bricks aren't crumbling or yellowed."

"I know."

"Do you think it's all a hoax? All of his discoveries?"

"I don't know," said Matt. "I just know that I hate him." He glared at the computer, looking as if he'd like to rip it from the desk and smash it against the wall.

Sarah opened her mouth, then shut it. Sometimes she was so mad at her parents for getting divorced she wished she could kick them, scream at them, throw them into a vat of boiling oil—or at least lukewarm. But she couldn't imagine what it would be like to grow up without them, not even knowing if they were alive, and being strung along like a puppet by someone else. She put her hand on his shoulder even though it was probably the wrong thing to do.

He shrugged it off. "I'm okay. I just need to know if he's alive or not."

"Maybe we can find out," said Sarah.

"Don't you think I've tried?" said Matt with a note of exasperation in his voice. "The only answer is in the lab or in the case. I think she keeps the keycard for the lab in the case. She never lets it out of her sight, day or night."

"Night would be the obvious answer."

"She locks it. I wouldn't be surprised if she swallowed the key, 'cause I've never found it."

"Then it'll have to be day. She must open it sometime," said Sarah.

"She's always at my father's office." He glanced out the window as if he could picture Nadine downtown in some cubicle, clutching the briefcase to her chest and smiling.

"Have you been to the office?"

"Yeah, sure, when I was five and she had no choice but to take me. Tight security there. I tell you, Sarah, there's no way." He was looking at her earnestly, but she didn't believe he would give up this easily. After all, this boy loved to defy his teachers.

"But you're his son," she said.

"She'd never leave me alone with it. You'd think she had classified information in the bag and it was attached to her wrist with handcuffs."

"Never say never," said Sarah with a spreading grin. "Even the wicked witch has to go to the ladies' room sometimes."

Matt eyed her sideways. The pained expression slowly dissolved.

"Where there's a will . . ." she said.

"There's a way." They slapped palms and started making plans.

At six-ten Nadine arrived home and slammed the front door on her way in. Sarah snuck down the hall and glanced over the stair railing to catch her first glimpse of the mysterious guardian.

Even before she had slid out of her glossy leather coat it became evident that Nadine was a mere twig of a woman. She had dips and hollows in her face that would be the envy of any skeleton, and she wobbled on stilted stork-legs as she thrust open the closet door. Her blonde hair hung in wisps from a taut chignon, accentuating the sharp bones in her cheeks and adding even more angles and less curves.

As Nadine's glance swept the mess of coats and hats, boots and mitts weeping water on the front tiles, she shook her head. She cast her gaze up the stairs, shocking Sarah into an instant retreat.

"Can't you ever pick up after yourself, you slob?" she yelled.

"Can't you get a maid?" Matt yelled back.

"Very funny." There was silence for a minute; then weary footsteps thudded on the wooden stairs. "So," she said. "Who's the guest?" Apparently she'd noticed the baby-blue parka.

"A friend," said Matt.

"You don't have any friends," said Nadine, a slight edge to her voice. She peered around the door frame, her eyes contracting suspiciously.

Matt glared at her.

Sarah smiled. "Hello," she said. "I'm Sarah."

"A girl?" Nadine said, gaping.

"Yes, that is my gender," said Sarah.

"I'm sorry. I didn't mean to be rude."

"Didn't you?"

Nadine looked taken aback. "I was just surprised, that's all."

Sarah smiled as if she were indulging a sweet old grandmother in a little eccentric behaviour. "Yes, that can happen. I was wondering if I could meet Matt's father. Have you seen him lately?"

Nadine's lips twitched. "He's on assignment."

"Guatemala?"

"Yes. Matt, those videos are confidential." She moved swiftly into the room, but slowed almost immediately as she began tripping over baseball gloves and sneakers, candy wrappers and old jeans.

"Why?" asked Matt. "There wouldn't be anything *artificial* about them, would there?"

"Of course not," said Nadine. "But they're only meant for your private viewing." She stumbled again, then couldn't contain herself any longer. Her face crinkled in distaste as she examined the half a Snickers bar that she'd impaled with the heel of her shoe. "This place is a pig sty."

Matt ignored her and continued in the same vein. "Don't you mean *designed* for my private viewing?"

Another wisp of hair fell out of her bun as Nadine glared at him. "I don't get your meaning."

"You wouldn't," said Matt.

"I was wondering," said Sarah, trying to cut the tension between the two, "if I could see some of your discs that you keep at the office.

Matt says you have a whole slew of videos from all over the world. I'm doing a project—"

"I don't think I can arrange that," said Nadine.

"Oh," said Sarah. This wasn't working. Maybe if she tried something else. "My dad's an MP in Ottawa. I think they're going to make him Minister of Finance."

Nadine's lackluster eyes sparked to life. "Oh really?"

Matt turned towards Sarah and smirked.

"He's always been interested in Professor Barnes's projects. My parents just got divorced, you know."

Nadine's pasty face bloomed.

"We live just down the street," said Sarah.

"Well, perhaps— But I really can't allow anyone in the lab. We're conducting some rather sensitive experiments. I could bring some of the videos out." She licked her thin lips, smearing the thick ruby lipstick over her skin.

Sarah tried to hide her frustration. This wasn't the solution she was seeking. "Well, maybe you could bring them to my dad's office on Parliament Hill. He has a viewing room we could use. Then maybe we could have dinner afterwards."

"On the Hill, you say?" Nadine's forehead creased in calculation.

"I know he wouldn't mind," Sarah continued. "If the lab is downtown, then you wouldn't have to travel far."

Nadine took a minute to answer, as if it was a difficult decision, but Sarah could have sworn she heard the woman purr. "If it's okay with your father," she said, "I would be happy to drop by after school on Friday and show you and your father the videos."

Matt had to bite his lip to keep from laughing. Sarah kicked him gently. He smoothed his face as best he could and looked out the window.

"That sounds great," said Sarah. "Thank you."

"No problem. Now if you'll excuse me—" Nadine backed towards the door.

"You must be tired," said Sarah.

The woman nodded. "Long days." She staggered as her foot connected with a buried baseball, but she quickly regained her balance, tugged her sweater down, and walked out into the hall.

Sarah rolled her eyes. "She's a shark."

"Takes one to know one," said Matt.

Sarah clobbered him with a shoe that was dangling off the desk.

"Hey, I loved it. But are you really willing to sacrifice your dad?"

"Dad's not that dumb," said Sarah. "I'll convince him to let her on the Hill. He's always been a fan of Professor Barnes. He'll be able to distract her while we make a grab for the briefcase."

"Right," said Matt. "You know, I don't think my dad's the genius, Sarah. You are."

Sarah smiled and bowed dramatically. Matt grinned as he ushered her out the door.

Later that night, while Sarah's dad was tucking her into bed, she broached the subject of the potential meeting on Parliament Hill. He'd just drawn the narrow slats of her beige blinds, walking easily over the spotless carpet. She had a couple of books on her nightstand and a clock radio, but otherwise every piece of sporting equipment she owned was neatly tucked in her closet, and every article of clothing had been folded and slipped into her drawers. She slid into the smooth, freshly scented sheets and began.

"Dad?"

"Yes, dear?"

"I made a new friend today at school. He even lives on our street."

"That's wonderful. See, Ottawa isn't as cold and miserable as you thought it was." He smiled and stroked her hair.

"Yes," said Sarah. "But there's more. He's actually Professor Barnes's son."

"*The* Professor Barnes?"

Sarah nodded vigorously. "And Matt—that's his son—and Professor Barnes's assistant would like to show us some videotapes of his discoveries. Isn't that exciting?"

"Absolutely," said her father.

"Only Nadine, that's Professor Barnes's assistant, can't let us into the lab." She explained about the sensitive nature of the lab environment and how she'd offered up her father's conference room and equipment. "Do you think that would be okay?"

He stroked his chin. "I suppose. Except you have school on Friday and I have a caucus meeting in Parliament."

"No, no. Not during school or work hours. After."

Her dad's forehead creased farther into his thinning hairline. "How did you manage to finagle this one?"

Sarah smiled. "Oh, you know me."

"I certainly do." His stern expression suddenly dissolved. He grabbed her into his arms and squeezed the stuffing out of her. Sarah glowed as she hugged him back.

"I love you, Dad," she said.

"Right back at you, kid. Sleep well." He stepped out of her room, rubbing his chin.

Sarah snuggled down into the blankets and sighed.

5

—— 🜂 ——

The Mission

THE NEXT FEW DAYS DRAGGED ON AS SARAH AND MATT PASSED NOTES back and forth in class, trying to avoid the eagle eye of Madame Leblanc. The thrill of the mission was upon them as they put their heads together during recesses and lunch hours. Step by step, they devised the cloak-and-dagger plan. Some of the people from their class were amazed at Matt's behaviour, or rather, his apparent disinterest in pranks. And they couldn't believe that another student preferred his company to theirs.

On Friday, Chelsea couldn't stand it anymore. She came up behind them as they laughed, whispered, and joked. "What are you doing with the jerk, Sarah?"

Sarah stood up. "He's not a jerk," she said. "If you got to know him—"

"Yeah, like I'd want to," Chelsea spat out. "He's a menace. Anyone with half a brain would steer clear of him."

"Well, I guess I've lost more than half my brain then," said Sarah.

"A lobotomy, I think they call it. Does someone with a lobotomy know what a lobotomy is?"

She looked at Matt.

"What's a lobotomy?" asked Matt.

"Exactly."

"Hey!"

"If you got my joke, you know what it is," said Sarah, giggling.

Chelsea huffed. "You guys are hopeless." She leaned towards Sarah. "You'll regret this, you know. With him for a friend, no one is going to want to hang out with you."

"Good. Then I can concentrate on my basketball."

"Humph. You're as weird as he is." Chelsea tossed the tassels on her toque back and stomped away.

Sarah sat back down beside Matt. "Why does she care?"

"I don't know. Maybe she's jealous."

"Did she try to meet your dad, too?"

"Once, two years ago. She slunk up to me and turned on the charm. Out of the blue. You think I would trust her? Ha!"

Sarah smiled. "But you trusted me."

"That's because you're different. You fought back when I slammed you down."

Sarah puckered her eyebrows.

"Yeah, I admit it. But you didn't give up. Not once. After what I did to you, you still wanted to get to know me. Not my dad, but *me*. You see, no one ever wants to get to know me. It's always about Dad. 'What's your dad like? Do you ever go to those cool places with him? Would your dad sign an autograph? What does your dad eat for breakfast?'"

"You're kidding."

"No, I'm not. Like who cares what he eats for breakfast? Only I would care about that stuff and I never knew." Matt dropped his gaze and kicked a clump of snow.

Sarah felt her heart go out to him again. The problems in her own life seemed microscopic compared to his. Sure, she missed her old friends and her mom horribly, but at least she still had her dad, stubborn as he was. As she tried to decide between reaching out to Matt or letting the awkward moment fade, a silence fell over the schoolyard. The buzz of students' chatter was dying down, which meant the bell must have rung.

"We have to go in," she said.

Matt got up. He brushed the snow off his backside. "Are we ready, do you think?" His face was brightening.

Sarah nodded. "It's a mission thumbs up."

Their next class was history, an hour-long lecture, dry and almost unbearable, as if they were plodding through a desert with no water. Sarah jotted down a few facts, but most of the time her eyes wandered outside. Mr. Fletcher kept pausing during his monologue. He'd turn to look directly at Matt, waiting for an interruption, but Matt was a model student today. Well, not model. He was snoozing, but at least he wasn't being disruptive. That would mean no detentions and they'd have no trouble escaping the school grounds.

When the final bell rang, Sarah expelled a sigh of relief. She turned around to shake Matt out of his stupor.

"Wh-what?"

"Freedom!" she exclaimed.

Matt grinned. With glowing faces, they raced out the double doors into the semi-circular driveway at the front of the school.

Sarah was thrilled to see her dad's car waiting for them. He'd left Parliament early, and he was acting chauffeur in his grand limousine—a cramped Saturn. She motioned for Matt to join her as she ran to the idling silver vehicle.

"You're early," she said. She wrenched the back door open.

"Got tired of the squabbling," he said. "Hop in."

Sarah leaped into the back seat. Matt joined her a little hesitantly. "Dad, this is Matt Barnes. Dr. Barnes's son."

"Pleased to meet you," he said, offering his hand over the front seat.

Matt shook, his spindly hand clamped tight in her father's huge paw. "Same here," he mumbled.

Sarah's dad turned around. He shifted the car into gear. "So where's this office of your father's, Matt?"

"Just off Sparks and O'Connor."

"Not far from Parliament, then. You told your dad's assistant to walk over to the Hill, right?"

"Right," he replied.

"Then if it weren't for you guys, I could have stayed at work, if you call it that."

Sarah frowned. "What do mean by 'if you call it that?' You're always talking about how hard you work."

"I do, sweetheart," he said with a smile. "Although sometimes I'm reminded of a pack of wolves fighting over a piece of meat."

"Do you mean to say that the parliamentary process, something you've praised all your life, something you made me learn when I was six years old, is a waste of time?"

"Oh, no, no," said her dad. "Not the process, dear. That's democracy, and it's our lifeline. But the politicians . . ."

"You're a politician, Dad."

"Yes. I guess I'm part of that sorry lot."

He darted onto the Queensway—the expressway to downtown Ottawa—and poured on the gas. "Suckers," he said, nodding where departing vehicles jammed the opposite side.

"It's not as bad as Toronto," said Sarah. "Those cars are actually moving."

Matt was looking out the window, studying the trees with glazed eyes. He didn't seem the least bit interested in Sarah's banter with her father.

"Are we boring you?" she whispered.

Matt shook his head. "I can't help but feel this won't work. How are we going to get our hands on that briefcase? Every time I've tried it's either been locked or she caught me snooping and kept an even closer watch on it."

Sarah gave his arm a pat. "Think positive. You've never had a partner before. Now you have two." She grinned, but she couldn't draw a smile out of Matt.

"I hate to interrupt," said her father, "but you're starting to remind me too much of the back-benchers in the House of Commons. Whispering usually means secrets, am I right?"

"Not really, Dad" said Sarah. "It means far more than that. Undercover operations, you know. It's far safer for you," she winked at the mirror, "if you don't know."

"My, you have been reading too many spy novels lately, haven't you?"

Sarah shrugged.

"So, Matt. Tell me about your family. What's it like to be the son of Professor Barnes?"

"I wouldn't know," said Matt. "I haven't met him."

Sarah poked Matt with her elbow, but her father merely chuckled. "I guess he's just Dad to you. Have you had any adventures with him?"

"This is the first," said Matt.

Sarah kicked him in the shins. "What?" he whispered. "What do you want me to say?"

"You're the son of a genius. Make it up." She was starting to get worried Matt was going to let something slip. They couldn't let her dad find out the truth. He might interfere with their plans. Then he'd be confronting Nadine instead of getting her to relax her guard.

"Well," said Matt. "He's really kind of a strange man, you know. Scientists are like that sometimes, I've heard. What's the word they use?"

"Eccentric," her father supplied.

"Right. So, when he's home, he just hangs around the house, doesn't say much, you know. But he's a great guy, I guess."

Now her dad was frowning. "I guess," he said. He looked at Sarah in the mirror, but she fled his gaze, turning quickly away. Her father was far too good at digging out secrets. She could sense the electrical storm in his brain already.

"And your mom?" he asked.

"Oh, she's dead," said Matt.

"I'm sorry."

"That's okay."

The drive continued in silence. At least Matt's abrupt response about his mother had stopped her dad from pressing further. He focused on the traffic for a while, at a loss for words. Finally he burst the swollen silence when he banked off the Queensway and turned down Nicolas Street, a major roadway to the city core. To their left, the sun was skewered on the pikes of steel and glass office buildings. "Lots of skaters out this evening." He pointed to the Rideau Canal.

Sarah looked at the shimmering ice surface and the colourfully-clad skaters gliding towards the palace-like Chateau Laurier hotel. She sucked in her breath as she gazed at the majestic buildings that crowned Parliament Hill. Even though she'd been to the capital before as a tourist or as a sidekick to her politician father, the elegance of the place never failed to enchant her. The hotel and the Parliament buildings reminded her of the pictures she'd seen of British castles like Westminster Tower sitting atop London with crusty old brick walls soaring into spires and battlements.

As the buildings loomed closer, more details emerged: elongated arched windows, stained/aged brown brick, peaked roofs that pierced the skyline. The seat of government was dominated by the stately Peace Tower where a clock chimed every hour—so much like Big Ben. These buildings were chips off the old British block. It was strange to see something that looked so ancient—Neo-Gothic it was called—in a frontier land.

"Beautiful, isn't it?" said her father.

She had to think of something disparaging to say about the city. After all, she was supposed to hate moving here. "Ugh, green roofs."

"You know it's tarnished copper."

"Someone should go up and polish them then. Mint green. They look like Barbie castles. Might as well paint the bricks pink."

Her dad sighed. "I remember when you used to goggle at the Parliament buildings. You said they reminded you of all the stories you'd read about King Arthur and the Knights of the Round Table."

Sarah rolled her eyes. "There are no knights in Ottawa."

"Maybe not now."

"Come on, Dad. I know better."

"They weren't exactly knights—"

"Da-ad, no history lessons, ple-ease."

The car slowed down as they vaulted the Laurier Street Bridge, a hoop of green metal spanning the Rideau Canal. Sarah looked down the length of the canal, the slender rope of ice that wound its way through the core of the city. Skaters dotted the ice like speckled paint on a window. Part of Sarah longed to join them, zooming over the frozen surface in her insulated leather skates, breathing in the crisp fresh air, and pirouetting on a smoother patch. But not today. She had far more important things to do.

After they'd crossed the bridge, the car edged through traffic into the midst of the office towers that comprised the downtown core. The Gothic flavour dissolved as the buildings impeded any view of Parliament. Here Ottawa became a modern city, full of exhaust and flying trash that curled through the wind tunnels of dense highrises. The sidewalks were choked with frantic men and women in suits and long coats rushing to catch a bus, coffee in one hand and a cell phone in the other.

With a swift twist of the steering wheel, her father maneuvered the car towards a gap between the tall buildings and cruised towards the West Block of Parliament, where his office was located. He pulled into the back parking lot, reserved for MPs, and slipped into a slot.

"Well, we're here. I hope you gave the lady the correct conference room number," he said to Sarah.

"I'm not that dumb," said Sarah. "I told Matt after you said it was okay. Hopefully she's already here."

"You can leave your backpacks in the car," he said. "Then we won't have the fuss of security."

Sarah heard Matt curse under his breath. He immediately dug through his backpack and withdrew a couple of discs and a memory stick. He tucked the discs into the waistband of his jeans, and slipped his sweatshirt over them, and jammed the stick into his pocket. She raised her eyebrows quizzically.

"In case we find something," he whispered.

She nodded just as her dad turned around to look at them. "Shall we go?" he asked.

Sarah and Matt leaped out of the car. They raced up the worn stone steps, leaving her bewildered father behind. At the top, they were halted briefly by security, then plunged through the broad double doors and slowed their pace only when some politicians with slicked-back hair and double breasted suits walked towards them.

"The conference room is at the end of the hall," said Sarah. As they approached it, they saw Nadine waving at them outside the door. This time her hair was impeccable, swept up, but loosely, so it softened her sharp nose and severe chin. Her glacier blue eyes twinkled like melting ice crystals. Sarah felt a chill slither down her back. She turned to find her father catching up to them, slightly out of breath. She reached out and grasped his hand protectively. He looked down at her with wide eyes.

"Just a little cold in here," said Sarah.

"Right," he said, but he still looked puzzled.

Nadine's face lit up at the sight of him. She still clutched the briefcase Matt had mentioned and an extra duffel bag hung over her shoulder. "Hello. You're the Honourable . . ."

"Just Donald. Donald Sachs," he said, holding out his hand.

She clasped it eagerly with her long scarlet talons. Her smile was so plastic it almost made Sarah gag. "Yes, of course. Sarah told me you were a—"

"A Member of Parliament," said Sarah, cutting in. "Representing Toronto Centre."

"I didn't catch your name." He gently retracted his hand. Nadine released it reluctantly.

"Nadine. Nadine Barnes."

"You're a relative of Matt's?"

"Distant cousin."

Matt glanced at the ceiling.

"I'm also Dr. Barnes's assistant. I run things for him while he's out of the country."

"Or out of this world," Matt whispered to Sarah.

Sarah scowled at him, warning him not to upset their plans, but Matt didn't look like Matt right now. He had the same tousled hair and sea-green eyes, but he was taller and fuzzy, not quite there. Sarah blinked. The illusion disappeared, leaving just plain Matt again.

"You sure you're not a corpse?" she whispered, leaning towards him.

Her father caught her eye. She clamped her lips and stood up straight.

Matt grinned at her. He seemed to love the joke.

They walked into the conference room, Sarah's dad leading the way. A large ebony table dominated the centre of the room, with matching leather chairs looping around the outside. A big-screen television was mounted on the far wall.

"Sarah told me you had some exclusive footage of the professor on assignment. We'd love to see it," said her father.

Sarah smiled. Straight to the point, Dad. Not falling for Nadine's sugar. She couldn't stand the thought of her father getting hooked up with this vulture, but she still needed him to distract the woman.

"Yes," said Nadine. "I have them in my bag." She placed the duffel on the table, flipped over the flap, and removed several discs. "Which one would you like to see first? There are the Mayans, the Alberta dinosaurs—that's a favourite of the children's—Egypt . . ."

"I'll let Sarah decide. She's the one with a fascination for archaeology and ancient history," he said. "In other countries," he added as an afterthought.

Nadine looked expectantly at Sarah.

"Um, maybe Egypt," she said. "I've always loved those mummies."

"Egypt it is." Nadine removed a disc and handed it to Sarah's dad. He slotted it deftly into a nearly-obsolete DVD player. "It's one of the professor's favourites, as well."

The giant screen sprang to life, displaying the pyramids as clearly as if they were right in front of them instead of viewed on film. The limestone blocks were vivid, eggshell-white, and perfectly shaped, as if they'd been freshly cut and spliced with no sign of crumbling stone or the stain of weathering. Professor Barnes stood in the foreground. He cleared his throat and began a narration of his new discoveries beneath the sphinx, including the secret burial chamber of Khufu, the builder of the Great Pyramid. Sarah was mesmerized, but at the same time she saw Nadine sidle up to her father and take a seat next to him. So far, so good.

Matt, however, watched with his head tilted, his mouth slack, trying his best not to fall asleep. They endured the next hour impatiently, Sarah continually glancing at the briefcase, but getting more and more exasperated as Nadine kept it close to her side. How were they going to pry it from her over-protective grip? But no opportunity presented itself, even with Nadine constantly making goo-goo eyes at her father.

After they'd watched a few videos, Sarah decided she would try a new tactic. Matt had his head buried in his arms, so she kicked him awake first.

"Wh-what?"

"Boy, am I ever hungry," she blurted out, looking at Matt. "These videos have been fascinating, but do you think we could have some dinner?"

"Y-yeah," said Matt. "I'm starved."

Her father raised his eyebrows and shot her a stern look, but she wasn't about to back down. "We could have some dinner at Chez Henri across the street. Ple-ease, Dad?"

"Why, that sounds like a great idea," said Nadine, jumping at the chance to dine with an MP at a fancy French restaurant.

Sarah's dad immediately agreed, since there was no diplomatic way to wriggle out of his daughter's trap, although he looked disgruntled. They left the West Block and strode across the street to Chez Henri, settling in at one of the elegantly draped tables of white. Nadine seemed to enjoy being instantly catered to by the haughty French waiter.

As they sat down, Nadine slid her briefcase under the table. Perfect. Then she excused herself to freshen up in the ladies' room. Even better. Maybe she thought it would look too odd to take the briefcase with her, so she left it behind.

Now was their chance. While her father chatted with Jean about the menu specials, Sarah reached under the table and snagged the briefcase. Then she rose from her chair, slipping it behind her back.

"I'm just going to get some fresh air while we wait for dinner.

Will you order for us, Dad?" she asked.

"All right," he said, obviously distracted by his discussion of the exotic herbs and spices in the *soupe du jour*. "What do you want?"

"The roast chicken breast sounds good. Matt?"

"Sure," he mumbled, his nose still buried in the menu.

"Be back in about half an hour," she said. "That's how long it usually takes to serve, right?"

"Um hum," said her father.

"Matt?" She nudged him with her shoe.

"Oh, oh yeah." Matt jumped up.

The two co-conspirators spun around and raced for the door.

As soon as they were outside, Sarah grinned at Matt and held up the briefcase triumphantly.

"Wow, girl, you're amazing," said Matt.

"Now we just have to open it."

They slipped into a side alley and Sarah tried to spring the latches. They flipped open with a *snap*. She looked up at Matt in astonishment.

"Nadine must have forgotten to lock them. Incredible. I guess your dad really has her off her game."

Sarah grimaced, but she wasn't about to downplay their good fortune just because of the barracuda.

Matt jumped for the case. Before opening it, he paused and caught Sarah's gaze. The corners of his lips were quivering. She smiled and nodded. Then he opened the Pandora's box.

His forehead creased in confusion as he stared at the contents. "It's just discs," he said. "And papers."

"What's on the papers?" asked Sarah.

Matt riffled through the stack, scanning as he went. "Formulas.

Mathematical formulas and scientific equations."

"Like what?"

"$E = mc^2$. That one's easy—the speed of light. But these: $d^2 = x^2 + y^2 + z^2$ and $d^2 = x^2 + y^2 + z^2 (1-v^2/c^2)^{\wedge 1/2}$ and $s^2 = x^2 + y^2 + z^2 - ct^2$. I have no idea what they mean."

"Let me see," said Sarah, pushing him aside and grabbing the papers. She shuffled through them. "This is all Greek to me. It's like that endless, unreadable code when you accidentally change the computer setting."

"I don't get it. Why all the secrecy?"

Sarah shook her head. "Your dad is a genius. We're just kids. But look here, it's Nadine's keycard." Sarah held up the slim plastic card. "This could get us into the lab, and maybe there we can find out more."

"Do you think we have time?" asked Matt.

Sarah glanced back at the restaurant. "You said the lab is just down the street." They might never get another chance, but what would her dad do if they took too long? She clutched the card tightly in her fist. "We've got to be fast."

Matt looked down at the keycard, his eyes glowing. "This may be the key to a lot more than the lab."

Sarah nodded.

"Let's do it."

6

The Lab

SARAH FOLLOWED MATT AS HE ZIGZAGGED THROUGH THE STREETS, hunching down in her plump winter coat. The wind whistled between the buildings as he plowed through several small drifts on the sidewalk, heading towards cobbled Sparks Street with its array of elegant boutiques. But he turned into a trash-cluttered back alley before reaching it. After walking a few steps, he opened a rickety wooden door with chipped paint and a network of spidery scratches in its surface. It looked like the neglected back door of a restaurant. He tramped through a narrow hall, climbed two flights of stairs, and stopped at a locked door with a security keycard slot to the side.

"This is it," he said, looking back at Sarah.

She smiled and took a deep breath. "Let's try the card." She inserted it into the slot. The lock immediately disengaged with a distinct *click*. She jumped back, though, as a loud *slurp* resounded in the stairwell and the door retracted.

"Oooh. Star Trek," she said.

They entered a narrow hallway that was tubular like the conduit ramp to an airplane. "I think Nadine's office is at the end, but the main lab is just up the hall," said Matt, advancing as if there were nothing unusual about the tunnel.

They passed a room labelled "Mailroom," another labelled "Finances." After several cautious steps, they came to a plate with the word "Lab" etched on it. The door was larger than the others, a dull grey metal rimmed with what appeared to be airtight sealant. It made Sarah think of the blast door of a bomb shelter, something she'd seen in old movies. The lock was different from the keycard slot at the entrance. It had a sheer glass front with no visible number pads, slits for a card, or inserts for a traditional key. Sarah paused. This was a problem.

Matt stared at the door, his forehead furrowed. "Any bright ideas? It's a fortress, you know."

"What kind of lock is that?" she asked.

"Looks like a retinal scan." He pointed to his eye. "I saw one once on a computer game."

"Figures."

"Was that an insult?" he asked.

Sarah didn't answer.

"Because if it was, I'll have you know that computer games can increase intelligence—"

"Can we stick to the problem? This was probably programmed for Nadine, right?"

Matt nodded.

"And who else?"

"No one."

Sarah turned to Matt and examined his face, so similar to the one in the videos of his father. "Had to be for your dad, too."

"So? That doesn't help us any."

"Here. Stand in front of it. I'll give you a boost."

"Don't be ridiculous."

"You look like your dad, Matt. And you have his genes. Just maybe, your eyes are similar, too."

Matt shook his head. "They'd have to be identical."

"Humour me."

"Fine. Here goes nothing."

Sarah boosted him with a grunt. As he placed his eye to the scan, a strobe light pulsed behind the glass. "Whoa," he said. She set him down as the lock clicked and a gentle gust of air escaped the seal. The door creaked open.

Matt and Sarah stepped into the laboratory.

"Welcome, Mr. Barnes. It's been a long time," said a monotone female voice within the room. Sarah and Matt froze, but not because of the digital voice. They looked up and up, their heads tilted back, their mouths hanging open. What they saw before them was a computer— the size of a church. It rose three floors in height and must have covered a city block in area. There were microchips by the millions, but only one console, with one chair.

"This is it? One gigantic computer?" Matt asked, looking bewildered.

"Hmm," said Sarah, equally confused. She scanned the room, but the only other unusual thing she saw was a curved metal door. "Maybe we're looking in the wrong place. Maybe the key to finding your father is in his work." She tapped the briefcase Matt still clutched in his hand. "What if you copied the discs? Then we could look them over on your computer at home."

Matt nodded, opened the case again, and removed a disc. He inserted it into the slot beneath the console of the immense computer. A tremendous *whirr*, followed by clicks and snaps, echoed throughout the lab as the entire driving engine of the machine awoke. It shuddered, sending vibrations through the floor. Then the strange metal door in the corner of the room parted in the middle. The halves slid apart like a pair of warped elevator doors. Inside they saw a hollow glass tube with two large metal plates on either side that were connected to a fringe of wires.

"What in the world . . ."

Sarah walked slowly towards the contraption.

"Don't go any closer," said Matt. "My dad was a genius, but he might be dead, too."

Sarah stopped halfway across the room as lights within the tube began to pulsate. The plates emitted a hydraulic hum and flew together until they clashed in the middle. Suddenly froth formed all around the interior of the tube. It grew and grew until it became one gigantic bubble and the tube seemed to disappear altogether. The light within it was searing; Sarah had to shade her eyes. When she glanced sideways at it, she saw a vision. It was distorted, but there was movement. A slim man with unkempt sandy hair seemed to shift in and out of view.

Sarah backed away. She clutched the desk for support as the room felt like it was oscillating. Small showers of dust floated down from the very top of the computer console. She saw an image clearly now, like on a movie screen.

An island expanded in front of her, growing larger and larger, as if she were being thrust into the scene, and on the island stood a city, with Roman pillars and marble-work houses. Except . . . they were falling. Everything was falling.

The ground rippled like a choppy sea and there were thousands of people, running, screaming, stampeding over one another. The earth cracked apart, widening into huge gashes that crumpled buildings. A wave as tall as the CN Tower cast its enormous shadow over the city.

Nathan Barnes watched helplessly as the tsunami rushed towards him. He flickered and winked out just before the wave crashed down. But the other people didn't. Sarah watched in horror as they were swept away.

The bubble popped. The vibrations ceased. Matt looked at her with bulging eyes. Was it real, or had they just witnessed another formulated video?

"Wh-what just happened?" asked Matt.

"That was your father," said Sarah, her chest heaving.

"But was this now, or some other time? Is he still alive?"

"I don't know. It looked like a movie I saw about Atlantis."

"But it wasn't like a movie," said Matt. "It seemed so real."

Sarah tried to sift through this strange event in her head. All Dr. Barnes's videos took place at ancient sites, but they didn't look ancient. How could that be? And then there was this strange machine in the corner of his lab. Maybe Dr. Barnes had discovered something extraordinary and maybe it had to do with the past. She wondered what Matt would say. "What if your father is trapped in some other time?"

Matt shook his head as if to clear it of cobwebs. "That's not possible."

Sarah grasped his shoulders. "Neither is a car going through a person. But I saw it. So don't deny it."

Matt didn't flinch. "It was a near miss. I get them all the time. People think I was born under a lucky star, or something."

"It was no miss, Matt. It was supernatural. So maybe this is, too. What was your dad working on before he disappeared? Did Nadine ever mention it?"

"No. It was top secret. James Bond stuff."

Sarah sighed.

"If what you say is true, then we just watched him die," said Matt. "He really is dead." He hunched over like he was in pain.

"No," said Sarah, taking his hand. "He winked out, disappeared—whatever you call it—just before the wave hit. I don't think he was there."

Matt met her gaze and straightened up, a glimmer of hope flickering in his eyes. "Then how do we find him?"

"Well, maybe the answer is in these discs. Try to copy them."

Matt nodded and turned back to the computer. The cursor was blinking as if asking for direction. He issued the copy command.

The computer said, "Are you sure you want this copied, Mr. Barnes?"

Matt said, "Yes."

"Thank you," said the computer. "Please insert discs for copying."

Matt slipped a disc out from under his shirt and placed it into the disc-writer. A dull grinding sound followed, and continued, as he inserted all the discs in the briefcase one by one. In seconds the computer had duplicated twenty. After it spat out the last one, Matt ejected his copy and stashed it beneath his sweatshirt again, tucked in at the waistband of his jeans. He jammed the originals into the briefcase and latched it shut.

"Okay, we're out of here." He headed for the door.

"Um, Matt. What about that?" Sarah pointed at the strange

bubble-making machine in the corner. "Shouldn't we close the doors again?"

"How?"

"I don't know. But you were the one who opened it. And if Nadine finds it like this . . ."

"I get your point." Matt strode back to the computer. "Maybe if I just tell it to close." He leaned into the microphone and cleared his throat. "Computer, close doors."

"Closing portal doors," said the synthesized voice. The curved doors slid silently together.

Sarah met Matt's wide eyes, her own blinking in confusion. "Portal?" he mouthed. There was no time to think about what it meant, though. They had to scram before her father came looking for them.

"Now, open the *laboratory* door," said Matt.

The blast door clicked open. Sarah poked her head out and scanned the corridor. It was still deserted, so they slipped out, closed the lab door and raced down the hall.

"How much time did that take?" gasped Matt once they reached the alley.

Sarah glanced at her watch. 6:38 p.m. She winced. "Looks like it's been longer than half an hour."

They didn't waste time chatting about it, but sped down the street clocking new records in the 100-metre dash. When they reached the restaurant, they stopped outside, trying to calm their breathing and smooth their disheveled hair and clothes. Matt slipped the briefcase behind his back.

They walked into the restaurant as casually as if they'd just been gone a few minutes. Both adults were seated at the table. Sarah's father had a cell phone pressed against his ear. He lowered it as they entered, his lips taut. Sarah's stomach clenched as she slid into her seat.

Matt sat beside her and made the case disappear beneath the folds of the tablecloth.

"Well," said Nadine. "We were about to send out the hounds. Of all the times not to carry your cell phone." She looked at Matt severely.

"I left it in my backpack," said Matt, glaring back at her. "As if you'd ever call me," he muttered.

"Why were you gone so long?" asked Sarah's dad.

"We took a walk along the locks by the river," said Sarah. "Then I felt queasy and had to sit down for a while. I'm sorry if we made you worry."

"Are you okay?" he asked, the frown leaving his face.

"Yes, I think so. But I'm not very hungry anymore. Can we go home?"

"Of course," said her father, rising from his chair. "I'm sorry, Nadine."

She gripped his hand, much to Sarah's dismay. "No need to be, Donald. We must do it again sometime."

He smiled and squeezed her hand in return. Sarah was about to toss her cookies for real this time.

"Great. Let's go," she said. She grabbed her father's hand, practically dragging him out the door.

"What about you, Matt?" asked her dad. "Are you riding home with your cousin?"

Nadine smiled, but her face appeared tight. "Would you mind dropping him off, Donald? I still have some work to finish."

"Not a problem," he said. "Come along, Matt. Thanks again, Nadine."

They hustled off to the car, Sarah and Matt climbing into the back seat. Sarah's dad watched her closely, so she did her best to moan and clutch her tummy. While they were speeding down the expressway to the outskirts of Ottawa, Sarah met Matt's eyes. He patted his shirt as if it concealed treasure. She grinned. Mission accomplished, but they were a long way from answers.

That night, as her father tucked her into bed, Sarah said, "I have a question, Dad."

"Shoot, my little invalid."

"What do you know about time travel?"

He blinked and looked taken aback. "Not much. Is there such a thing?"

"That's what I wondered. Has there been any research, any break-throughs? Do you know?"

Her dad tapped his head. "I'm brilliant, Sarah, but I'm no phys-icist. Look it up on the Internet. You know how to research a topic."

"Okay. I just thought you might know something. You know, gov-ernment, top secret experiments."

He laughed. "You must get off the spy novels, sweetheart."

Sarah grinned, happy to be joking with her father again. Then she remembered the look Nadine had given him just before they parted ways, and she lost her smile.

"Do you like Nadine?"

Her father tilted his head. "Sure."

"Oh." She twisted the covers in her fists.

"Good night." He started to get up.

"I mean, do you *really* like her?"

"Now, what's this about?" He sat back down on the side of her bed.

"I just wondered. You seemed to be having fun while I was gone."

"We were starting to get worried about you, Miss Invalid. Don't think I don't know that you're up to something with your new friend."

Sarah put on her sweetest smile. "Whatever do you mean?"

He leaned in closer. "Don't forget, I read spy novels, too. Now go to sleep."

He kissed her lightly on the forehead, then added a quick wink as he ducked out the door.

Sarah bit her lip. Her dad was much too smart. They'd definitely have to watch their steps from now on.

7

Verse

SARAH WOKE UP SATURDAY MORNING TO THE RATTLE OF HER WINDOWS and the fizz of snow driving against the glass. The wind howled. It made her hunker down under her duvet. Her dad's cheerful whistling, the sizzling of bacon, and the sweet smell of pancakes summoned her, but she wasn't yet ready to poke her nose out of the covers. Finally, the thought of the mystery she had to solve made her scoot out of bed and dash for the shower.

The sluice of warm water made her forget about the wind and the snow outside. She couldn't wait to meet up with Matt again and investigate his discs. Everything she'd witnessed so far told her that Dr. Barnes was involved in something very unusual and, by the looks of Nadine, maybe even sinister. She let the water splash over her as she thought about Dr. Barnes in the midst of what looked like the Atlantis catastrophe. The panic in his eyes—it had seemed so real. Maybe he really was in some ancient past. And maybe, just as Matt suspected and feared, he was dead now. She hoped not.

She slipped out of the shower and dried herself absentmindedly. The wind screamed outside. She shivered, but she wasn't really cold anymore.

Sarah drifted to the kitchen, her mind still far away. Her father placed a steaming plate of pancakes in front of her.

"I see you're wide awake," he said.

"Hmm," she nodded, sawing off a piece of pancake. She popped it into her mouth.

"It tastes better with syrup, you know."

"Hmm," she said, gnawing on the next slice.

He snapped his fingers in front of her face as he sat down with his own plate. "Are you sleeping, or are you just somewhere else?"

"What? Oh, I was just thinking."

"Deeply, by the looks of it."

Sarah smiled and bit another piece. "Oh! Is this ever *gross*." She grimaced.

Her dad couldn't help but laugh. "Like I said, syrup would help." He handed her the bottle. She smothered her pancakes with the thick golden liquid.

"Now that's the Sarah I know. What's on your mind, dear, that you forgot all about your sugar fix?"

"Oh, just things. Can I go over to Matt's?"

"If it's okay with Nadine."

"Matt said Nadine was working today. I'm sure she wouldn't mind if I kept him company."

Her father gazed out the window, lines developing on his forehead. "That boy seems to be alone an awful lot."

"Yeah," said Sarah. "But not anymore. He's got a friend."

"Yes, he does, doesn't he?" He turned back to her with a buoyant smile. "Well, it's okay with me, as long as you check in for lunch. Bring Matt along, if you like."

"Great," said Sarah as she stuffed the last bite into her mouth. "Gotta go." She leaped up from the table.

"What about some bacon?"

"No room," said Sarah, launching towards the closet. She grabbed her parka and boots.

Her dad followed her, munching on a slice of bacon. "Might I just say something first?"

"Sure."

"I know you're getting involved in some sort of mystery, but keep the spy stuff to a minimum, please. Nothing dangerous or illegal, okay?"

"I'm an angel, you know that." Sarah winked.

He pursed his lips and leaned over. "Don't fly too high, if you get my drift."

"Oh Dad, you're so sixties." She turned and ran out into the blinding snow.

"I'm not that old," he yelled after her and shut the door.

Sarah covered the block in seconds and tramped through the thick snow to Matt's house, shaking her head at the drift-covered driveway that rarely saw a shovel. As she approached the door, the shutters flapped against the brick; the windows rattled so ferociously she was sure a poltergeist inhabited the old mansion.

Ignoring the slithery feeling the house gave her, she climbed the porch steps and rang the bell. No light lit up in the quiet house. No curtain was thrust aside. She rang again. Not a peep, except for the eerie rattling and clapping of the shutters. She knocked. Nothing.

With clenched fists she gave in to her frustration. She started pounding.

The blinds on the upper level were tweaked apart. Two jade eyes peered out.

Sarah pounded again. "Come on, Matt."

A few minutes later the door creaked open. Matt's pale face poked out of the doorway. His hair was spiked up on one side and crushed flat on the other. He stepped aside and gestured with a sweep of his hand for her to enter.

"You know," she said, "if I didn't know you already, you'd scare the heck out of me."

"Why?" asked Matt, yawning.

"Because you really do look like a corpse in the morning."

He grinned as he scratched his scalp, raising more porcupine quills in the tangled mass. "What time is it, anyway?"

"I don't know. Nine or ten." She swept in, carrying a swirl of snow with her. "Were you going to sleep the day away?"

"I usually do," said Matt.

Sarah shrugged out of her coat. She heaved it at him while she took off her boots. Matt caught the coat, looked at it oddly, and tossed it to the floor beside his.

Sarah wrinkled her nose. "You really are a slob, you know."

"Uh huh," said Matt. "Your point is?"

"Never mind. Is Nadine home?"

Matt walked into the kitchen. He glanced at the empty coffee cup in the sink. "No, she must already be gone. I think she'd rather be anywhere than here with me."

Sarah shook her head. "How can you live this way?"

"Oh, I've survived. Self-reliance and all that rot. Come on. I'll get dressed while you boot up the computer. We have work to do."

Sarah followed him upstairs. Halfway down the hall, she peeked into Nadine's immaculate bedroom, just to be sure the woman was gone, and . . . because it drew her eyes. The bed was satin-smooth, not a fiber out of place, and adorned with a lacy violet bedspread. A dark mahogany headboard and matching armoire added a touch of the macabre. But what troubled Sarah the most was how clean it was. There wasn't a stray blouse or bra anywhere, not even a speck of lint on the creamy carpet. Nadine's makeup and perfume were assembled on a vanity in neat colour-coded rows. She turned back to Matt's room. It was hard to believe it was the same house. She had to wade through the clothes to get to his desk, which was made of cheap clapboard. As she tossed aside faded jeans and ratty sweatshirts, she began to see an evil stepmother comparison.

"Doesn't she ever buy you anything new?" asked Sarah.

Matt grunted. "No. I just get hand-me-downs from a friend of hers. Even the cell phone and my computer are her cast-offs."

"Why? She can afford it, can't she?"

"Of course she can. She's rich because of Dad's videos. Everything *she* owns is new. But that doesn't mean I should get any of the money. I owe her instead, 'cause Dad left her with a spoiled brat to look after while he gallivanted around the world."

Sarah touched his shoulder. He shrugged her hand off. "It's okay. I've learned to live with it. I used to think she cared a little. Whenever someone interviewed her about a new discovery Dad had made, she would hold hands with me and tell everyone what a wonderful kid I was. But as soon as the cameraman walked away, she'd drop my hand, shoo me into the house and forget about me again. When I made her a drawing or a present at school, she'd smile, pat my head, and I'd find it in the trash a day later."

"Oh, Matt. How awful. But she must have looked after you as a baby."

Matt snorted. "Right. She had nannies look after me when I was younger. And those ladies actually showed me what a parent might be like. But as soon they started snooping or asking where Dr. Barnes was, she fired them." He wrenched open a drawer, and yanked out a clean pair of faded jeans and a hockey sweatshirt.

Sarah didn't know what to say. How could anyone be so mean?

"Let's not talk about it anymore. We have better things to do than talk about Nadine." Matt grinned and winked, as if he'd dismissed her from his mind. Without a second thought, he pulled off his pajama top. When he reached for his bottoms, Sarah flushed and turned away.

"Matt," she admonished.

"What?" he said.

"You really like to shock people."

"So?"

"So, you don't have to shock me. I'm your friend, so don't try to drive me away."

"I'm not," said Matt. "I just don't see what all the fuss is about. Are you blushing? I mean I'm not that cute."

Sarah giggled. "You're crazy." She heard him zip up his jeans. She flicked on the computer, then turned back to him, relieved to find him fully dressed. "I'm surprised you weren't trying to work on this last night."

"Too risky," said Matt. "If Nadine had walked in, all that work we did would have been for nothing."

"I guess you're right," said Sarah. "Funny thing. I didn't really look at it as work."

Matt smiled. "Neither did I." He sat down in the swivel chair and motioned for her to sit beside him.

Sarah sat. She noticed the strange book again, perched on the corner of his desk. "Matt, I have to ask. Why do you have a book about the First Nations? You don't seem to care about anything in history class except catching up on your sleep."

Matt sighed, shook his head, and swivelled towards her on the chair. "You're awfully nosey today, aren't you?"

"But it just doesn't make sense."

"It was my dad's, okay? I found it in the closet in Nadine's room one day when I was looking for some clue that would tell me where he'd gone, and what had happened to him. I found this book in a box—something she hadn't gotten around to throwing out. I thought it might have meant something to my dad. Even if it didn't, it was the only thing I had left of him, you know?"

Sarah nodded. No wonder the book looked like it had been spun through the washing machine and then through the dryer. He'd probably read it over and over, just because his father had thumbed through it, maybe only once. Sarah touched his arm.

"It's okay," Matt said. "It's just a book. Now let's stop talking about it and start figuring out what dad was up to. Reading that book never helped me find him. But this might."

He turned back to the computer and logged on.

"Verse?" she asked, when she saw him type his password.

Matt gave her a sidelong glance. "You really are a snoop."

"Sorry." She shrank down in her chair.

"Never mind," said Matt. "I guess I can trust you with this. I've trusted you with everything else."

"What does it mean?"

"It's something I heard in Dad's videos. He repeated it a few times, but it didn't fit in with his commentary on the Mayans, or the Romans."

"Verse," she said, contemplating. "I wonder if he was referring to poetry."

The computer played a note that told them it was fully alert. Matt inserted the disc. The screen came alive with equations and computations. Matt studied it. Sarah tilted her head.

"Anything?" she asked.

"Nah," he said.

He scrolled down through the jumbled mathematics. The equations were endless.

"Is this making any sense to you?"

Sarah shook her head. "It has to have some meaning, but we're not scientists. How are we supposed to figure it out?"

"There must be something to it," said Matt. "It's guarded like a bank vault."

Sarah stared until her vision blurred, but she got nothing. "It's not helping. Let's check something else."

"Okay. What next?" He looked at her expectantly, his eyebrows hooked upward.

"The Internet."

"If you say so." Matt turned back to the computer, clicked on his direct access and engaged the Internet. "What exactly are we looking for?"

"Let's try some of your equations."

Matt plugged in the first few. "Pythagorean theorem for distance," he said. "Einstein's relativity. The third one here says it equates time with distance and distance with time. I think it means time is relative to speed and distance. Einstein said the faster you go, the slower time passes."

"But you'd have to go awfully fast to go backward in time. Faster than we can travel."

"Hmm," he said noncommittally. He typed out another equation. "Planck's constant. I think we're getting into quantum physics."

"Forget it," said Sarah. "Let's look for something less technical."

"Like what?"

"Time travel."

Matt squinted at her. "That might give us a list of novels."

"Try it, okay?"

"Okeedoke." He entered the subject, then waited. There were four hundred and sixty-six million listings. "Where do you want to start first?"

"Well, I guess we should narrow the search. How about 'science of time travel?'"

Matt tried again. That reduced it to 1500.

"This one," said Sarah, pointing to an ABC Science News article.

"*Star Trek*? Sarah I don't think—"

"Do it," she insisted.

Matt complied, his face puckered in doubt. "My dad isn't into science fiction."

"No, he's into science," said Sarah. As she scanned the article, she felt like she was getting mired in mud. "This is too deep for me. More quantum physics. We haven't even finished photosynthesis in school."

"I thought you were smart," said Matt.

"Hey, I like history. Math too. But advanced science is not my thing."

"Well, it's mine," he said. "I'm not my father's son for nothing. See this here. It explains the theory that there are multiple universes. Not just one, but many overlapping. So if that's the case, for real, then maybe different times can be happening at the same time as ours. Get it?"

Sarah scrunched her nose. "Different times along with our time?"

"Yeah. You see the other earths are all the same earth, only in different universes. So similar things are happening but not always at the same time as our present. So you could step from one time to another, only in a different universe that looks, acts, and smells the same. We're in a multiverse."

A light bulb snapped on in Sarah's head. "Verse, Matt. That's where you got your password."

Matt blinked. "You're right. Multiverse. It is the word Dad mentioned. It must be the key." He studied the article again. "It's all theory, though. But this is interesting. They say that the closest universes will have almost identical histories. Maybe an atom or a photon that's different. A photon is a small particle of light," he added, probably because Sarah couldn't keep the confused look from her face. "But the ones farther away will have different pasts—like maybe we lost World War II, or 9/11 didn't happen. And there's supposed to be this quantum foam between the universes, like tiny wormholes. If you can tap into it, enlarge a wormhole with some sort of negative energy, you could slip from one to the other"

"Huh?" said Sarah. "What is negative energy?"

Matt scratched his head. "Well, they say here that all ordinary matter has positive energy. But exotic matter with negative energy can be made by squeezing energy out of a vacuum created in a tiny gap between two metal plates. Just like what we saw in the lab. So when you bring these two plates close together, photons of long wavelengths can't exist between the plates, so it excludes some of this energy from the system. And as they get closer, a force takes over and pulls the plates together. That means the energy density between the plates has to be negative."

"Right," said Sarah rolling her eyes. "I totally understand."

"Just think of it this way. That machine must tap into this quantum foam with negative energy and then creates a wormhole that might be large enough for a human being to pass through."

"So you think your dad turned on the tap?"

"I'd say he broke the dam. Imagine if he's discovered time travel. It sure seems like he's travelled to the past, with all his videos from strange and ancient-looking places, but why hasn't he come home?"

"Maybe the experiment turned sour. Maybe somehow he became trapped." Sarah crushed her cheek on her hand. "So now we know how. Sort of. The question is how do we help your dad?"

"Assuming he's still alive," said Matt, his mouth tightening.

"It just doesn't make sense. If this machine could transport him into another time through a wormhole, it should be able to transport him back. But he just seems to jump to different times and different places."

"This is hopeless," said Matt. "We finally found the answer to one puzzle, but we have dozens more to solve."

Sarah slipped her hand onto Matt's shoulder. This time he didn't shrug it off. "It's a start, Matt. We have an idea of what happened to him now. If we work together, maybe we can get him back."

"Where do we go next, though?"

"Where your dad went. The lab, of course."

"So how do we get into the lab, with eagle-eye Nadine always perched there?"

"At night," said Sarah. "When she's tucked away in bed dreaming of *my* dad."

Matt grinned. "She's quite interested in him, isn't she?"

"As long as the feeling's not mutual," Sarah snapped. "God forbid that I end up with her for an evil stepmother, too."

They both laughed. "So when should we carry out our secret mission?" asked Matt.

Sarah tapped her lips. This was going to be tricky. "I don't know. Dad has bed-check every night. He was kind of suspicious of our vanishing act yesterday. We'll have to wait a few days just to lull him into complacency."

"Lull him into what?"

"We'll get him to relax. Hopefully the Prime Minister will spring some delicious scandal and keep him busy up on Parliament Hill."

"Where did you learn to talk?"

"My dad's a politician," said Sarah. "Where do you think? And I read a lot. You should try it more often." She glanced at the book beside the computer, but she didn't get any response from Matt other than a grin.

"I'd rather fight Zargocian the Sphinx in *Battle of the Planets*."

Sarah sneered. "See, that's what I mean. At least you're up on science or you'd be a brainless twit."

"At least I'm not a nerd, like my dad. Look where it got him."

"He's probably had more excitement than any of us will ever have," said Sarah. "Nerds are often geniuses and either make a lot of money or," she smiled, "travel through time."

"And die," said Matt, his grin disappearing.

"And live," said Sarah.

The wind howled outside as if to emphasize her words. Both of them shivered, but their eyes were sparkling.

8

The Bat Cave

MATT TRIED TO KEEP A LONG FACE AS HE TRUDGED ALONG WITH SARAH to her house. Secretly, the invitation for lunch thrilled him. As they arrived, he looked up at the two-story, red and beige brick construction. The white trim was freshly painted, and the windows sparkled from a recent application of Windex. The driveway passed between twin mountains of shovelled snow, creating a wide valley to the door. It seemed so welcoming, almost as if a hand was beckoning him in.

Having lunch *with* other people—not beside them, like at school—was an entirely new experience for Matt. Sarah told him they'd be having hotdogs and milk, which was better than the peanut butter sandwiches he usually had to throw together. It was strange, but Matt felt he could actually let his guard down, until Sarah's dad tried to fish for information.

"Nadine seems to work an awful lot," he said.

"Um," said Matt, stuffing his face with a hot dog.

"Are you home by yourself all the time?"

"Not always. Besides, I'm almost thirteen."

"Self reliance," said Mr. Sachs. "A very admirable quality. Well, in case you need a little advice sometimes, I'm here quite often."

"Too often," said Sarah, smirking.

He scowled at her. "Lucky for you, little lady, or you'd be starving."

"I can cook," said Sarah defensively.

"Well, macaroni and cheese is not on this year's list of most nutritious foods."

"Um," said Sarah, holding up her hot dog.

"Hmm. I suppose you've got me there."

Matt watched in silence as Sarah sparred lightheartedly with her father. He tried to laugh when they exchanged jokes, but it was hard not to be jealous. Sarah had a relationship that he envied. Even though her mother didn't live with her anymore, at least she had a father who seemed to care for her deeply. He'd give anything to have that himself.

"Well, any plans for tomorrow?" asked Mr. Sachs.

"Not really," said Sarah.

"Computer games," suggested Matt quickly.

He wasn't quick enough for the politician. "I was thinking," said Sarah's dad, looking at the swirling snow as if he could see past it to the dark silhouette of the Gatineau Hills across the river. "Would you be interested in a little spelunking?"

"Spelunking as in caves?" asked Matt. A thrill coursed through him.

"You bet," said Mr. Sachs.

"Will we have to crawl through tunnels?"

The older man shrugged. "Maybe."

"With spiders and bugs all over the place?"

"Quite possibly."

Sarah shuddered. She didn't seem quite as thrilled with the idea. Then she crinkled her eyes. "And will you be *teaching* us about caves?"

"Is there anything wrong with that?" asked her dad, trying his best to keep a straight face and look innocent.

"He's setting us up," said Sarah.

"I don't care," said Matt. "No one's ever taken me to a cave before."

Sarah's eyes assumed a thoughtful look that he was beginning to recognize. "Are there caves open in the winter?"

"Yes," said her father. "They're actually quite spectacular. Icicles dangle from the stalactites, and they glitter in the light of the flashlights. It makes the caves seem magical."

Sarah's face flushed. "Okay. I'm in."

"Great," said her dad, rubbing his hands together. "When you get home tonight, Matt, make sure you ask Nadine for permission. If it's okay with her, you can meet us here first thing in the morning."

Matt nodded. He hid a flinch at the mention of Nadine. He had no intention of telling her anything of his impending adventure. The woman always made his life miserable. There was no way he'd allow her to spoil another day spent with a real family.

The next morning, Matt slipped out of the house before Nadine was awake. An empty wine bottle sat on the counter, so he guessed she'd sleep till noon, at least. He'd dressed in a ragged old ski jacket, another leftover in his father's closet from the days when he'd actually inhabited the Barnes's house. He wore thermal-weave long underwear and scruffy old jeans, of which he had plenty. He'd been warned to dress warmly and to dress down for crawling through tunnels layered with bat guano. He shivered with excitement as he rang the doorbell to Sarah's house.

Mr. Sachs opened the door. "My, we're up early."

"Yes, we are," said Matt, looking at Sarah's dad. The man was clear-eyed and bouncing with energy. "Is Sarah ready?"

"Not yet. She was more enthusiastic yesterday, when she had to scoot out the door before breakfast. Obviously, today's adventure is more appetizing for you, Matt, than for our history buff. What was it that had her so keen yesterday?"

Matt looked down. He shuffled. "Oh, nothing much. Just some old computer discs I had to show her." He found it harder to lie to this man than he'd ever found it to lie to an adult before. Maybe because this was the first adult he'd ever liked, aside from his kindergarten teacher. At least it was only half a lie.

Sarah's father nodded, although his squint said something quite different. "Well, those discs seem awfully interesting to my daughter. She can't seem to focus on our conversations anymore."

"Pretty boring stuff. Just some math and science," said Matt.

"All right," he said, placing a hand on Matt's shoulder.

It felt strange, but Matt resisted the urge to shrug it off.

"I won't ask again, unless I'm worried that you're going to wind up in trouble. Secrets can be pretty important." He invited Matt into the kitchen. "Did you have breakfast?"

Matt shook his head.

"You need to eat, you know. I thought about bringing a slingshot with us today. We could eat bat roasted over an open fire. But I didn't think Sarah would appreciate the pioneer approach as much as you."

Matt laughed. "Well, I am a little hungry. But roasted bat?"

"It's probably a delicacy in some countries."

"I'm not that adventurous."

Mr. Sachs winked as he spooned thick oatmeal into a bowl.

Matt stared warily at the mush. "I eat dry cereal mostly."

"Sticks to the ribs, Matthew, my boy. Hearty spelunker fare. Besides, I don't think you eat right. You're much too thin."

"You sound like . . ." He was going to say a mother, but he had no one with whom to compare.

"Like a bossy parent?" said Sarah's dad. "Which is what I am. Eat. No arguments. I can't have you passing out in the cave. I may be young at heart, but the idea of dragging you up steep cliffs and through twisting tunnels just doesn't appeal to these flabby muscles."

Matt glanced at Mr. Sachs as he plopped down in the chair and started eating. He didn't see an ounce of flab on the man. He tried to grimace as he chewed, but gave up trying to fool Sarah's dad as he shovelled spoonful after spoonful into his mouth. The thick porridge had been lightly sprinkled with cinnamon and brown sugar. It was delicious. It filled a hole in him that had been empty for years.

Mr. Sachs smiled as he slopped a spoonful into his own bowl. He sat down across from Matt. "Shall I don my chef's cap now?"

"I wouldn't go that far," said Matt, grinning. "But it's not bad." A ferocious yawn made him jerk his head up from his bowl.

The stairs protested as Sarah tramped down them, her russet hair tousled, her eyes cloudy. She looked from her father to Matt with arched eyebrows. "What are you doing here so early?" She stifled another yawn.

"Early to bed . . ." said Matt. "You know the saying."

"You may be healthy," said Sarah, smiling crookedly, "but you sure aren't wise."

"Really," said Matt. "Why do you say that?"

"Because you're still wearing your pajama top." She tugged on the Spiderman flannel that poked out of the sweatshirt he'd jammed on in haste.

Matt flushed. "Oh. I guess I was in a hurry."

"For what? We have all day."

"To get out from under—you know," he said. Except he shouldn't have.

Mr. Sachs's sharp gaze swung back and forth between Matt and Sarah. "Out from under what?" he asked.

"Under the covers," said Matt.

The man frowned. "Nadine does know that you're spelunking with us today, doesn't she?"

"Of course," said Matt, too quickly.

"Should I call her?" he asked. He rose from his chair and reached for the phone.

Matt jumped up from his own chair. "No, you can't. She sleeps in on Sundays. If you wake her up, she's like a bear."

Sarah bit her lip. Her eyes locked with her father's.

"I think," he said, "that we'd better stop by your house on our way out."

Matt's chest tightened in horror. "It's not a good idea," he said. "She's kind of scary when she gets up. Her hair's all over the place and the skin under her eyes is sort of pouchy."

"Matt," said Sarah.

"Her eyes are bloodshot and she's got a wicked temper. It's better if you just let her sleep. She won't mind if I go out. She's happier when

I'm gone anyway."

The creases in Mr. Sachs's forehead deepened with each word Matt said. "I see. Be that as it may, we need her permission. Don't worry. I can be very persuasive. And, can I give you a little advice? There's a word called 'diplomacy.' Try to be a little less honest when discussing your cousin with other people."

"Less honest?" said Matt.

"You must remember," said Sarah, "my dad's a politician."

"Oh. Gotcha," said Matt.

Mr. Sachs looked unimpressed. "Maybe I've been teaching you the wrong things," he said to Sarah. "Sit down and eat."

Sarah sat and obeyed. She protested just a little over the oatmeal—it wasn't her favourite—but clamped her lips when her father eyeballed her.

After breakfast Sarah went upstairs to get dressed. Her father cleaned up the dishes while Matt nibbled at his nails till he tasted blood. He tried to come up with some other excuse to avoid confronting Nadine, but his repertoire of lies was exhausted. When Sarah bounded down the stairs again, he was having trouble breathing.

"Ready?" asked her father.

Sarah nodded.

"Matt?"

"Uh-h no," he choked out.

"It'll be okay, Matt. Trust me," said Mr. Sachs.

After donning their coats, the trio slogged through the snow to Matt's house. Sarah and her father took the lead. Matt plodded behind, each step heavier as he approached the door. Mr. Sachs rang the doorbell three times before the curtains were thrust aside upstairs and a frightening face peered out. Matt had not exaggerated. Nadine's bulging bloodshot eyes peered through clots of tangled stringy hair. At first no recognition registered on her face. Then her eyes protruded even more. "Right down," she yelled.

At least ten minutes passed before she appeared at the door. Her hair had been brushed, makeup dabbed on, but she could do nothing about her red eyes.

"Donald, what brings you here?" She smiled, but as her gaze came to rest on Matt, there was fury in it.

"Nadine," said Sarah's dad. "We're on an expedition today. I just wanted to let you know where Matt was off to, so you wouldn't be worried."

Matt stared at Mr. Sachs. The man wielded diplomacy like it was a magic wand.

Nadine's eyes softened as she met the politician's.

"Expedition?" she inquired.

"Actually we're spelunking in some caves north of the city. Nothing dangerous, I assure you. I'll be with them the whole time."

"You'll be with them? Why that sounds quite exciting. In fact, *I* was quite a spelunker as a child."

"Were you?" he asked. "You'd be welcome to join us, if you like."

Matt blinked. The pressure in his chest grew as he saw exactly where this was heading. Sarah grimaced openly.

"Yes. Well, I'm not exactly dressed."

"We'll wait, of course," said Sarah's father.

"That would be wonderful," Nadine trilled. "Come in while I get changed. It sounds like an adventure. Had Matthew mentioned it yesterday, I would have had much more time to prepare. But I'll do my best to hurry."

She ushered them in and dashed upstairs. Mr. Sachs looked intently at Matt. Matt looked away.

"She wouldn't have let me go," he muttered.

"You didn't give her a chance," he said. "She might surprise you, you know."

Sarah scowled. "'You'd be welcome to join us, if you like?'" she mimicked. "Dad, ever the diplomat."

Her father lowered his head and growled, "You have to give people a chance, Sarah. She might be a lot of fun."

"Mom was a lot of fun, too," said Sarah, "but you dumped her."

"I didn't dump—" He gritted his teeth. "Things didn't work out, that's all. I was away too much. Your mother couldn't handle—"

"Couldn't handle me?"

"Of course not," he said. "She loves you."

"So much that she made me leave."

"Must we discuss this here? I'm sure your friend Matt is not interested in our personal matters."

Matt shrugged. He made his eyes wander, to give them some privacy, but he didn't really care.

"There," said Nadine, coming down the stairs. Sarah gaped. Mr. Sachs's eyes opened wide in appreciation. Nadine was dressed in jeans, a flannel shirt that still managed to hug her curves, and a faded jean jacket. Her face was slathered with makeup, which made her eyes looked haunted instead of tragic, her severe face softer instead of jagged. Her hair was swept back in a ponytail, and she had what looked like an authentic Indiana Jones hat on her head.

"You look like you're ready for a treasure hunt," said Sarah's father. "But I must warn you, the only treasure we're going to find is rock and bat guano."

Nadine's smile flickered, but it didn't go out. "Sounds interesting," she said. "Shall we?"

Mr. Sachs held Nadine's coat for her. Sarah scowled and turned away. As they headed out the door, Matt tried to reignite his initial thrill, despite being roped into inviting Nadine along. He doubted very much that she could keep up with them anyway.

Sarah still grumbled as she brought up the rear. "He'll just never understand. He's so bullheaded. Can't he just make it up to her?"

Matt swung around. "Maybe he can't. Did you ever consider that? At least you still have a father."

Sarah staggered back. "I . . . I . . . suppose you're right. I guess I'm lucky, eh?"

"Sure are," he muttered. "You could have been stuck with her." His thumb extended furtively towards Nadine who was just getting into the car.

Sarah agreed. "How are we going to keep her nose out of what we're doing? And how are we going to keep her greedy claws off my dad?"

"First things first," he said. "Let's get through the day."

In the car Nadine giggled and flirted incessantly in the front seat. Her hands kept fluttering onto Mr. Sachs's arm. Sarah's face turned an odd shade of olive. She flung her hand up to her mouth.

"Don't upchuck in my lap," whispered Matt.

She smiled and took a deep breath.

Matt returned a quick grin, then gazed out the window as they hurtled through downtown to cross the Ottawa River at the Mac-donald Cartier Bridge. When they reached the exit for the bridge near the Chateau Laurier Hotel, Sarah's father looked in the mirror and spoke to him.

"See the statue?" He pointed to the imposing figure of a man dressed in a seventeenth century tunic and sash, and holding a sextant in one hand. "Samuel de Champlain."

"Dad?" said Sarah.

He pretended he didn't hear her. "He was the first European to explore this region. He befriended the Algonquin people. Ottawa was named by the Algonquin, you know."

Sarah rolled her eyes.

"It was called *Odawa*, meaning 'traders.' That's what the French first did here, trade kettles and utensils for furs with the Algonquin. Champlain was scouting the land for riches and resources. He also made first contact with the aboriginal people of New York State, the Iroquois, although he decided to go to war against them because they were bitter enemies of the Algonquin."

"I know," said Matt.

"Really?" said Sarah's dad. "Do we have another student of history in the car?"

"Not exactly," said Matt. "I just know something about that stuff. You know, First Nations history." A lump formed in his throat when he thought about his father's book.

Sarah slipped him an understanding smile.

"That's great," said her father. "You've read up on it a bit?"

"And how," he said.

"Well, I'm glad someone in this car is interested in *local* history, rather than just European or African history." He looked pointedly at Sarah in the rearview mirror.

She shrugged.

The Saturn swung onto Sussex Street, where the Prime Minister and the Governor General resided in elegant stone mansions, and cruised towards the Ottawa River. The river swept from west to east separating the province of Ontario from the province of Quebec. At this time of year, a thick crust of ice covered the water and made it shimmer like a jewel. Across the river in Gatineau, the Museum of Civilization, a construction of glass and steel squares and triangles, reflected the stray beams of light that pierced the cloud ceiling. Its windows winked at them like a bewitched ice castle.

"Now just imagine the Algonquin traversing this river in their birch bark canoes," Mr. Sachs continued. "Over there—" he pointed to the boiling rapids half obscured by a dam upstream from Parliament Hill, "—an effigy of one of their sacred spirits, Nana'b'oozoo, presided over the river."

"I don't see anything," said Matt.

"That's because the city built a dam to harness the rapids' power. The backwash buried the figure."

"It seems sort of disrespectful," said Matt.

"You'd be the expert on that," whispered Sarah, smirking.

Matt ignored her. He stared at the rapids still rumbling through the river beyond the layer of ice. "What really happened to them all? The First Nations, I mean."

"Some still live around here, but many of them were killed by the Europeans. Surely you know this," said Sarah's father.

"I do. But it still doesn't make sense. If they were so fierce, why would they allow themselves to be wiped out?"

"It was the European diseases mostly. They had no immunity to them. So eventually there weren't enough of them left to fight. You must have read about the land grabs. The British, French, and Dutch governments bequeathed land that wasn't theirs to begin with to their citizens who settled here. They also forced many tribes to sign treaties that tricked them into giving up their rights to vast tracts of land, while they were pushed into tiny reservations. It's the saddest, cruelest part of our history."

Matt grimaced. "I remember reading that an Iroquois chief warned his people in the 1700s. He said, 'Can you not see that it makes no difference whether these white men are of the French or the English or any other of the peoples from across the sea? All of them threaten our very existence. All of them! When they came here they had nothing. Now, like a great disease they have spread all over the east until for twelve days' walk from the sea there is no room for an Indian to stay and he is made unwelcome. Yet this was not long ago all Indian land. How has it gone?'"

It grew strangely quiet. Matt looked up and noticed the others watching him with wide eyes.

"Did you memorize that?" asked Sarah.

"I . . . well, I read it a few times."

"Good for you," said Sarah's father. "I'm glad at least one young person has found the time to read about our land and feel compassion for the original people. It was a shame, what happened."

"Such a shame," said Nadine, piping up for the first time since Sarah's father had begun to talk about the First Nations.

Matt rolled his eyes. As if *she* would have sympathy for anyone.

They all fell into a heavy silence as the car rocketed over the bridge and left drowned Nana'b'oozoo behind. It careened over slushy highways and quickly climbed the snow-shrouded Gatineau Hills. Matt's gaze followed the bouncing trees and shifting shadows as the car bobbed up and down—like a roller coaster ride through a tunnel of dense branches. An hour later Sarah's dad turned down a snowy path through the woods to emerge in front of sheer rocky slopes. Sarah gripped Matt's hand, her eyes glittering with excitement. He smiled at her and didn't release her hand until the car came to a stop.

As soon as they got out of the car, a guide stepped from a shack at the base of the hill. He wore ski apparel and a miner's hat. He introduced himself as Guy.

"Great day for spelunking, *non*?" he said.

The kids nodded mutely. Nadine kept glancing at the hole in the mountain.

Guy shook Mr. Sachs's hand. "Great to see you again, Mr. Sachs. I'm glad you called yesterday. We don't have many reservations in winter, but it is well worth the trip out here."

"Yes," said Sarah's dad. "I'm sure it is. The kids are very excited."

Guy turned to Matt and Sarah. "You will not be disappointed. Now, we all must wear the *chapeau*." He pointed to his head, then motioned for them to follow him into the shack. He distributed miner's hats with headlamps to each of them and a heavy battery pack to wear like a backpack. Nadine had difficulty adjusting her chinstrap, so, of course, Sarah's dad had to gallantly step forward to help.

"It is very cold in the caves, especially in winter. You are all dressed warmly?" He surveyed the group critically, smiling and nodding at their ski jackets and double layers. When he got to Nadine, he frowned. "That does not look warm." He nodded at her jeans.

"They're a thick material," she explained, her nose jutting into the air. "I'll probably be warmer than you."

Guy elbowed Matt knowingly. "Never argue with a woman," he said, chuckling. "Let them find out for themselves."

Matt chuckled, too. "This might be fun."

Sarah sputtered out a laugh.

"What's the joke?" asked Nadine, rounding on them.

"Oh, nothing," said Sarah. "Just looking forward to this."

Nadine's eyes shifted back and forth, from Sarah to Matt. They shuffled uncomfortably under her gaze and could only escape it by looking into the woods. With one last withering glance, she grasped Mr. Sachs's arm as they proceeded to the wooden doors in the side of the mountain.

"What makes a cave?" asked the guide.

"Water," said Sarah. "I think."

Guy smiled. "Exactly. In what type of rock?"

This time Sarah looked stumped.

"Isn't it limestone?" asked Matt.

"Right," said Guy.

"But limestone's made from seashells," said Sarah. "There are only a few lakes around here."

Guy leaned forward as if to impart the closest-held secret in the world. "This used to be an inland sea."

"You're kidding," said Matt, studying the gigantic trees and well-established flora.

"We're talking millions of years. It created the limestone, which in turn, created the caves." He opened the doors, revealing a drafty tunnel six feet in height leading downward.

Matt tilted his head. Was this it? "It looks kind of small."

"You were expecting maybe the Mammoth Caves in Kentucky?"

Guy chuckled. "It was a small sea."

Sarah's dad placed his hand on Matt's shoulder and leaned down. "Smaller caves are more interesting. Only a true spelunker will crawl around on his hands and knees."

Matt looked at Nadine. He turned away to hide his grin. This was just too delicious. He couldn't wait to see her crawling around in a spider-infested bat-cave.

They entered the cave, headlights on. The walls were slick and smooth, shimmering in the odd spot with icicles and tiny crystalline sculptures created by the ever-present moisture. At first they could walk upright and admire the fairy-quality of the cave, but soon they found themselves ducking and walking hunched over as the tunnel narrowed and closed around them. The light from the entrance disappeared quickly as they penetrated deeper into the network and the air grew denser, mustier. Eventually they reached a shaft downward, shaped like a funnel, where a ladder had been fixed to assist in the descent. More icicles dangled from the ceiling here, and bulbous extrusions of limestone stippled the wall.

"Wow. Cool," said Matt.

"Yes, it is cool," said Guy with a grin. "But we must be cautious. It's a steep climb down."

He descended the ladder first, then gave a hand to the rest of the group. Sarah was thankful for his assistance when she nearly slipped off the ice-coated rungs. But when he steadied Nadine as she faltered on the ladder, she slapped his hand away in contempt.

"That's gratitude for you," Matt whispered to Sarah.

Nadine behaved quite differently to Sarah's father, though. When she teetered on the scattered rocks at the bottom, she clutched his hand. In fact, she sidled so close to him that Sarah dug her nails into Matt's arm.

"Ouch," he said.

"Oh, sorry," said Sarah.

"Everything okay?" asked her father. He slipped out of Nadine's pincers and turned around.

"Yeah," said Matt. "Just a spider bite."

"Spider?" said Nadine anxiously.

Guy waved his hand. "Harmless," he said. "They don't usually bite. They are . . ." He paused, searching for the word. He snapped his fingers. "Sluggish in the winter."

Nadine shuddered. She nestled closer to Mr. Sachs. Sarah scowled and shot a glance at Matt, who merely shrugged and tried to hide his grin.

"What's down those tunnels?" asked Matt, pointing to some tubules split off from the main cavern.

"Those are secondary shafts," said Guy. "A maze, really. Dangerous without a guide."

"And with a guide?" asked Matt.

"Well," said Guy, looking at Sarah's dad, "it's a belly-crawl in places."

Mr. Sachs scrutinized the tunnels, then looked at Nadine. "It might be difficult."

"Not for us, Dad," said Sarah. "We're tough."

Nadine, who'd been casting nervous glances all over the cave, probing every nook and cranny for a spider's nest, turned towards Sarah. She pressed her lips together. "Of course we can go. We've come this far."

"Are you sure?" asked Sarah's dad.

"Yes, Donald." Nadine mustered a partial smile.

"All right. Let's do it," he said.

"Yay!" shouted Matt and Sarah simultaneously. They both leaped for the nearest shaft.

Guy caught them by their coats. He yanked them backward. "Not that one, *mes amis*. You end up in the middle of the mountain and then you get lost forever."

Matt was undeterred. "Not a bad way to go."

"Only we're not *going* today," said Mr. Sachs. "You listen to Guy, or the only place you're going is home."

"Gotcha," said Matt, saluting.

They aimed for the left-hand tunnel, the one Guy indicated with his hand. Nearly giddy from exploring this otherworld, Matt eagerly scrambled behind Sarah on his hands and knees through the narrow shaft. It slithered left, then right, angled up, then down. Guy shouted at them to ignore the offshoots, branches that intersected with the main tunnel every other metre. Behind them, Nadine muttered curses as she scraped her knees or broke a fingernail. She screamed once when a spider dropped from the ceiling and landed in her hair.

"If only I had a video camera," he whispered, sharing quiet giggles with Sarah.

Their progress slowed as the tunnel tapered down to the size of a heating duct. Soon they were slithering through the cave like snakes, measuring distance in centimetres instead of metres. The rock closed around them like a fist. Matt's throat tightened in the confined space, but it was amazing, too, to wriggle like a bona fide caver into the heart of the mountain.

"Now listen, *mes amis*," said Guy, crawling right behind them. "At the end of the tunnel—"

A loud scream drowned out his words and nearly blew out their eardrums. "Oh no! What is that! It's a . . . snake! A snaaake!"

Sarah snorted. Matt hooted. He'd never heard Nadine freak out like this before. It was awesome! They both continued crawling as the tunnel expanded, belling outward and becoming broader and higher. Soon they could stand and walk again.

"It's okay, *Madame*. Stay calm." Guy tried to console the hysterical woman.

"This is incredible," said Sarah, looking back at Matt as she stepped forward. Matt's smile instantly fell as she dropped out of sight.

"Maaatt!" she shrieked.

He leaped towards her and jammed his runners into the rock. He'd come to the edge of a cliff and teetered there, as Sarah dangled from her fingertips on a narrow ledge sixty centimetres below him. Beneath her feet, a gaping black void waited to swallow her.

"Hang on!" he yelled. He called for help, but Guy and Sarah's father couldn't hear him over Nadine's screams. He braced himself against a rock and leaned over the side. "Grab my hands."

Sarah swung a hand up to grip Matt's. He caught it and hoisted her up, but her body scraped against the soft rock where Matt was standing. The limestone quivered, shuddered, then crumbled away.

"Oh noooo!" she screamed, as they both plunged downward.

9

Stalactites and Spears

SARAH SHOOK HER HEAD AND SAT UP. SHE TRIED TO LOOK AROUND, but it was as wholly dark as a black hole in space. What? Why? Maybe the light from her helmet had shattered, when it had crashed against the rock on the side of the cliff. And maybe Matt's had, too. Spikes of pain jabbed her just about everywhere, but her bones didn't crunch as she tried to move. Nothing broken, at least. When she probed beneath her, she found out why. A soft cushion of what felt like mud, but was probably bat guano, layered the ground in this section of the cave. They must have stumbled into a roosting area. Thank goodness, or they both might have been seriously injured or killed.

"Matt," she called anxiously. Matt groaned somewhere nearby. "Are you okay?"

"Okay?" he said groggily. "Define 'okay.'"

"Alive?"

"Barely."

"Able to speak?"

"Obviously."

"Able to move?"

"Not so sure."

Sarah crept towards the sound of his voice. She dusted the ground with her hands until she touched his torn and rumpled jacket. "Oh, there you are. Any broken bones?" She felt along his limbs until he swatted her away.

"Just bruised," said Matt. He sat up slowly. "I guess *you're* okay."

"Yes," said Sarah. "Lucky for us we landed on bat poop."

"Oh, that's what this is," said Matt. "Never thought I'd say I was lucky I landed in a pile of poop."

Sarah giggled. "Me neither."

"Sarah!" her father called from above. "Sarah, Matt, are you okay?"

A pencil of light penetrated the inky darkness over their heads. It revealed the dim outline of Matt minus his helmet. He must not have had it strapped on.

"Dad, I'm here." Sarah waved. "We're all right. We had a cushioned landing."

"That's a relief," he called down with a sigh. "Guy says we can't get you out from up here. We have to go around. What happened to your lights?"

"They must have broken." She touched the top of her helmet and discovered cracked plastic.

Some mumbling trickled down from above. Her father yelled, "We'd throw you down a flashlight, but Guy thinks it will break, too. Can you hang tight until we get there?"

"Sure, Dad. We're tough cookies."

"Well, I'm not," he said. "You scared me to death. I'll be right there." His voice faded. Sarah's chest grew tight as the light shrank and eventually blinked out. This left them in a total blackout.

"I hope it won't take them long," said Sarah.

"Not afraid, are you?" asked Matt.

"Me, afraid? Never." She gulped.

He clasped her hand and squeezed. "You're shivering."

"Just the cold."

Matt snuggled closer to her. He put his arm around her shoulders. It made her feel better but she couldn't suppress fear creeping down her spine.

"Do you feel eyes on us?"

"Now that you mention it."

"Hundreds of eyes?"

"It's a bats' nest, for goodness' sake."

Sarah chewed on her lip. "I guess they're not vampire bats."

"Your garden fruit variety."

"Harmless, right?"

"Of course."

She shivered again. "Well, I suppose we could search for your helmet. If the light still works, we'd be able to see something at least."

"And explore some more, too."

Sarah gave him a shove.

"Aren't you tired of exploring after falling off a cliff?"

"Never," said Matt. "I guess I have a little of my dad's blood in me, after all."

They hunted around on their hands and knees, feeling rocks and guano and a trickling stream, but no helmet. Matt's voice drew farther away, so Sarah hurried in his direction.

"Wait up," she called.

"I'm not going anywhere. Ow!"

"What?" asked Sarah, trying to peer through a wall of black for some sign of danger.

"I don't know. Something sharp." Matt had stopped, but Sarah didn't know it until she rammed into his back and sent him sprawling.

"Hey, watch out," said Matt, sitting up and spitting out what could only be bat droppings. "I really didn't want to eat this stuff."

"Sorry," said Sarah. "What was sharp?"

"Hold out your hand."

She did and Matt placed a stick in her hand. She ran her other hand over it. There were soft feathers on one end and a sharp triangular point at the other. "Arrow?"

"I think so," said Matt.

"Like in First Nations?"

"Well, they used to live here."

A wind swept through the cave, chilling Sarah's face. "I wonder where that wind came from?"

Matt didn't answer.

"I mean, it's strange, you know, so deep in a cave, to have such a strong wind."

Matt stayed quiet.

"Matt?"

The silence was tomblike.

"Yoo-hoo." Sarah reached out. She swirled her hand in empty space. Suddenly she shrank back as a light appeared in the dark cave—a pearly pale light that swelled into a gigantic sphere. It encased Matt.

His eyes bulged; his mouth formed an oval that looked like a scream, although no sound escaped.

Then the silence snapped, like a tree hit by lightning. Wild chants and shrieks flooded the cave. A swarm of First Nations people emerged from the shadows, unleashing arrows into the sphere. This time she heard Matt screaming. The sound knifed into her heart. And there was blood, so much blood—

The bubble burst.

"Matt!" she cried, her voice echoing madly off the cavern walls.

"What?" he said.

"Are you okay?" She dropped the arrow. Desperately, she probed and prodded the soft earth until she found him. "Are you hurt? Are you bleeding?"

"No," said Matt. "Are you nuts?"

"Don't make fun of me, Matt," she said. "You weren't here two seconds ago. When you were, you were in that bubble, like the one in your dad's lab. There were First Nations people everywhere. You were bleeding . . . all over. . . ."

Matt grabbed her arm even as she still frantically searched his body for penetrating wounds. "I'm okay," he said. "Maybe you were dreaming."

"It was no dream."

"Then maybe you hit your head when you fell."

"Matt, it was real. I saw it. I heard them."

"There are no First Nations people in here, Sarah." He gently released her arm.

Sarah fell silent. Finally she said what she'd held back since they'd met. "Matt, that bubble follows you around."

"What?"

"A car passed right through you, and I saw it then. When we opened your father's lab, it was there. And now, you were in it."

"What the heck does that mean?"

"It means that you're connected to your father's invention. Whether it's a spirit or your father himself, whether in the future, the past, or the present, *it's with you*. Maybe even *part of you*. And it scares me. It scares me to death."

Matt didn't reply. At first Sarah was afraid he'd disappeared again. "Matt?"

"I'm still here. Do you think," he said, taking a deep breath, "that my father's protecting me?"

"I hope so. But what I saw today didn't look like protection."

"A warning, maybe? If he knows the past, maybe he knows the future."

"The future? What does the future have to do with First Nations?"

"They're still around. There's reservations not too far from here."

"Maybe some First Nations people are still around, but they're not dressed in feathers and buckskin. They don't carry bows and arrows."

Matt shook his head. "I don't get it, then."

"Neither do I," said Sarah.

The gloom gave way to a piercing light. Sarah leaped backward, terrified it was a repeat episode of the bubble attack. She stumbled over some rocks and crashed to the ground.

"Sarah!" shouted her father. "Are you there?"

"Here, Dad," she said, scrambling to her feet. She waved with one hand and shielded her eyes with the other, so she could see the advancing rescue party. Three human shapes with bobbing lights approached. She eagerly stepped forward, but flinched as something sharp jabbed into her foot.

"Ouch!"

She bent down. The arrow jutted from the sole of her boot. "Not this thing again." She wrenched it out and whisked it up to the light. A droplet of blood trickled down the head.

"Sarah," said her father as he swept into the cavern. "Sweetheart."

She looked up, about to cast the arrow aside, when the third person in the rescue party stepped around Guy. It wasn't Nadine. It was a black-braided, fur-wrapped member of the First Nations.

"Sarah, this is Chief Annawan. He's an Algonquin . . ."

Her knees buckled. The world went black again.

10

More Visions

SARAH BLINKED. HER FATHER'S WORRIED FACE LOOKED DOWN AT HER, and a wave of relief washed through her. He was patting her hand.

"Are you sure she's awake?" asked Matt, giving her face a playful tap.

"Hey," said Sarah. "Have you been slapping me to wake me up?"

Matt chuckled. "I suggested it, but your dad wouldn't let me."

Sarah tried to sit up, but her head still spun like a wobbly wheel, so she sank back down. She shivered in the damp, frigid air, which sent slivers of pain shooting through her foot. "I thought I saw a First Nations person," she muttered.

"You did," said her dad. "He's gone back down the tunnel because he thought he might have frightened you, although I can't imagine why. I thought you'd be thrilled to meet an aboriginal person from this region. He's one of the guides here at the caves. When he heard about your fall, he offered to help. I've been told that he knows these caves better than Guy."

"Oh," said Sarah. "I feel a little silly."

"It's not really her fault," said Matt. "We found an arrow. Then Sarah had some weird dream."

"Dream?"

"Something about arrows and First Nations warriors. Maybe she hit her head when she fell."

Her father's lips pulled taut. He inspected Sarah's head but found no break or bump. "We'll have to get you checked out," he said.

"Aw, Dad. I'm okay, really."

"Just the same, I don't like the sound of this."

Sarah glared at Matt.

"You do realize, sweetheart, that the First Nations don't shoot arrows anymore. And when they did, they were just hunting or defending their land. Let's get you out of here."

He put a protective arm around Sarah and helped her to her feet. "I'm okay, Dad. I can walk by myself." She tried to disengage his arm from her shoulder, but he held fast.

They hobbled out of the cavern, Guy leading the way. He seemed very quiet.

"It was our own fault," said Matt, loud enough for Guy to hear.

"What?" asked her father.

"The fall. We weren't looking where we were going. We were listening to Nadine panic, and we were stupid. We promise we'll be more careful next time."

"There won't be a next time," he said.

"But—" said Matt.

"I don't like this cave," said Sarah. "I think it's haunted."

Her dad frowned.

As they walked, the path seemed to broaden and heighten. They stepped into an amphitheater with what looked like glittering chandeliers dangling from the ceiling. Sarah stopped and gazed around her. Matt paused and spun a 360-degree circle, open-mouthed.

Pearly white stalactites dripped from the ceiling in waxy cones. Stalagmites extended spindly fingers from the rocky ground. Everything glistened with a thin layer of condensation, reflecting the beams of the flashlights and bathing the cave in a soft glow. A burbling stream rushed through the centre, carving a new path in the limestone. It was a spelunker's dream come true.

"This is amazing," said Matt.

"I guess it's not such a bad cave, after all," said Sarah.

"It is incredible, isn't it?" said her father. "On my first rush through here I really didn't care to appreciate it. And I still think we'd better get Sarah to a hospital."

"Hospital? Dad, that's crazy. There's nothing wrong with me."

"You're limping."

"That's because I stepped on an arrow."

"You stepped on *what*? Let me see."

Sarah rolled her eyes and pulled off her boot. She steadied herself on her father's arm as she lifted her foot for him to examine it. "It's just a scratch," she said.

"Looks more like a gash. Where is this arrow?"

"I think I dropped it when I fainted."

"Well, it must have been pretty sharp to penetrate your boot."

Her father opened his pack and withdrew a first aid kit. He sat Sarah on a rock and wrapped her foot.

"Is everything all right?" boomed a voice from the other side of the cave. Chief Annawan stepped into the dazzling light of reflections.

Sarah started, but she was determined not to faint again.

"Much better," said her dad. "Sarah seems to have stepped on an arrow."

"Yes," said the chief. "I saw it on the ground where she fell." He turned to the side, revealing a Roots backpack cinched over his fur coat. It looked so out of place, yet the arrow he held up did not. "Must be three, maybe four hundred years old. And not a scratch on it." He spun it around in his hand. The feathers fanned out at an angle like the wings of an aircraft. "Very unusual."

Sarah's father had finished wrapping her wound. He gingerly slid the boot over her foot before he stood up to examine the culprit. First he studied the wood of the shaft. Then he inspected the gleaming copper head. "I thought most Algonquin used flint arrowheads."

"Some chiefs traded for copper with the Ojibwa," said Annawan.

"Interesting," he said. "But this wood looks almost new."

"Like it was made yesterday," said the chief.

"Is it a fake?"

Annawan shook his head. "Algonquin to the letter. Not something we make for souvenirs today. The real thing."

Matt sighed. He sank down to the rock beside Sarah. "Hey, I could use a Coke."

Sarah's dad smiled. "We all could. You seem to have stumbled onto a mystery, but it can't be solved today. We'd better head home."

Matt readily agreed and sprang to his feet. He helped Sarah stand with a supporting arm around her shoulders. Sarah was having trouble digesting the enigma of the arrow. She couldn't take her eyes off the chief. His ebony braided hair and fur-clad body made her quake. His soft chocolate eyes did nothing to dispel the images in her mind—the arrow in his hand even less so. She had to get out of here.

Sarah grabbed Matt's hand and tugged him towards the wide mouth of the cave that opened up at the head of a steady incline. Thin threads of light penetrated the gloom, giving an impression of the world outside, maybe even sunlight. What she wouldn't give to feel sunlight on her face again. This chilly cave and its weird secrets made her feel like she was coated in ice.

Guy strode alongside them, still wearing a worried frown. Her father trotted behind, his breath hot on Sarah's neck. He'd be hovering over her all week after this. The chief didn't join them. He must have stayed behind to continue his examination of the arrow.

They emerged higher on the cliff face than they'd entered. Blessed sun shone all around, making the snowy landscape shimmer. Forest matted the land below, wrapping its wild arms around rivers and lakes. Up here on the rock, where the world opened up, Sarah could finally breathe again. She was so relieved she almost threw herself into Nadine's arms, but she caught herself just in time.

"Oh, dear," said Nadine. "Are you all right? I was so worried, but I couldn't bring myself to go back in there again." Her eyelashes trapped crystal snowflakes, which melted down her cheeks in tiny streams. Sarah wasn't fooled. Even more disturbing was how the false sympathy seemed directed all her way. Not a word or expression of concern for Matt. He'd fallen off a cliff and Nadine didn't even care.

"Let's get out of here," said Sarah.

"I agree," said her dad.

Matt braced Sarah nobly as they hobbled down the steep path.

He held the door open for her and helped her into the car. Her father smiled as he suppressed his own paternal urges.

As Matt sat down beside her, Sarah grinned feebly. "I thought chivalry was dead."

"I'm no knight," said Matt. "I'm just worried."

"You don't believe me, do you? I mean, you think I hit my head."

"I don't know. It would make more sense."

Sarah leaned closer. "Tell me that that thing in your dad's laboratory makes sense."

"All right. I'll give you that one."

Sarah met his gaze, then felt other eyes drilling into her. She looked up. Nadine had just gotten into the front of the car and was staring intently at her. The woman's eyes had narrowed until the crow's feet around them seemed ready to walk away.

"Yes?" asked Sarah.

"Just wondering what you're whispering about," said Nadine.

"Nothing," she replied.

Matt's jaw hardened.

Sarah's dad squeezed into the driver's side of the Saturn and started the car. As he began driving down the snowy lane, Nadine said, "Secrets can be dangerous things. They can lead to accidents."

"That's right," said her father, focused on the road, unaware of the look on Nadine's face. "We don't want any more of those, do we?"

Sarah met Nadine's eyes. "Is that a threat?"

Her dad coughed. "Sarah, how ridiculous . . ."

"Of course not, dear. It's just a warning, something every good parent should give."

"Ha!" said Matt. He coughed and cleared his throat as Nadine's glare lanced through him.

Nadine turned around gradually, like the second hand of a clock. Matt fell into convulsions on the back seat, but Sarah failed to see the humour in it. "This is no joke, Matt," she said.

Matt swallowed his laughter, shrugged, and looked out the window. Sarah looked out the other side. A few birds fluttered by in the woods, flashing brilliant feathers of yellow and blue. A trio of crows sat on a wire—not a good omen. A deer shot out of the forest like a fully-flung javelin and leaped right in front of their car. Her father slammed on the brakes, skidding from side to side on the narrow road, and came to a stop. Somehow, the doe managed to bound across without being hit.

What her father didn't see—what no one seemed to notice except Sarah—was the tall young warrior who sprang after it. He drew back his arrow—a fine new arrow with fleecy feather tufts and a smooth shaft—and let it fly. The arrow arced, then angled down and penetrated the deer's soft belly. She bleated as she fell, dying, but the warrior wasn't finished. He turned in their direction, searching for new quarry. He found it sitting peacefully beside Sarah in the back seat. Matt studied the doe's path into the forest. He didn't seem to notice the carcass it had become. His eyes seemed glazed; his skin translucent. The backseat swirled in a fuzzy haze.

"Matt, watch out!" cried Sarah. She dived on top of him. The arrow zinged past her ear and flew out the opposite window. Matt squirmed underneath her, but she held him down. A car door clicked open, and then another. A strong pair of hands grabbed her coat from behind and dragged her outside.

"No, you can't!" she screamed. "They're going to kill him!"

Her father wrapped his arms around her, holding her tight as she struggled. The world became grey, then black.

"Daddy," she whispered. "Save Matt."

She slumped in his arms, unconscious.

11

What Really Happened

SARAH AWOKE IN A BRIGHTLY-LIT HOSPITAL ROOM BENEATH PRISTINE starched sheets. The smell of disinfectant filled the air, making her feel like gagging.

"Where . . . ?"

"You're in the hospital, sweetheart." Her father's face shone like an angel's over her bedside, or was he simply haloed by the fluorescent light above him?

"Dad? What am I doing here?" She looked in dismay at the bed opposite her. A bandage-clad girl lay in it with her left leg elevated in traction. "We weren't in an accident, were we?"

"Not a car accident, Sarah. Do you remember the cliff?"

"How could I forget it?" The fog in her brain retreated as her memory of the trip home suddenly became crystal clear.

"Matt!" She grabbed her father's shirt. "Where's Matt?"

"He's at home. He was here for hours, but they had you sedated, so I thought he should get some rest."

"You can't leave him alone, Dad. He's in danger."

"From whom, Sarah?" he said firmly. "He's safe in his own bed."

"Th-the First Nations, of course."

Her father shook his head. He smoothed her hair and kissed her forehead. "No one's going to harm Matt. Trust me."

Although still unconvinced, Sarah let go of her father. No one had seen what she'd seen. She must sound insane to her dad. The more she persisted, the more chance the doctors would call it a delusion and keep her locked up for good. Even scarier, maybe she was crazy.

"When can I go home?" she asked.

"Not for a while. I've asked some specialists to look at you."

"You mean shrinks?"

"They're called psychiatrists. And yes, along with a neurologist."

Sarah bit her lip. "You won't let them drug me, will you?"

"Of course not," said her dad. "They're just going to check out your noggin. Then we can go home."

"And I can see Matt?"

"Yes. Let me assure you, there wasn't a scratch on him when I dropped him off."

She sighed as she drifted into a peaceful sleep again. She should call Matt first, just to be sure, but she was too tired.

Sarah spent two days going through CT scans and MRIs. The doctors quizzed her and showed her ink blots to determine her mental status. Much to Sarah's surprise, they pronounced her sane. Matt had visited her twice, so she knew he was all right. She didn't discuss the visions with him either. She thought it best to erase them from her memory, although that was easier said than done. Only one thing disturbed her more than the visions she'd had—a phone call from her mother.

The phone had rung between scans the day before. She'd picked it up and was happy to hear her mother's cultured voice.

"Sarah, sweetheart! I heard you had an accident."

"Yeah, Mom. I had a little fall in a cave."

"My goodness. What was your father thinking of, taking you into a dangerous cave?"

Sarah winced at her mother's tone. "It wasn't really Dad's fault. I was sort of careless. Anyway, I'm doing okay now. Are you going to come up and visit?"

"Dear, I would love to, but I have mountains of work to do. We're getting the spring and summer fashion line-up ready for showing. Your father called me to let me know that you were in the hospital. If it were serious, I'd be there in a flash. But he assured me that you're fine."

"But, Mom. I miss you."

"I miss you, too, sweetheart."

"And I want to come home." Tears welled up in her eyes.

"Oh, um . . . I know it's been hard. It's an adjustment. But I think you have to give it more time."

"Mom . . . ?"

"It would just be too difficult here for you. I've been working until ten or eleven at night. I wouldn't have the time to spend with you that you need. Dad was always there to help you with your homework and make supper before he became an MP and had to travel to Ottawa. I'm sorry, Sarah. It's just not possible."

"Why is it possible for Dad to be a single parent, but not you?"

"Don't be silly, dear. He's always had more time than I have.

Now I have to go. There are clients on the other line. But I'm so glad to hear that you're all right. Love you."

"Sure," she said. "Bye."

The line clicked hollowly. Sarah swiped at her tears, all the anger and hurt of the past year resurfacing. She was stuck here. Her mother didn't want her. She couldn't even come to visit while Sarah was in the hospital. She threw the phone down on the night table in disgust.

That night she had trouble sleeping, but she tried her best to fake it when the nurse did her rounds. The next day was torture, as she kept mulling over the conversation. But eventually, she decided to thrust it from her mind. Stranger things were happening here and she should focus on them.

Her father picked her up on Wednesday morning when the doctors signed her release papers. She skipped school that day. He played hooky from Parliament. She loved her dad dearly, but his hovering was darned annoying. On Thursday, she insisted on going to school. Even Madame Leblanc was better than this constant pampering. Her dad reluctantly agreed. But he insisted on dropping her off at the door, so she didn't walk with Matt. She ignored the stares and whispers as she entered the classroom. Madame Leblanc nodded pleasantly to her. Sarah slipped past Matt with a sidelong wink, slid into her seat and turned towards him.

"Hi," she said.

"Hi yourself," said Matt, grinning. "You look like a ghost."

"I saw one," said Sarah, the ghost of a smile on her face.

Matt chuckled. "Hey," he said, leaning forward. "When are we going to break into the lab again?"

Ice prickled through Sarah's skin. "I don't know if that's a good idea anymore."

Matt's face fell. "I know you've been sick, but this is important."

"I know it is, but after what happened and Nadine's threat—"

"What *really* happened?" he asked.

Would he understand? Did *she* even understand? "We'll talk about it later," she whispered as Madame eyed them sternly.

The morning dragged on. The weather had turned mild, and it was raining, so they were forced to spend recess indoors. Madame insisted they read or do homework, and keep silent. It wasn't until lunchtime that Matt brought up the weird stuff again.

"Okay," he said, munching on his ham sandwich. "Tell me what happened to you."

"I don't know," said Sarah. "Maybe nothing. Maybe everything. A premonition or an omen. Something bad, whatever it was. Matt, I really saw a First Nations person outside the window in the car. He was shooting at you again. I like adventure as much as the next girl, but I don't want to see anyone die. Especially you."

Matt grinned and grabbed her hand. He didn't care that half the class was watching and giggling. Sarah did, but she ignored them. She squeezed his hand back.

"I'm not going to die," said Matt firmly.

"Your dad might have."

"Yeah," said Matt. "Maybe. But I'm not my dad."

Sarah took a deep breath. This probably wasn't the right place to discuss this, but she had to know. "Matt, I think it's time you told me the truth."

Matt wrinkled his forehead as if the concept was confusing. "Truth?"

"About the car and the bubble. About you."

He looked down and ran nervous fingers over his desk. When he met her eyes again, he nodded as if he'd finally admitted something to himself. "All right. The thing is, sometimes I do have these weird feelings, like I'm not real."

Sarah tilted her head. "Go on."

"It's like I look at myself and my body is all fuzzy. When things happen—" He stopped and grimaced as if what he had to say was just too crazy to put into words. She knew the feeling.

"Like the car," she prompted.

"Like the car. I black out."

"You don't remember what happens?"

"More than that. It's like I'm not there. I'm somewhere else."

"Where else?" asked Sarah.

Matt chuckled. "It's just so crazy."

Sarah leaned forward. "Tell me."

"Atlantis," he said. "Egypt. Alberta."

"Alberta?"

"In the Jurassic period. At least I think it's Alberta, 'cause of the number of dinosaurs. It's only a glance, anyway. Just for a second. I really am seeing the strangest things."

"What about First Nations people?"

"No," said Matt. "Nobody like that."

Sarah caught a flash out of the corner of her eye. Chelsea had stretched her skinny neck and red head awfully close to their desks. She scowled at her, and Chelsea retracted her head like a turtle.

After that, the afternoon seemed incredibly long. She yawned through geometry and napped through Shakespeare. The only time she perked up was when Mr. Fletcher continued his history lesson on Samuel de Champlain and the Algonquin Nation.

"As I mentioned before, the Algonquin were at war with the Iroquois," said Mr. Fletcher. He wrote the word "Algonquin" on the board. He scratched some arrows, extending from it.

"Weren't they the First Nations people who shot me?" Matt whispered in Sarah's ear.

"Not funny," she whispered back.

"They enlisted Champlain in attacks against the Iroquois." He drew a line to the word "Iroquois."

"Maybe they thought I was Iroquois."

"Stop it, Matt."

"But they weren't accustomed to the organized attacks that Champlain tried to employ, so despite now having the French and some guns, they didn't win every battle. Eventually, the Dutch and British supplied the Iroquois with firearms and they began to push the Algonquin even farther back," Mr. Fletcher droned on.

"See, they got creamed."

"Before this time, the Iroquois had banded together as the Five Nations, a confederacy of tribes who wanted peace—the Mohawk, the Oneida, the Cayuga, the Onondaga, and the Seneca—actually forming a blueprint for the confederacy of the United States. But they couldn't come to terms with the Algonquin—they were always at war."

"And they just keep coming," said Matt.

Sarah couldn't suppress a giggle.

Mr. Fletcher stopped. "Is there something you would like to share with the class?" He locked eyes with Matt.

"No," said Matt, meeting the teacher's stern gaze.

"Miss Sachs?"

"No, Mr. Fletcher," said Sarah softly.

"They were talking about the First Nations people who attacked Matt," Chelsea piped in from across the aisle. "The ones that Sarah keeps seeing outside her window." She tossed her head at Sarah.

All the other students in the class hooted. Sarah opened her mouth, then slunk down in the chair. Her face flushed as she blinked back tears.

Mr. Fletcher cleared his throat. "Well, it seems that my history lessons have been making some impact. But now we'll return to the war between—"

Chelsea, usually the model of cooperation, was not ready to let it go. "Look, Sarah. Arrows. Outside the window. Everyone duck!"

The students shrieked and dove for cover. The cacophony rattled the windows. *How could she? The witch!* Sarah wanted to grab her backpack and stomp out the door, but that would bring phone calls and questions and maybe more doctors. She wiped her eyes and rode out the laughter. Eventually it died down, but as she turned to look at Matt, she caught him in the act of snapping an elastic band across the room, where it whacked a student in the back of the head. She smiled. A valiant effort at revenge. But Chelsea wasn't finished yet. She'd saved her final nastiness for the next day.

12

The Unauthorized Visitor

FRIDAY MORNING, SARAH WALKED WITH MATT TO SCHOOL. THEY TRIED to keep a distance between them, so they wouldn't be jeered as they crossed the schoolyard. Luckily the bell rang before anyone could start harassing them. As they entered the classroom, Madame Leblanc moved to one side of her desk to let them pass. Behind her, between the chalk and brush on the ledge of the board, rested an arrow. Sarah gasped and shook her head. "Matt," she choked.

"I see it," he said.

She staggered to her desk and clutched it to keep steady. A hoarse snigger came from the desk opposite her. She turned. Chelsea smirked and drew her hands back across a toy bow.

"Are you going to faint, Sarah?"

Sarah grabbed for the bow. "You evil witch!"

Chelsea clung to it, stubbornly refusing to let go. The two had a tug-o-war until Madame Leblanc marched down the aisle. She wrenched the bow from their hands. "I really think this is quite enough," she said. "Chelsea, did you bring this into school?"

"*Oui, Madame,*" said Chelsea, bowing her head.

"This was not very nice."

"It was only a joke," said Chelsea.

"It is something Monsieur Barnes would do."

"I would never," said Matt, protesting a little too loudly. Madame gave him a severe look that stopped him short. "Well, I wouldn't," he whispered.

"I know," Sarah whispered back.

"How could you compare me to that . . . that insect?" said Chelsea.

"How could you be so cruel?" asked Madame.

"I . . . didn't . . . mean," Chelsea whimpered. "I didn't think. . . ."

"Indeed you didn't," said Madame. "All right, then." She turned to walk back to the front.

"That's it?" Sarah burst out, her face burning. "We get detentions. She gets '*all right?*'"

Madame Leblanc swung around. "That will be quite enough, Sarah."

"But it's not fair. Something like this should at least get a blackboard full of '*I'm an idiot in a world full of prodigies.*'"

"You are not the teacher," said Madame. "Besides, Chelsea is not an *idiote.*"

"Could have fooled me," said Matt.

"Monsieur Barnes, I did not ask for your opinion. If you don't keep out of this, you will be heading for—"

"Detention. I know."

Sarah shook her head. "I don't understand this."

"*Assois-toi!*" said Madame.

Sarah took a deep breath.

"Sit down!" Madame repeated.

Sarah sank into her seat, her mouth clamped shut. At the same instant, the national anthem began to play. The entire class stood at attention except for Sarah. She remained seated, slumped in her chair with her arms crossed, daring the teacher to challenge her again. But Madame Leblanc ignored her. She looked flustered, fingers fluttering over her hair and face, like when she'd argued with Matt, but Sarah felt no pity for her this time. After the anthem finished, Madame immediately began the lesson without reviewing their homework from the previous day as was customary.

Sarah sat through the hour with her arms crossed, not taking notes, just glowering at her teacher. When she got tired of glowering, and Madame ignoring her, she looked outside. The rain had stopped overnight, the fields and trees had frozen into an eerie kingdom of ice sculptures, and now snow sailed past in a blind sweep with the wind. Drifts were piling up fast over the road and sidewalks. Maybe the students would be sent home early for a snow day. That was her only hope of salvation.

The wind picked up the snow and hurled it against the glass, periodically erasing Sarah's view of a nearby spruce tree. Suddenly she saw a shape in front of the tree. It was covered in fur like a bear, but black braids protruded from beneath the hood. It couldn't be.

"Matt," she whispered.

Madame Leblanc paused in her lecture and frowned.

"What?" he whispered back, frowning as well, but directly at the teacher.

"Look out the window," she said.

Chelsea smirked across the aisle. Matt glared at her before he looked.

"Am I seeing things again?" Sarah asked.

"Lots of snow," said Matt. He squinted and fed a hand through his hair. "You may be right. But he's not going to shoot me, so don't worry." He patted her shoulder.

"How can you be so sure?"

"Because that's Chief Annawan."

"Really?" She studied his shape, distinguishing a tan face and trim body under the skins. He did look familiar.

Madame Leblanc paused again. "The whispering must stop," she snapped.

Sarah turned towards the front. "So should the cruel jokes."

Madame's eyes bulged from their sockets. Sarah thought they might pop out with the slightest whack to her back. "Mademoiselle Sachs is learning lessons from Monsieur Barnes in rude behaviour."

Sarah folded her arms in front of her. "Mademoiselle Sachs is only interested in justice."

Madame Leblanc shook her head. "This is unacceptable. Totally unacceptable. I will have to—"

"Chelsea," said Matt. "Look out the window."

Chelsea scowled, but she did look. It would have been impossible not to. Her eyes expanded, like two inflating sticks of bubble gum. Her mouth dropped open; her muscles tensed. The fur-framed face was two centimetres from the glass. "No," she whispered. "It can't be."

"I don't think he wants to shoot us," said Matt. "But I wouldn't blame him for shooting you."

Chelsea jumped off her seat. She stumbled over the seat behind, toppling a couple of desks and sending some students sprawling to the floor. She came to rest on the floor herself, and stayed there, looking petrified.

"What is happening?" cried Madame Leblanc. She turned to the window. "Oh," she said. "Who is that?"

Chief Annawan had pressed his leathery face against the pane as snow swirled around him. Sarah met Matt's eyes. They couldn't suppress their giggles.

"This is not funny," said Madame Leblanc. "We have a stranger peering in our window. I think I should call the office."

"No," said Sarah. "We know him."

"Actually, I think he's cold," said Matt. "We should let him *in*." He jumped up from his desk and hustled to the door.

"Monsieur Barnes. Don't you dare!" said Madame, her face flushed cherry-red.

Matt was already gone.

"I don't believe this," said the teacher, squeezing out from behind her desk. "It's not safe to let strangers in. Why will that boy never listen to me?"

Within seconds Matt returned, towing Chief Annawan with him. The Algonquin entered the chaos of the room with an air of complete calm. He walked over to Sarah, lifted the upended chair across from her and eased his large frame into the small chair without a crack in his dignity. He shrugged the fur coat from his shoulders.

"Do not be afraid," he said softly.

Sarah attempted a smile as the room settled down. "I'm not," she whispered.

Chelsea rose from the floor and brushed herself off. "I'm not afraid," she said. "You're just a man in a costume."

Annawan looked at her. "*You* should be afraid. I am Algonquin, and you have insulted me and upset my friends with your petty bow and arrow joke."

Chelsea stepped back. She sucked in some air.

"You should show more respect." His eyes narrowed.

Chelsea's lips quivered as she backed up another step. She squeaked like a mouse, then turned and bolted out the door.

The chief nodded. "Better, Sarah?"

"Yes, thank you," she said.

"The least I could do."

Madame Leblanc, who'd remained poised at the front of the room, her face crushed in a frown, hesitantly stepped forward. "I'm sorry to be abrupt, but guests need to sign in at the office and clear it with me to visit the classroom."

Annawan waved his hand at her, still looking fixedly at Sarah. "I'm sure the right honourable Member of Parliament, Mr. Donald Sachs, would be happy to provide you with a reference, but I'd hate to bother him when this will only take a minute."

Madame Leblanc huffed, but she settled herself in her chair and held her tongue.

The chief leaned forward. He clasped Sarah's hand. "I know the arrow was a shock, but you have nothing to fear."

"But Matt?"

Annawan shifted his gaze to Matt. "Matt looks fine to me."

"You don't understand."

"Oh, but I do. You've seen visions. Can you tell me about them?"

Sarah took a deep breath. "I've seen warriors," she said, "attacking Matt."

"Describe them."

Sarah described the buckskin-clad warriors with crimson and black war paint who'd fired flint-tipped arrows at her friend.

Annawan raised his eyebrows. "What about their hair?"

Sarah paused. Why would he ask that?

"Were they in braids like mine?" He pulled a tightly wound braid out in front of him.

"N . . . no. I don't think so."

Annawan stayed quiet, waiting.

"They had half their heads shaved. They had mohawks."

"Exactly," said Annawan. "They *were* Mohawks. Part of the Iroquois or the Five Nations, as your most knowledgeable professor has told you." He pointed at the board where Mr. Fletcher's history lesson had not yet been erased from the day before. "*People of the Flint*, as they liked to call themselves. Our warriors did sometimes shave their heads and stiffen their hair with grease so that it spiked up, in times of war, but if these men were on the warpath in *this* region, they weren't Algonquin."

Sarah chewed on her lower lip. "So the warriors were Mohawk?"

"Yes." Annawan smiled.

Matt met Sarah's eyes. He cocked his head to one side. "What difference does it make if they were Mohawk or Algonquin?"

"Nothing anymore. The Mohawk are often on the warpath with the government nowadays—like the Oka crisis when they stood against the desecration of their burial ground with a golf course. But now they use guns, not arrows. And I don't imagine they'll bother with you. You have nothing to worry about." The Chief smiled again.

"Ah, okay," said Matt. "They're Mohawk and that's that. It explains everything. Except *it doesn't explain anything!*"

Sarah touched his shoulder to calm him. Matt took a deep breath.

"It doesn't explain Sarah's visions. It doesn't explain the arrows. It doesn't explain my getting skewered."

Annawan sighed. "It's always so difficult to understand from your scientific viewpoint. Theory and logic must explain everything in this world. Some things you have to accept on faith.

"Obviously what you saw, my dear, wasn't real, or at least not currently real. Some people believe that you can connect with a disturbed spirit, or even have visions from residual imprints in the land—spirits of an ancient battle that remain behind—but what you saw were Mohawk or *cannibal* warriors, if you will. Not the nicest translation, I know. It was just an odd Algonquin name that stuck, when we weren't too fond of each other. We used to call them *dog meat*, too, when we were at war."

"So you think she was seeing the Mohawk on the warpath years ago?" asked Matt.

"Possibly. In the past the Mohawk did attack the Algonquin in this region. I thought at first that the arrow was Algonquin, but I was wrong. And it can't be from modern times, although it is a bit of an enigma. If you saw a vision of a centuries-old battle, triggered by falling on the arrow, then that's likely all it was. It can't harm you today." The chief placed his hand on Sarah's shoulder.

"Or Matt?" asked Sarah.

Annawan laid his other hand on Matt. Then he dropped his hands abruptly and rose from the chair.

"Wait," said Sarah, rising too, and touching his sleeve. "Why did I see it and not Matt?"

Annawan leaned down and whispered, "Perhaps you have a gift."

He paused for a fleeting second. "Or you are one to someone else." He winked surreptitiously at Matt.

The Algonquin straightened, smoothed out the ripples in his fur coat and walked briskly towards the door. But he paused at the threshold and swivelled back on the heel of his Kodiak boot. Madame Leblanc watched with wide eyes as he strode to the front of the class. At the blackboard, he pulled down the map that was dangling halfway over the history lesson. It showed the St. Lawrence and Ottawa River region.

Annawan seized a marker from Madame's desk. He drew a line through the words Quebec and Ontario. He wrote "Tenakiwin." For New York State, he added "Kanienke." He stroked out the word "Algonquin" on the board and inserted "Kichisippirini—The People of the Great River" and "Anishnabe—The Original People." For "Iroquois," he wrote "Five Nations" and replaced "Mohawk" with "Kanienkehaka—People of the Flint." At the section of the Ottawa River below Parliament Hill he spelled "Asticou—Boiling Kettle." He drew an effigy of a stone-faced giant in the centre and called it "Nana'b'oozoo."

"The Algonquin sacred spirit," he said. He glowered at Madame Leblanc and added in a growl, "Your government has desecrated a holy land."

Madame's hand flew to her breast.

Annawan swung about, still scowling, and left the room.

Sarah slumped in her chair. She stared incredulously at Matt. "Did you understand any of that?"

"Like anything that's happened since I've met you makes sense."

Madame Leblanc tried to restore order to a class that was abuzz with excited chatter. She had little luck, so she called an early recess.

"And you," she called after Matt and Sarah as they headed for the door. "No more surprise guests!"

Sarah and Matt burst out laughing. When they ducked out into the hallway, Sarah turned to Matt, the pressure within her subsiding like the slow leak from an inner tube, and leaving behind a spreading warmth. Despite the visions and the sinister laboratory they'd seen, she didn't feel afraid anymore. Maybe Annawan had been more reassuring than she'd realized.

"Let's do it," she said.

"Do what?"

"Find out what's behind that door."

The grin faded from Matt's face, but it still maintained a faint glow. He grasped her hand and nodded. They both knew what door she was talking about. It wasn't a school door, or even a steel door to a laboratory. It was a door through time.

13

Caught in the Mousetrap

IT WAS FRIDAY NIGHT, NEARLY ZERO HOUR, AND THE HOUSE HAD finally grown quiet. Sarah's dad had flicked off the TV to turn in for the night. When he peeked in the door, Sarah snored at headboard-rattling volume. He snuck in, smoothed the covers, kissed her lightly on the forehead, then tiptoed out again. Her eyes flashed open.

She lay in bed, waiting. It seemed like hours, but only thirty minutes had passed when she heard slow rhythmic breathing coming from the master bedroom. She heaved the covers back and pulled on a black sweatshirt and a matching pair of jeans. *Hey, if you're going to do the spy stuff, you might as well dress the part.* Silently, she donned her parka and boots, grabbed her backpack, which she stuffed with mitts, a scarf, and a water bottle, and crept out of the house.

Matt was waiting for her. He tiptoed from the mansion like a cat burglar, barely leaving impressions in the snow.

"Ready?" he asked.

"I guess," said Sarah. "Is she asleep?"

"Dead to the world. As I wish she really were."

"Let's go."

They set off down the street, which slumbered like their guardians—hardly a car invaded the quiet suburban neighbourhood. At the end of the block stood the lone glass bus shelter beside an open field. The wind swept in over the corn stubble and snowdrifts and whipped through their coats, making them shiver and stamp their feet. Hopefully, they wouldn't have to wait too long.

After fifteen minutes of huddling together to keep warm, the garish-looking city bus finally appeared. A travelling billboard, logos and advertisements crammed every available white space on its broad exterior. Inside, the seats were practically empty, except for a couple of giggling passengers in the back. The driver raised his eyebrows as Matt and Sarah climbed aboard, but didn't ask any questions. People rarely did.

They transferred twice before they reached downtown. When they arrived at Laurier Street, a main thoroughfare, they got off the bus and trotted uphill towards the steel-girded fortress of the city centre. More people wandered the street in this part of the city—club hoppers and night crawlers. Sarah was surprised to see so few homeless people, but Matt explained that they usually haunted the ByWard Market area because it was popular with tourists.

A few minutes later, the co-conspirators reached the alley. Matt stopped in front of the door and motioned Sarah to follow. He slipped his hand into his pocket and extracted the keycard.

"How did you . . . ?"

"I took it from her briefcase while she was in the shower tonight. She doesn't lock it as much since she's been mooning over your dad."

Sarah clenched her fists, but she willed herself to relax. After all, Dad didn't seem the least bit interested in Nadine, especially after she'd revealed how little she cared for Matt when they'd fallen in the cave.

Matt inserted the card, disengaging the lock with a resounding *snick*. The Star Trek doors slid open.

As they stepped through the doors, they found the lights on, but not a whisper of activity in the silent halls. The only sound was the squelch of their boots on the carpet.

"The lights probably activate remotely when someone opens the door," said Matt. "They were on last time, remember?"

"Yes," said Sarah. "I hope you're right. I hate to think what Nadine would do to us if she caught us in here."

"Danger is my middle name," said Matt, creeping up to the solid laboratory doors.

"Right." Sarah rolled her eyes. "Let's do it."

Matt placed his eye in front of the retinal scanner. The mechanism flashed and the seal snapped, popping the steel door open.

"Welcome, Mr. Barnes," said the computer in her synthesized voice.

"Thank you," said Matt.

He fumbled with his backpack as he approached the computer and withdrew the sacred disc.

"Here goes nothing," he said, as he inserted it.

Loud clicks and whirrs echoed in the chamber. The portal doors slid open like a pair of metal curtains. The machine hummed.

As Matt stared intensely at the portal, something flashed on the screen behind him. Sarah turned to the computer.

"Failsafe," she said. "What do you think that means?"

Matt blinked and swivelled back around. He gazed thoughtfully at the monitor. "It's a backup."

"For what?"

"How should I know? I didn't program this thing."

The word blinked out.

"Where would you like to go, Mr. Barnes?" asked the computer.

Matt raised his eyebrows and looked at Sarah.

"Atlantis," she suggested. "That's where we saw him last."

"Atlantis," said Matt into the microphone.

The computer hummed. "Repeat destination."

Matt cleared his throat. "Atlantis," he said loudly.

"Time?" the computer asked.

Matt looked at Sarah again. "I have no idea," he whispered.

"Ten thousand BCE. Hopefully we can catch him before the earth-quake and the tidal wave."

Matt nodded and stated the time period. The computer flashed a series of strange codes. In the corner, framed by the metal doors, the machine rumbled. A dazzling light appeared between the two plates as they slammed together and a large translucent film developed.

"Step into the foam, Mr. Barnes," instructed the computer.

Matt froze. "I don't want to go there. I want to find my father, Dr. Nathan Barnes. He's in Atlantis. You have to bring him back."

The computer rattled annoyingly, like tumbling coins in a dryer. "Very well. I will find him. Retrieving him will be more difficult."

The bubble swelled. Multiple images eventually became one, as if the machine could focus, but more likely it was expanding into the other time and place. Once again monumental pillars rose out of an island surrounded by a churning sea. People dressed in silky robes were ferrying in and out of this island metropolis on boats. A silver aircraft flew overhead and landed on a strip just outside the city.

"Did they have planes twelve thousand years ago?"

"We don't know," said Sarah. "Atlantis was supposed to be a myth."

"We know now," said Matt. The bubble enlarged and the image was magnified. Sarah and Matt stepped back. The last thing they wanted was to be sucked into Atlantis. They'd both seen what had happened to it.

In Atlantis a flurry of activity jittered before their eyes. Weird amber contraptions with exposed gears and miniature rotors throbbed and quivered along the streets as they trundled people throughout the city. The sounds suggested motors, but the vehicles weren't belching exhaust.

The city, itself, was constructed of stone, from the cobblestone pavement to the skyscrapers in the centre. People here created—buildings, vehicles, and roads. Boats departed the docks empty and returned laden with raw material.

Matt was glued to scene, taking it all in, from the quarried rock to the gleaming metals.

"Hey, isn't that uranium?" he asked, pointing to the silver-white chunks of metal that some men were handling very carefully.

Sarah studied the material, perplexed. "I wouldn't know uranium if it came up and bit me, but I'll take your word for it."

"I saw some pictures of it on the Internet when I was doing a science project on nuclear energy. Atlantis sank, didn't it?"

"That's what it looked like."

"Or maybe it blew apart."

"You think they tinkered with a Manhattan Project?"

"Could be. Looks like they advanced way beyond their intelligence."

"A little like now."

"Too much like now. Just like this time machine. Dad figured out how to build it, even figured out how to go back in time, but he was too stupid to make sure he could return to the present, first."

"That doesn't make sense," said Sarah.

Matt shrugged.

"I mean, he's a genius."

"Even geniuses have their failings. Look at me."

Sarah did look at Matt. She studied his intense green eyes and determined mouth. She examined the crease of his brow where intelligence teemed. She knew he wouldn't set foot in that machine unless he had a sure-fire way of getting back. "It just doesn't add up."

"Maybe it was an accident," he suggested.

"I suppose," she said. "But even if it was, don't you think he'd have a backup?" She and Matt looked over at the computer screen, remembering the flashing word.

"If he did, it didn't work," said Matt. The babble from the scene made him turn back to Atlantis. "I think I see him."

Sarah gazed through the portal. There were so many people, milling about, like the packed halls of a crowded sports arena. Where could he have seen the professor?

"There," said Matt, taking a step forward. Sarah whipped a hand out to prevent him from getting any closer to the machine. "He's walking back from the jetty. I recognize his hair."

Sarah scanned the pier, but it was like looking for a single ant in a swarming colony. Then she spotted him. Tawny hair, a scruffy beard sprinkled with grey. The vision grew. The computer had enhanced the image or perhaps redirected and enlarged the wormhole.

"Dad!" Matt yelled at the film.

The man turned around. His eyes connected with his son's—a shocking moment that should have been sentimental but wasn't. He goggled at him and his face turned white.

"Can you get him out?" Matt asked the computer.

"Of course, Mr. Barnes. We must destroy him first and recreate him here."

Matt paled. "Destroy him?"

"Dr. Barnes is trapped in the quantum foam. The wormhole will not allow him to pass back into this lab. The only way I can extract him is to recreate him. Shall I do it now?"

"Wait," said Matt. "What if you can't recreate him?"

"I have his DNA," said the machine snidely, if a machine could be snide.

Matt turned to Sarah. "What do you think?"

"This is crazy. What if he has part of his memory missing when the computer puts him back together, or the machine omits some crucial piece of his DNA? What if he's just a clone?"

"But if it's the only way of getting him back . . ."

Interrupting their thoughts, the man inside the bubble spoke. His words were faint and barely intelligible but he was obviously trying to communicate through the wormhole.

Both Sarah and Matt leaned forward and strained their ears, their noses centimetres from the film.

"Matt," he said.

He waved and gesticulated. He mouthed words they couldn't hear.

Sarah squinted, trying read his lips. His gestures seemed so urgent.

What was he trying to say?

She got it! "*Danger.* He's saying we're in danger."

"From what?" asked Matt, scanning the room. The computer didn't pose a threat.

"From me, Matt," said a voice behind them.

Sarah and Matt whirled around. The voice that scraped their eardrums, like nails on a blackboard, was unmistakable.

Nadine stepped from behind a bank of processors, her mustard hair loose and wild, her eyes narrow and hard, her mouth tight and malevolent.

Sarah and Matt stepped backward, almost into Atlantis.

"Do you think I'm a fool, boy? Do you think I would let you bring him back after all I've done to keep him bottled up?"

Matt's mouth dropped open.

"Do you think I would let him interfere again? He was never a father to you, anyway. Why would you want him back?"

Matt shook his head, but he drew himself up. "Anything would be better than you."

"Matt," Sarah warned, but he was beyond listening.

"It was *you*, wasn't it!" he yelled. "*You* kept him trapped in this time machine all my life! *You* were the reason he couldn't come back!"

Nadine smiled crookedly, her head tilted to the side.

"You cooked the machine, didn't you? You kept him in the past so you could take all his money. *You even took his son.*"

"The only thing I didn't want," said Nadine. "But you don't understand the full story, little man. Yes, I may have wanted a better lifestyle than my ratty old apartment. I may have been jealous, but it was your father's arrogance that drove me to extreme measures.

I argued with him about all of this." Her arm swept the room. "But instead of listening, he was going to fire me."

"Probably what you deserved," said Matt. "How did you keep him away from me? How did you mess up the machine?"

Nadine laughed. "Oh, Matt. You think you can just bring him back and life will be rosy. You'll finally have a daddy. But he never really cared about you. He was too busy with his pet." She stroked the computer console. "It was all he cared about."

The bubble behind them rippled as Dr. Barnes's image ballooned. "Not true!" he shouted.

"Isn't it? Let me show you something. Computer, activate tape 537." She smiled. "Dr. Barnes at work."

A video projected onto a screen at the far side of the room. It showed Dr. Barnes hard at work on his equations in front of this very computer.

"*Dr. Barnes,*" a stout grey-haired woman interrupted. "*They called from the hospital. Your wife just went into labour.*"

"*Humph,*" said Dr. Barnes.

"*Should I send flowers?*"

"*Humph,*" said Dr. Barnes.

Matt gripped Sarah's arm. His eyes were riveted on the screen. His muscles stiffened into tight cords.

As the video played on, the woman disappeared and Dr. Barnes resumed his typing. A self-satisfied smile bloomed on his face.

"*We're almost there.*"

The door banged open again. "*Dr. Barnes?*"

"*I'm working, Gena,*" he barked.

"*Your wife is having difficulties, Nate.*"

Dr. Barnes looked up. "*My wife?*"

"She's having a baby."

"Very good."

"And she might not make it."

"Quite right," he said.

The dreamy expression returned to his face.

"I've got it," he exclaimed, once again hunching over the keyboard.

"Seen enough?" asked Nadine, stopping the film.

Matt glared at her, his fingers digging into Sarah's skin. "I don't believe it." He looked back at the bubble, at his father, who was shaking his head with his hands outstretched.

"Even with proof? You're as bullheaded as he is. No matter. You'll be able to sort it all out yourself. Computer, scan the two minors and program the wormhole to transport them."

A beam of light projected from the computer and traced the pattern of Matt and Sarah's bodies. It was just a light brush of warmth, like that of a sunlamp, but the roar in the room grew louder. Goosebumps sprang up on Sarah's arms and legs as energy charged between the two plates in the machine.

"This should only take a few minutes," said Nadine. "Goliath here is quite fast." She patted the processor.

"My name is Isabelle," said the computer in a haughty voice. "Opening wormhole. I have Matthew Barnes's DNA already on file. Should I collect the female's in case we have to reconstruct?"

"What?" said Nadine. "How can that be?"

Matt blinked repeatedly, but Sarah understood.

"Your dad logged your DNA, Matt. That's why you could get into the lab."

"But why would he do that? And when?"

"I don't know," she said. "It might have been when you were a baby. Don't believe what Nadine's saying. He must have cared for you to do that. Anyway, it doesn't matter right now. We have to get out of here."

They raced for the door and tugged at it repeatedly, but it was sealed tight. "Computer!" Matt yelled. "Open lab door."

"Unable to comply. Wormhole is activated," said the machine.

"Open it, you bucket of bolts."

"Unable to comply. There's no need to be rude, Mr. Barnes."

The rumbling resumed. Sarah met Matt's eyes, seeing her own panic reflected there. What were they going to do?

Nadine laughed. "You really think I could let you walk out of here after you've seen all this?"

"Wormhole at full width," said the machine.

"Very good," said Nadine. "Program the foam to slide them into Atlantis, same time. It's a very good time," she said. "Just before the flood."

Sarah and Matt turned. They tugged at the door again, to no effect. Nadine grabbed their shoulders and tried to shove them towards the portal. They kicked at her legs and beat at her arms until she lost her grip. But she'd brought them closer.

Nadine charged at them, her teeth bared. She catapulted Sarah to the edge of the portal, tipping her into the foam. Matt leaped and grabbed Sarah's hands. He wrenched her backward, but she didn't pull free. The wormhole was like a magnet, dragging her inward. The two opposing forces were tearing her apart.

The babble of people and the roar of engines threatened to rupture Sarah's eardrums. Matt yelled at her, but his voice had grown fainter. Then the bubble burst. She tumbled to the lab floor, every muscle in her body aching.

Nadine screamed and kicked a chair. "Darn that quantum foam," she yelled. "Computer, re-quantify."

Sarah felt a flicker of relief. When the bubble had collapsed, Atlantis had disappeared, along with its crowds, machines and Matt's father.

"He's shifted the foam again. Just when I've found him," snarled Nadine.

Matt suddenly grinned. "So you don't have absolute control. Dad can shift from time to time, can't he? He's even come back here before, to protect me."

"He was too late," Nadine said. "He discovered my adjustments, but he was too late to reverse them. All he can do is float in and out of different universes on the quantum foam. He can never stay anywhere for very long, especially here, because the computer can't enlarge the wormhole the amount of time needed for his return."

"Then why does he do those videos," asked Sarah, "if he knows about your double-cross?"

Nadine smiled. "Because I have a hostage." She smirked at Matt who bristled immediately.

"*You cheating, lying, double-crossing snake!*"

Nadine's smile broadened. "Well, I suppose I won't be able to lock in Atlantis, with his tampering. Where and when else should I send you meddling pests? Oh, I have it. Sarah seems to like the First Nations so much, how about Odawa in 1615? Computer?"

"Searching."

"We'll make it summer. No need to freeze before the Algonquin get you. And let's see." She tapped her chin. "In a cave. The Bear Creek cave. Even better." Her eyes glittered.

"Oh no," said Sarah.

"Wormhole dilated," said the machine.

Sarah glanced behind her. The bubble spewed out of the plates again. She shuddered as the image swelled, because it wasn't an image of anything. Just darkness. "Not again," she whimpered.

Matt grabbed her hand. They tried to bolt for the door, but Nadine barred their path. She charged like a bull, tumbling them backward. Matt lost his balance and his hand plunged into the bubble. The suction was incredible; it pulled him irresistibly towards the void.

Sarah gripped and yanked, using all her power to pull him out, but this time she couldn't break the bubble's hold. She quaked from the effort, every muscle straining, and she managed to pull him back a few centimetres. But Nadine's hands captured her ankles and upended her into the wormhole.

In one last desperate act, Sarah kicked backward, making contact with the bony woman. Nadine slammed to ground, Sarah's boot in her hand, but Sarah had slipped out of it and into the rippling bubble. The room spiralled and she fell, downward, outward, inward, crushed beyond belief, but still holding Matt's hand. She couldn't find air, couldn't snatch a breath, for the longest minute of her life. Then she landed, with a thud, on the soft limestone ground layered with bat guano.

14

Where the Deer and the Bear Roam

Matt groaned and opened his eyes. There was nothing to see, of course, because they were back in the bat cave.

"Sarah," he said. "Are you there?" He tried to sit up, but a wave of dizziness washed over him, and he sank back down.

"Here," she said in a shaky voice.

Matt fumbled around in the darkness until he found her backpack, and then slid his hand down her arm to her hand.

"My head hurts, though."

"Tell me about it," said Matt. He rubbed his throbbing skull. He tried to sit up again, taking it slowly and swallowing some bile. A sudden rustling noise in the cave made him tense. He could sense the presence of other creatures, but he couldn't see anything.

"Those vampire bats again," said Sarah.

"Fruit," said Matt, but he didn't feel as brave as he had the last time they were in this situation. For one thing, there was no rescue effort under way. Secondly, he had no idea how they were going to get back, or if that was even possible. Thirdly, they had no light.

"Wh-what are we going to do?" asked Sarah.

Matt gulped. "I don't know. Get out of this cave, for one." He struggled to his feet, then leaned down to help Sarah up.

"Which way?" she asked.

A gurgle and the mightier rush of a stream came from his left. "This way," he said. He led her forward, shuffling to avoid rocks, grazing the side wall with his fingertips, until he splashed into some water. Sarah held back at the water's edge.

"I'm missing a boot," she said.

"Oh," said Matt. "That's not good. You should avoid the stream, then. It's still pretty cold."

Sarah murmured agreement and gave the stream a wide berth. They walked with their arms outstretched, stumbling occasionally over scattered rocks. Matt followed the stream against the flow until the walls gave way. He blinked when he realized he could see. Diffuse light spilled from the cave mouth and reflected off the stalactites, creating wavy patterns on the ground. Relieved, they sat on a rock to rest.

"We're almost out," said Sarah.

Matt squeezed her hand.

"What do we do once we're out?"

"Avoid First Nations camps," said Matt.

"Do you think we're really in the seventeenth century?"

"If Dad was in 10,000 BCE, then we're in the seventeenth century."

Sarah sighed. "How do we get back?" Her eyes glittered in the ghostly light, most likely from budding tears. Matt blinked his own away.

"We don't," he said. "We just have to concentrate on staying alive."

Sarah sniffed. "Why were we so stupid? After he warned us. . ."

"Who warned us?" asked Matt.

"Your dad, of course. What do you think the arrows meant? He was telling us about the First Nations, that we might end up in this time period if we kept snooping in the lab."

"How did he know?"

Sarah shook her head. "For someone so smart, you sure can be dense. He's travelling through time. If he knows what happened in the past, maybe he can also travel to the future. Then he showed us what he saw through a wormhole. Maybe he can lock onto you some-times, because the computer has your DNA. But he couldn't stop what happened, since Nadine has control over the computer."

"I suppose it's possible," said Matt. "After this, anything's possible." He coughed and cleared his throat. The cave rumbled in reply.

"Be quiet," whispered Sarah. "You don't want to bring the whole Five Nations down on us."

"That wasn't me."

The rumble occurred again, thunderous, sending vibrations through the cave and shaking stalactites from the rock ceiling. They exploded into hundreds of slivers on either side of Matt and Sarah. His heart flapping wildly against his chest, Matt met Sarah's eyes.

"What lives in caves besides snakes and bats?" she asked.

"Bears," Matt mouthed.

They leaped up and raced for the entrance. Near the lofty archway, Matt tripped over a rock and crashed down on his left knee. A scream ripped through his head that he suppressed by biting his lip. Sarah tugged on his arm and pulled him to his feet.

Another roar blasted through the cave. They ran faster, Sarah pulling, Matt limping, until they reached the opening and dashed through. They ran headlong into an enormous black bear rearing on its hind legs. They both ricocheted backward and fell to the ground.

The bear opened its mouth, displaying a jagged row of sharp teeth. But it was the spike-length claws that drew their attention. Before the creature could snap their necks, or maul them with its powerful claws, something whistled through the air. It thudded into the beast, throwing it backward.

The bear stumbled and groaned, an arrow jutting from its chest. It roared and swiped with its claws, centimetres from Matt's face. *Thud. Thud.* Two more arrows struck the bear, one in the throat, the other in the chest. The creature did a clumsy dance and fell over, blood welling from the puncture sites.

Matt and Sarah rolled away as the bear roared in agony. They looked at the forest, where a boy, no older than they were, stood holding a bow. He had braided black hair, deep brown eyes, and a deerskin shirt and leggings. He nodded to them, then disappeared into the forest.

"Wait!" called Matt, bouncing to his feet.

"Are you crazy?" said Sarah, standing groggily.

"He saved our lives." Matt nodded at the bear, which had stopped groaning and lay still.

"But he's . . ."

"Probably Algonquin, like Annawan. If we're going to survive here, we'll need allies."

Sarah sniffed.

"Do you think we can hunt and eat berries and survive without help?"

She shook her head. Her lips quivered as she gazed at their surroundings.

Matt understood her fear, but he didn't know how to help her. They were encircled by a sea of trees and brush that probably swept all the way to the Gatineau River to the west and the Ottawa River to the south, although they'd have different names in this time. The trees were in full bloom, their emerald leaves shivering in the early dawn.

"At least she didn't leave it winter," said Matt.

"It's beautiful. Except I hate it."

"We wouldn't last a day if it was winter," he said, ignoring her comment. "Especially you, without a boot."

Sarah looked down at her stockinged foot. The sock was damp and caked with dirt and crushed leaves. It was the same foot that an arrow had pierced less than a week ago. She kept wincing, so it must still hurt.

"You could borrow mine," he said. "But I don't think we're the same size."

Sarah compared his size eight boots to her size fives. "It wouldn't work," she said. "Besides, one injured person is enough."

"Hey, you didn't see my knee." He rolled up his pant leg. The kneecap was swollen to twice its normal size, scraped, bloody, and bruised.

"We are a sorry pair, aren't we?" she said.

Matt grinned. "Might as well laugh as cry."

The hint of a smile touched her lips. "Okay. I'm open to suggestions."

"I suggest we find our arrow-shooting friend."

"And if he suggests that we aren't friends," asked Sarah, "with his arrows?"

"Then we can cry," said Matt.

"Right." Her voice sounded strong and steady. She drew up her chin and faced the New World.

Matt joined her, taking in the view. Fire swept through his veins. He intended to make the most of this adventure and do his best to ignore the fear that bubbled beneath the surface. Besides, they could just as well have been thrown into Atlantis. This world might be untamed and wild, fraught with hazards, but it was still Canada. No tidal wave threatened to sweep them away. No earthquakes would swallow them into the sea. They were going to survive, if only to show Nadine that she hadn't won the war. In fact, the war had just begun.

15

———— ⟁ ————

An Aboriginal Encounter

SARAH TRUDGED ALONG BESIDE MATT AS THEY WALKED INTO THE forest to look for the First Nations boy. They weren't trackers, so they had no idea where the boy had gone. Their loud rustling progress through the bush startled rabbits and squirrels, who scampered away. Thousands of birds twittered and sang, replacing the silence of the cave. Sarah jumped every time a chipmunk dashed out of a pile of leaves. This place teemed with wildlife, so different from the steel, concrete, and human-packed streets of Toronto.

"Please tell me there'll be no more bears," she pleaded.

"Roarrr," said Matt.

"Not funny."

"Look, Sarah. You have to admit this is pretty amazing. I mean we get to see the world before they had skyscrapers and combustion engines. We get to hike through the forest before they cut down acres of it. We even get to see the first people who lived here. I mean, I'm no aboriginal person, but deep down, I've always had this secret longing to be one."

Sarah looked at him, dumbfounded. Then she tripped on a tree root and fell flat on her face. She sat up and swatted leaves out of her hair.

"The adventure of a lifetime," she muttered. "What a great opportunity. Let's hike through the forest, get eaten by bears and, if we're lucky, run into the sharp point of an arrow."

Matt held out his hand to help her up, but she brushed it aside.

"You're a pessimist," he said.

"You need a reality check."

"I'm just making the best of a—"

"Bad situation," she completed. "I know." She stood and wiped the dirt and leaves from her jeans. "I'm just sort of scared, you know."

Matt nodded. "That makes two of us."

"If we had only—"

"Shh," said Matt. His eyes swivelled to the side.

"You're not helping any," she said.

Matt growled and clamped his hand over her mouth. His eyes darted left and right, but nothing moved or rustled nearby, nothing happened except for birds flitting from tree to tree.

"Someone's watching us," he whispered in her ear.

Matt pulled his hand away and tiptoed forward. He crept around a massive pine trunk fringed with ghost lilies and edged near a tire-sized hole in an oak tree. As he tipped his head to peer around the tree, a fox leaped from the hollow, grazed his cheek and dashed away. Matt fell on his backside as the red fur streaked through the woods.

Sarah burst out laughing. "That was the scary watcher?"

Matt's face flushed. His jaw hardened. "That's the thanks I get for trying to save your life." He cast her a murderous glance.

Sarah kept giggling. "I don't think *he* was dangerous."

"That doesn't mean you have to laugh."

"I was just trying to make the best—"

"Of a bad situation. I know. Darn it, don't throw my words right back in my face."

"It's better than—"

"Shh," said Matt.

"Not again." She fell silent as his eyes locked with hers, transmitting a stern warning. At the same instant, thick clouds scudded across the sun, deepening the shadows among the trees. A hoot in the woods sent a current down her spine.

"Matt?" she whispered. "Owls don't come out during the day, do they?"

"Don't think so."

Matt got quietly to his feet. The two stood back to back and searched the woods. The friendly forest full of harmless creatures turned ominous. A sudden breeze stirred the leaves and boughs of the trees. Every shadow was a possible hiding place for a lurking enemy.

Matt tugged Sarah forward cautiously, clutching her hand. She didn't want to keep going, but what choice did they have? They tiptoed around bushes and stepped over deadfall, cringing every time the branches snapped or leaves crackled. Another hoot rang out.

"Maybe we should go the other way," whispered Sarah.

"I'd rather face an arrow head-on than take one in the back."

"Seriously?" she said. "Fine. Let's head right on into the hurricane."

She boldly marched forward—although her every fiber screamed this was madness—and tripped and fell onto a pile of leaves. The leaves exploded, flying outward and scattering like a volcanic eruption. An extremely disturbed black and white animal scuttled out of the pile. He snarled and hissed, then whipped around and raised his tail.

"Oh no," said Sarah.

"Oh yes," said Matt, backing away from the disgruntled skunk.

Before Sarah could scramble away, it spewed noxious mist all over her. She screamed. She covered her face, choking and sputtering as the cloud enveloped her. Matt hacked, too, a few steps away. But all the noise they made couldn't drown out the sound of laughter coming from a nearby maple tree.

The laughter grew louder and wilder until the black-braided boy fell from his leafy camouflage on a quivering branch, and rolled over and over on the ground. Tears streamed down his face. He held his belly in a fit of giggling.

Sarah met Matt's eyes. They were both still choking and coughing, but eventually they caught the laughter bug. Their screams turned to chuckles. Their chuckles became hoots. They rolled on the ground beside the boy, and let all their fear and frustration explode into giggles.

They laughed until there was no laughter left. Then all three sat up and wiped away their tears. The First Nations boy nodded. They nodded in return. The boy's eyes travelled over them, now wary again. Sarah copied his perusal. Abruptly, he stood and tapped his chest.

"*Chogan*," he said.

"Choke on," Sarah and Matt repeated, smiling.

The boy glanced at the sky and shook his head. "Chogan," he repeated. He pointed at the maple tree, where an intrigued blackbird tilted its head at them from a branch.

Sarah brushed herself off and jumped up. "Got it. Chogan. I think it means 'Blackbird.'"

The boy grinned.

Matt clambered upright and pointed to himself. "Matt," he said. "Sarah." He jabbed her arm.

"*Tu n'est pas français.*" The boy stated the obvious fact that they weren't French.

They shook their heads. Matt's eyes grew wide.

"*Hollandais?*" asked the boy. Dutch?

"*Non,*" said Matt, elbowing Sarah in the ribs.

"Ouch. What did you do that for?" she whispered.

"He'll think we're Dutch or British."

"I know," she said. That wouldn't be good. If this boy was Algonquin—with Mr. Fletcher's lessons and Annawan's reference to this region, it only made sense that he was—then the Iroquois and by association the Dutch and British were their enemies. Or were they?

"I'm no idiot," said Sarah. "But who do we say we are?"

"*Suede,*" said Matt to the boy. Swedish.

The boy chuckled. He was no idiot either.

Matt shuffled from one foot to the other, chewing on his lip. The boy approached him. Matt stepped back. Chogan shook his head, pressing a finger to his lips.

"I think he'll keep our secret," said Sarah.

"Or he'll turn us in as spies."

Sarah held out her ragged shirt and raised her stockinged foot. "Do we look like spies?"

Chogan giggled. He shrugged a deerskin bag from his shoulder and pulled out a dry pair of moccasins. He offered them to Sarah. "*Makasin*," he said.

Sarah gaped at the moccasins. How extraordinarily generous. She accepted them, bowing her head in thanks.

"*Merci.*"

The boy nodded.

Sarah slipped the soft-soled shoes onto her feet and stashed her other boot in her backpack. She looked down at the moccasins Chogan was wearing. They were muddy, worn, scuffed, and torn in patches. He'd offered her a new pair.

"Wow," said Matt. "That was nice of him."

Sarah murmured her agreement and brushed away a tear. For the first time since they'd landed here, she didn't feel cold.

"You know if I had another pair of shoes I'd give them to you."

"Of course, you would," said Sarah, unable to take her eyes off Chogan.

He gestured north, somewhere deeper in the woods, and started off in that direction.

Matt watched him go, his eyebrows perched high on his forehead, but he didn't move. "Should we follow? I mean he probably thinks we're British. What if he takes us to Champlain?"

"We can trust him," said Sarah, traipsing assuredly after Chogan.

"I hope so," Matt said, matching her strides.

"What choice do we have? You wanted to follow him after he shot the bear."

"That was before I knew he spoke French, and before he knew we were English. He could be leading us into a trap."

"Or he could be saving our lives." Now she remembered. Matt had it all wrong. It had to do with dates. "Look, Matt. Nadine sent us to the year 1615. The British hadn't even arrived here yet. You should know that if you read that book on the First Nations."

Matt opened his mouth to answer, but Sarah cut him off.

"Think about it. Captain John Smith had just landed and established Jamestown in Virginia in 1607. You know, the Pocahontas story. The Iroquois haven't even met the British yet. And the Dutch are just settling in Albany, New York. That's probably why Chogan mentioned the Dutch. Besides, he already saved us from the bear. And he just gave me his best shoes to protect my feet. I say we've made a friend."

As Sarah closed the distance to Chogan, the boy turned around and smiled. When she drew alongside him, he pinched his nose and edged away.

"*Cigag*," he said.

"I thinks he's talking about the skunk," said Matt.

"I got that," said Sarah.

As he passed an evergreen tree, Chogan popped a nodule from the bark. It released a trickle of sap, along with a potent, refreshing pine scent. He took Sarah's hand and smoothed the sap over her skin, motioning for her to coat herself with it. Sarah confidently followed his instructions, although the sap was very sticky. Soon the repugnant skunk smell abated, and they could all breathe easier.

After that, they walked in silence for almost two hours. Sarah should have been wilting from exhaustion after such a long hike, but the moccasins trod like air on the forest floor. She hadn't even realized the sun was going down until shadows crept around the trees. Chogan didn't stop. When they began to trip over exposed branches, he held out his hand. Sarah grasped it, and clutched Matt's fingers with her other hand, forming a chain. They trudged onward until they came upon a steep slope, where gurgles and splashes promised a river and rapids down below. The canopy of the forest peeled back, allowing the setting sun to break through and bathe the travellers in a waxy light.

Chogan tapped his lips with his forefinger and motioned for Sarah and Matt to stay behind the wall of trees. He strode down the slope towards murmuring voices. Sarah clutched Matt's hand in a tight squeeze. He grinned, reassuring her, but he didn't obey Chogan's instructions. He pulled his hand free and crept towards the edge of the pitch.

"Matt," she whispered. "Matt!"

But he wasn't listening.

16

Hiding

GRITTING HER TEETH, SARAH SLUNK BEHIND MATT AND PEERED DOWN the slope. Despite their situation, he was still so rebellious, flagrantly disobeying instructions as if he were back in Marshland Elementary.

"Matt," she whispered, but he waved her to be quiet as he studied the activity below.

Chogan had just stepped into a clearing, which was lit by a number of small fires. Birchbark wigwams encircled a central fire and a totem pole engraved with a solemn wolf.

A tall scowling Algonquin man stood by the fire with his arms crossed. Women with long black braids and buckskin clothes tended the smaller fires. They were using clay or copper cooking pots to stew vegetables and braise skinned rabbits or fish. Other men sat cross-legged before the fires, savouring the smell of the evening meal. They bounced small children on their knees or chased older children around the camp. Some men smoked from long-stemmed clay pipes.

Most of the people were chattering or laughing—except the stern man in the middle of the camp. His eyes were coal-black, his lips a solid slash. He glared at Chogan and spoke rapidly in the musical Algonquin tongue, the words incomprehensible to Sarah, but the tone unmistakable.

Chogan shrugged his shoulders as he pointed in the direction of the cave. The man's eyebrows arched as Chogan drew pictures in the air with his hands, tracing a massive girth and a great height. He bared his teeth and said the word "*makwa*" loudly enough for Sarah to hear. He was clearly giving a description of the bear.

The man's gaze softened as he strode towards Chogan. He spoke so comfortably to the boy, in tender buttery tones, he had to be his father. Chogan lifted his bow and scratched out an imaginary height two and a half metres in the air. His father rolled his eyes. The boy smiled and readjusted his level to the two-metre size of the bear. This time his father nodded. He called over to some of the men around their respective fires.

First Chogan spoke to them. Then they murmured amongst themselves. One burly man fetched a large deerskin cloth from inside a wigwam, while two others lit torches made of birchbark coiled around a stick. Another warrior attached a short stick to his headband, with what appeared to be fungus inserted in a notch at the top. He lit this also, releasing a stream of smoke. Perhaps it was a way to repulse the miserable black flies and mosquitoes that swarmed as soon as the sun went down. Already the insects were feasting on Sarah and Matt, who tried to swat at them as quietly as possible.

All four men headed up the slope, the torches flaring brightly and driving back the darkness like the light of an oncoming train. They aimed straight for the crest where the time travellers were watching. Sarah and Matt quickly shrank back into the shadows of the trees and ducked beneath a large shrub. Sarah caught her breath as three of the Algonquin immediately brushed past their hiding place, disturbing the bushes around them. She puffed out a sigh as the last Algonquin skirted their shelter, but a crackle centimetres away froze the air in her throat. She'd forgotten the fourth warrior.

The man peered through the leaves, an odd glint from the moon reflecting off the whites of his eyes. His bowstring was stretched back, his arrow aimed directly at her heart. Sarah's stomach clenched; her chest tightened. This was it. They were going to die.

The man's gaze shifted from her to Matt. His arrow traced the same pattern. Abruptly, he lowered the arrow and chuckled. He shook his head, his deep rumbling laughter startling the birds above him out of the trees. Chogan's father called out to him. He mumbled something and winked before he followed the other men.

Sarah looked at Matt and gripped his hand even tighter. They waited to see if the warrior had still tipped off Chogan's father to their presence, but nothing happened. Matt parted the leaves of the bush, nodded as if he was satisfied that the men had left, and crept closer to the edge of the slope. Since Sarah's hand was still attached to his, and she doubted a crowbar could pry it off, she had no choice but to join him. She looked down into the clearing again.

Chogan and his father had returned to the main fire and were sitting beside it. A petite woman in a buckskin dress and leggings brought them a brimming container of food to share. Even from this distance, Sarah could see that she resembled Chogan. She had the same slouching round cheeks and crescent-shaped eyes. The only feature Chogan had inherited from his father was his prominent nose

Sarah touched her own nose and smiled. *At least I'm not the only one.*

As the trio shared their meal, a younger version of Chogan scampered up to the woman and climbed into her lap, completing the circle around the fire. It was an idyllic family scene. The four Algonquin sat together eating and chatting. Chogan's mother smiled proudly at her son. With exaggerated gestures, he described his defeat of the monstrous bear.

Matt seemed satisfied and crawled backward to their little shelter under the shrub, dragging Sarah with him. They sat back and shared a relieved sigh. Sarah, now exhausted, leaned her head on Matt's shoulder. He put his arm around her.

"Why do you think the man left us alone?" she whispered.

"I don't know," said Matt.

"He really looked like he was going to shoot us."

"I guess we're not much of a threat."

"True," said Sarah. "But he didn't even turn us in."

"Look at it this way," Matt whispered. "We're two dirty shivering kids, huddled down in the dark outside their camp. There's no danger of our mounting an attack on their village. Maybe the chief has no sympathy for strange starving children. So, he thought, I'll let them go. If they do cause a problem, well, fifty strong-armed warriors should be able to take care of them."

"You think?" Sarah smiled.

Matt rested his head against her hair. "I know."

"Matt. You almost make getting thrown into a time machine by a wicked witch, getting attacked by a bear, and being nearly impaled by an arrow seem like a great adventure."

"Really?"

"Almost."

The hours dragged by. Soon the darkness thickened; the Algonquin must have extinguished their cooking fires. The men, women and children had likely crawled into their tents, since silence settled over the camp. Sarah and Matt were numb with fatigue; energy seeped out of their weary bodies like yogurt through a sieve. They stretched out on the carpet of pine needles, their stomachs groaning from hunger.

Sarah was almost asleep when a hand shook her shoulder. She blinked and sat up. A dark creature loomed over her. She clapped a hand to her mouth.

"*Repas*," whispered Chogan. Supper.

"Oh, it's you," she said with a sigh.

He placed a wooden bowl in her lap. He seemed much smaller, now that he wasn't hovering over her.

Chogan turned to Matt and shook him awake. He shoved another wooden bowl into his hands. "*Mangez*," he said, making a chewing motion with his mouth.

Matt dipped his hand into the bowl and pinched a small morsel. He sniffed it. His face lit up as he bit down. "Fish," he said.

Sarah grasped an even smaller portion. She chewed gingerly, savouring the soft flakey texture and little gushes of juice. Matt eagerly crammed more food into his mouth.

"This is delicious," he said. "I think it's trout."

"There's some kind of vegetable and wild rice, too," said Sarah, poking the food with her fingers. Before long, she was stuffing her mouth full. The hole in her stomach slowly filled.

"*Merci*," she whispered to Chogan. The Algonquin boy grinned and rubbed his tummy. He flipped a bearskin blanket off his shoulder and handed it to her. Sarah smiled as she accepted it, speechless with gratitude. Chogan touched her shoulder, then crept back to camp.

Sarah and Matt crawled under the bearskin and snuggled down to sleep. Sarah would have tumbled headlong into her dreams, but Matt wouldn't let her fall. Obviously the food had perked him up.

"How long do you think Chogan can keep us a secret?" he whispered.

"I'm not going to worry about it," said Sarah, through a jaw-cracking yawn. "He's keeping us alive right now."

"What if that older warrior comes back and slits our throats in our sleep?"

"Then we won't know it, will we? Go to sleep, Matt. We can worry more tomorrow. Right now I don't have the energy."

Matt pulled the skin up around his chin. He fell silent. Sarah was so exhausted, she didn't care if a whole band of First Nations people impaled them in their sleep. Or if the French and British armies clashed right here in this clearing. Anyway, it seemed quite secure between the trees, with their stomachs full and the blanket tucked around them. Chogan was looking after them. What could possibly happen?

She didn't notice the four Algonquin return with the carcass of the bear. They dragged it right past their den in the forest. The fourth warrior turned his keen eyes towards them. He grinned as he saw the glint of Matt's pale hair in the moonlight.

17

Matt and Sarah's Totem

DAPPLED SUNLIGHT BROKE THROUGH THE BRANCHES OF THE WHITE pine and tickled Sarah's nose with its warmth. She sat up immediately, reenergized after the sleep and meal, and crawled to the edge of the slope to spy on the active camp below.

Three Algonquin women were busy skinning and smoking a bear. Sarah shuddered. Could it be the same one that had tried to attack them yesterday? The coarse black fur and sharp pointed teeth looked hideously familiar. Other women in the camp were preparing breakfast over the cooking fires. The men huddled together around the main fire, voices raised in a heated debate.

A shiver rippled through Sarah at the sound of their angry tones. Were they discussing what to do with the orphaned children just outside their camp?

Matt stirred, yawning and stretching, letting the bearskin slip from his shoulders. He propped himself up, blinked a few times, then crawled on his hands and knees towards her. When he reached her side, he peered down the slope. "Hey, that looks like our bear," he whispered, scratching his head.

"I think it's Chogan's bear," said Sarah. "I'm just glad that they're eating *it*, instead of it eating *us*."

"You said it," said Matt.

"What do you think the argument's about?" Sarah motioned to the adults in the centre of the camp.

"Whatever it is, I don't think it's about us."

"How do you figure?"

"Well, for one thing, we're still here, not down there, being tied to a stake."

"Good point."

"Since we're still undiscovered, what do we do next?"

Sarah gazed at the dense woods around them and the fast-flowing river behind the camp. It was all so foreign, even though they were just a few kilometres from Ottawa. This river must be the Gatineau River, but no houses lined its banks, no highways ran alongside it. A thickness developed in her throat. Tears prickled her eyes.

"I just want to go home."

"Don't we all," said Matt. His jaw tightened, as if bothered by her homesickness. Maybe he thought if he surrendered to it himself, the hard shell he'd built around his feelings might crack. "I'm looking for realistic options."

Sarah bit her lip and turned away.

"I'm sorry," he muttered, "but we have to face the truth. There is no way back. Nadine made sure of that. Even Dad couldn't find a way back from the past."

She knew he was right. But how could she just accept that they were never going home? Her thoughts trickled to the warm cozy house on the outskirts of Ottawa, protected from pests and the harsh climate. Her father was likely preparing a stack of pancakes for breakfast, only she wouldn't be there. He'd find her bed empty, and he'd start to worry. He'd call the police, they'd scour the neighbourhood, but they wouldn't find her. No one would find her.

Sarah looked at Matt through a haze of tears. His image shifted and blurred. His outline seemed vague. She blinked away the tears, but he didn't come clear.

"Matt?" She reached out and touched his sleeve. Her hand swept through his wispy image as though through a holograph.

"Oh no!" She pushed closer and slammed into his body, solid as steel.

"What in the world are you doing?" he asked.

Sarah threw her arms around him.

"Sarah, what are you getting all mushy about?"

"Y-you weren't here, two seconds ago."

"What are you talking about? I haven't budged from this spot."

"I mean it, Matt. I couldn't see you clearly, so I reached out to touch you, and you were nothing but air."

Matt patted his arms and legs. "Doesn't feel like air to me. Though I did feel a bit weird."

"Don't you ever leave me," said Sarah.

"Not a chance. You're serious, aren't you?"

"*Dead* serious."

"Don't say that word."

Sarah smiled. "You're still *the walking corpse* to me."

"I almost forgot about that," said Matt, grinning. "What do you think it means—this vanishing stuff? Can we get back?"

"I don't know."

"Well, you thought it was Dad before. Maybe it's him now, too."

"He could still be around," said Sarah, "protecting you, somehow."

"My guardian angel."

"That's reassuring. Only if he can't get home, it probably doesn't get us home, either."

Matt nodded. "Even his warnings with the arrows didn't help. It was kind of drastic, wasn't it? Showing you visions of someone shooting me with an arrow just to keep us from the lab."

"I think it was the only way he could communicate," said Sarah. "Maybe when he opened a wormhole into our time in the quantum foam, he had only seconds, so he had to do something wild to get our attention."

"Yeah," said Matt. "I suppose." His eyes shifted to the village below and popped wide.

"What is it?" asked Sarah.

He hushed her and pointed. The Algonquin men had stopped their debate as they admitted a visitor into their camp. A tall young white man with a wiry black beard strode to the centre, near the totem pole. He sat down across from Chogan's father and greeted him in French. Matt strained forward to hear what they were saying.

"I think it's all about trade," he said.

"I hope so," said Sarah. "If they start talking about shooting strange kids, I'm out of here."

Matt waved her to silence and leaned forward again. The Frenchman made slashing gestures with his hands. He pointed to the south.

"What are they saying?"

"I think we're in trouble," said Matt.

"They're talking about war on the Five Nations, aren't they? Is that Champlain, do you think?"

Matt shook his head. "It doesn't look anything like the statue."

"What statue?"

"You know, the one your father showed us. The great discoverer."

"What's to discover? This is an occupied land."

"I'm sure Chogan would agree with you. The problem is that the Algonquin wound up helping the French, and since we're English, I doubt if the French would treat us kindly. Especially if they're trying to get a toehold in North America one step ahead of the British."

"Chogan's not going to turn us in," said Sarah.

"Maybe not Chogan, but what about the other Algonquin who saw us?"

"I don't know, Matt. He hasn't done anything yet."

"Yet. Maybe he's just taking his time. I don't think we should stick around to find out."

A tap on Sarah's shoulder gave her a jolt. Her heart thumped wildly as she looked behind her, but it was only Chogan. What a relief. She tried to talk, but he clapped a hand over her mouth.

With an urgent wave at Matt, beckoning him to follow, Chogan quickly slunk backward towards the denser part of the forest. But his lightning movements stopped when his eyes lit upon the oak tree just behind Matt.

"What? Do you see a ghost?" Matt whispered, slipping easily into French.

"*Do-daim*," whispered Chogan.

Matt frowned. "Do-what?"

"*Do-daim*," said Chogan with more emphasis.

Sarah squinted at the tree that disturbed him so much. A carving was etched in the bark—a roughly drawn image that resembled a boot.

Matt finally got the idea that they weren't staring at him. He twisted around. "What's this?"

"*Do-daim*," said Chogan again, his voice getting sharper. The unspoken words were "you idiots."

"Totem," said Sarah, snapping her fingers. "Maybe he's saying that's your totem."

"Wow," said Matt. "Except I didn't draw it. What kind of a silly totem is it, anyway? I mean a bear or a wolf, even a moose, would be better than a boot."

"A moose would be more like it," said Sarah.

"Hey!"

"Wait a minute." The totem struck a chord, but what was it? Sarah looked down at her own feet.

"D'you know what it means?" asked Matt.

She didn't answer. Instead she dug around in her backpack and unearthed the muddy winter boot. "What do you think?"

Matt looked at the boot, then at the drawing. "I suppose it could be. So your stupid winter boot is my totem?"

"No, silly. It's not just *your* totem, it's *ours*. Besides, I don't think it's a totem at all. I think it's a message from your father. Remember when you felt weird a few minutes ago and you disappeared? That's when he must have left the message."

Matt's brows crushed together. "A message. What exactly does this message mean?"

Sarah rubbed her forehead, as stumped as he was. "Darned if

I know. Let me think about it."

"You do that," said Matt. "In the meantime, maybe we should get out of here."

Chogan nodded as if he grasped the gist of their conversation. "*Allez!*" he said. He crept deeper into the woods, urging them to follow.

Sarah and Matt hunched down and slipped between the feathery ferns and stiff pine boughs that echoed their passage with crisp rustles. They trod carefully, to avoid tripping over arching roots or stepping on any dry twigs that would surely give them away. Gradually, the sound of conversation from the camp faded. They could breathe easier.

"Chogan." Sarah caught up to him. "Where are we going?"

Chogan muttered something in Algonquin and slapped her gently on the side of the head. "*En français, si tu veux vivre.*" In French, if you want to live.

"*Je suis désolé. J'ai oublié.*" I'm sorry. I forgot.

Chogan smiled. "*D'accord. Tu apprends.*" All right. You're learning.

They chuckled, even though it was an odd time to be joking. Chogan took her hand and wound his way down the slope, guiding them in a wide semicircle around the camp. Water gurgled and splashed, an obvious clue to his heading—the river.

They emerged from the trees beneath a series of rapids, leaping and crashing water over bulging river rocks and boulders. Chogan disappeared into nearby bushes and hauled out a birchbark canoe, the shell composed of thick strips of bark teased around curved wooden ribs. In the hull sat two sets of paddles and a buckskin backpack similar to the one Chogan had worn the day before. He shoved the canoe into the current and held it steady for the two time travellers to jump in.

Matt leaped aboard, but Sarah held back.

"Hurry," said Matt.

"I'm not so good with boats."

"Can you swim?" asked Matt.

"Of course," she growled. "I finished Level Eight in swimming lessons, at the top of my class."

"So what's the problem?"

"Well, that was in a swimming pool."

"You mean you've never been in a river or lake before?"

"Well . . . no," she said, searching for some way to explain. "There aren't many of them around Toronto."

"Lake Ontario?" he said sarcastically.

"That's just too big. And polluted," she hastened to add. But she couldn't meet his gaze. It seemed silly that she'd lived next to a Great Lake her whole life without ever swimming in it.

"You mean your dad never took you camping?"

"Mom hates bugs," said Sarah. "She's not very outdoorsy." She wanted to say *neither am I*, but held her tongue.

Matt rolled his eyes. "City slickers. Okay, just think of this as a big pool."

Sarah took one step towards the canoe, biting her lip. Chogan raised his eyebrows, clearly growing impatient. She didn't want him to think any less of her, so she tried to force herself forward. Her feet seemed glued to the mud on the bank.

"Sarah," said Matt.

"Pools d-don't have r-rapids," she said through chattering teeth.

Chogan, looking exasperated, muttered something in Algonquin, let go of the canoe—which started to drift away with the current—and grabbed Sarah around the middle. He hoisted her into the air like a sack of dirt and tossed her into the canoe. Sarah shrieked as she landed in a heap in the bottom. The canoe rocked savagely and nearly capsized. Before she could untangle her legs, Chogan had leaped aboard behind her and pushed off into the current.

"I don't believe it," said Sarah, grasping hold of the ribbing and struggling to sit up. "I thought he was nice."

Chogan ignored her as he dug his paddle into the river. Within seconds he had the canoe sailing through the fast flowing eddies.

"*Tu n'es pas gentil*," she shouted at Chogan. You're not nice.

Chogan grinned and shrugged. "*Tu vivras*," he said. You'll live. His paddle hovered in midair as he shouted at Matt: "*Arrête!*" Stop!

Matt stopped paddling. He glanced back at Chogan, who scanned the banks with microscopic focus. Sarah tried to ignore them, still fuming at Chogan's rudeness.

"He's such a jerk," she muttered.

"Be quiet," said Matt.

Sarah fell silent. The boys were too tense, too wary. She studied the forest. Nothing to see but tall trees and dense shadows. Four beetle-black crows flapped over their heads. A skunk waddled out of a thicket. There was no sign of a French invasion force. After thirty seconds, Chogan commenced paddling again and instructed Matt to do the same.

Sarah heaved a sigh. They'd faced a new challenge at every turn since they'd landed here, but had ended up with no damage except a few scratches. Why should their luck change now? Chogan must be jumping at shadows.

As she turned to face forward again, something whistled through the air, followed by an abrupt *thud*. Matt let out a bloodcurdling yell and tumbled backward. He lay there, in the bottom of the canoe, twitching and moaning, an arrow jutting from his shoulder. Blood welled from the puncture site and trickled down his blue shirt. Sarah gasped, then screamed.

Chogan yelled in Algonquin and booted her in the back. He motioned to the paddle that Matt had dropped. Sarah shook her head, but Chogan snarled and kicked again. She scrambled forward and gripped the paddle. Chogan grabbed Matt under the arms and hauled him backward to the middle of the boat, where he laid him down. The canoe rocked as if caught in the clutch of giant waves. A shower of arrows fell into the water beside them.

Chogan set to paddling, all the while yelling at Sarah. "*Allez! Allez!*" Go! Go!

Sarah sliced through the water with the paddle, even though she couldn't stop shaking. She had to attack it, the same way she'd attacked a basketball on her old Scarborough court. She couldn't think of Matt, groaning behind her, blood pouring from his wound. She'd be no good to him if she were dead.

The arrows soared through the air and splashed into the river behind them. The warriors gave chase along the riverbank, their painted faces and war shrieks coming closer, but as Sarah and Chogan paddled like Olympians, their attackers dropped back, their feet becoming entangled in the shrubs and weeds along the bank. Chogan ignored everything around him. He grunted and stabbed the river. Soon the sound of skittering water swallowed the horrid shrieks.

Sarah's arms screamed from the effort, but surprisingly she kept pace with Chogan. Just ahead, a strange rumbling sound swelled, but she paid no attention to it. They had to escape. Suddenly she looked up and her heart skipped a beat. They were approaching rapids, a jumble of rocks and cascading water as long as a soccer field.

"Chogan," she yelled, over the rising roar.

Chogan shook his head and aimed the canoe straight for the middle of the rapids, where a narrow gap split the rocks. The water poured through this gap with explosive force.

"Portage!" she shouted.

Chogan shook his head again. He pointed backward. They were still being pursued.

"But this is suicide," she gasped.

Matt groaned. Sarah risked a glance back at him. His eyes were pinched and tearing from the pain. "You . . . can . . . do it," he said, through gritted teeth.

Sarah nodded and turned back to face the white water. She thrust her paddle into the current as they headed straight towards the gap in the rocks. The waves buffeted the canoe, tossing it from side to side. Sarah braced herself against the sides of the boat to keep from being tossed out.

"Hold on tight," she shouted back to Matt.

"H . . . holding . . . on."

The canoe shot through the gap like a cannonball from a cannon. It soared in the air, then slapped down into the water again. An electrical jolt zapped all the way up Sarah's spine. She plunged the paddle into the water, trying to keep the rocking canoe upright and its nose straight.

Boulders rose up on either side of them, as if they were mountains and the canoe was rocketing through a pass. Mist whipped up from the water blinded her. She blinked. A devil of a rock stood right in their path.

Sarah jammed the paddle deep. Chogan grunted behind her, so

he must have done the same. The canoe twisted sideways. It scraped the side of the rock, tilting and nearly capsizing. Sarah and Chogan compensated by swinging their body weight to the opposite side. The canoe righted and dashed farther down the river, where the number of rocks eventually dwindled. Sarah sighed. Calmer waters were just up ahead.

"I think we're out of the woods," she shouted back.

"Nothing but woods," said Matt, in a frighteningly weak voice.

They splashed down the final length of the rapids. As the canoe swept into a gentler current, Sarah wiped the sweat from her brow.

"We made it."

Then the nose of the canoe caught in an eddy spun off from a small whirlpool. It torqued and yawed. Despite Sarah and Chogan's frantic efforts keep it upright, it flipped over, tossing all its passengers into the icy water.

18

———— ⬦ ————

Enemies All Around

SARAH GASPED. SHE BOBBED ABOVE THE WATER FOR AN INSTANT, THEN sank. The shock of the ejection from the canoe into the frigid river had paralyzed her. The backpack still clung to her shoulders and weighted her down. She tried to swim upward, but the cold sapped her strength with every kick, every stroke. Was it time to die, here in the past? Would Dad ever know what had happened to her?

She saw a figure deeper in the water—a flash of blue and a shock of yellow hair. It had to be Matt, wounded and incapable of fighting for his life. Suddenly power sizzled through her. She stripped off her pack and let it float away. Then she kicked off into the depths of the river.

Matt swirled deeper and deeper, but Sarah determinedly gained on him until she could almost touch him. He floated in front of her, ghostly, with pasty skin and wide dark eyes. She reached out, grasped his shirt by the back collar and tugged him towards the surface. Her strokes with one arm were ruthless, her kicks as strong as that of a ninja in a desperate battle. This was one fight she was going to win. She broke the surface and gasped, still gripping Matt tightly. He bobbed up beside her, slack and lifeless.

Fear clutched Sarah's heart as she glanced at his inert body. Ignoring it she swam boldly towards the shore. Chogan stood hunched over on the riverbank, breathing heavily and watching her approach. He showed no emotion, just reached out for Matt when she brought him near. Chogan pulled Matt onto the grass and dropped him there. He turned to help Sarah from the water but she was already out—hair plastered to her head, shrunken from the cold. But Chogan must have seen the fire in her, because he stepped back.

She knelt down beside Matt and tilted his head.

"*Il est mort*," said Chogan. He's dead.

"*Non*," said Sarah.

Chogan shook his head, but he continued to watch, his eyebrows perched so high on his forehead they almost met his hairline. Sarah bent her lips to Matt's and breathed into him. He had to live. He had to. She felt for a pulse in his neck, but there was none. With her hands clasped, she compressed his chest, forcing the blood through his heart. She bent to breathe into his mouth again. *He had to live. He had to.* Minutes passed that seemed like hours. Her shoulders ached; her arms trembled. She couldn't stop. At last her arms wouldn't pump anymore. She stopped to check for a pulse again. There was none.

"*Live, you genius. You stupid, silly boy. I'm not going to call you a corpse. You're not a corpse!*"

Chogan stood back, mystified.

"*And where were you!*" she yelled at the sky. "You're his father, his guardian angel! You've saved him so many times! *What's wrong with you!*"

She pounded Matt's chest in frustration, which caused an explosive ejection of water from his blue lips. He gasped suddenly and started coughing. Sarah wiped her eyes. He was alive! She rolled him over so he could expel more water from his lungs. Despite the fact that he'd drowned, that an arrow was still embedded in his shoulder, he was breathing and trying to talk. Sarah turned him onto his back again.

"N-not a c-corpse," he said. A smile flitted across his face. Sarah couldn't help but hug him.

"Ow."

"Sorry." She backed off. "It's just . . . You almost left me, you know. Right here, in the middle of nowhere, in the middle of who-knows-when, surrounded by hostile people."

"One n-nice one," Matt corrected.

"Yes, one nice one," said Sarah, looking up at Chogan. After his frantic attempt at traversing rapids to save them, and all the help he'd given them so far, the anger she'd felt towards him when he'd thrown her in the canoe had completely dissolved.

Chogan stared at Matt with a deep frown. He pointed at Sarah. "*Shaman?*"

Sarah shook her head. "CPR," she replied. "Rescue breathing, lesson number six."

"And . . . y-you were a-afraid of the water," said Matt. "She was conning us," he said to Chogan.

Chogan's forehead looked like it would crumple into his skull. He nodded uncertainly and turned towards the forest.

Matt tried to get up, winced and sank back down. "We have to go," said Matt. "Chogan has his ears perked up again."

Sarah glanced at Chogan. His eyes darted here and there; his head was cocked to one side. She turned back to Matt, whose face was pasty, with dark smudges under his eyes. The arrow protruded from his shoulder, where blood still oozed.

"You're in no condition to move," said Sarah.

"If we don't move, we'll all be dead," said Matt, reverting to French.

Chogan agreed. He pointed at the woods. "Mohawk. They're coming."

Sarah nodded at Matt. "He can't move. He still has an arrow in his shoulder. We have to take it out first."

"Not me," said Chogan. "I am not a *shaman*." He examined the riverbank downstream and gestured towards a pile of rocks. "He will be safe there until I bring one back."

Sarah gazed doubtfully at the jumble of rocks beneath a sheer cliff. A shadow nudged between the rocks, perhaps a hole but barely the hint of one. "Some hiding place." When she looked back at Chogan, the urgency in his face made her scramble to her feet.

Together, they put their arms around Matt and boosted him up. Sandwiched between them and stumbling over riverside debris, Matt managed to stagger to the shelter. Sure enough, a crawlspace angled into the cliff, just under the pile of rocks. Sarah and Chogan dragged Matt backward into the hoop-like opening.

Matt grunted as his arrow-torn shoulder bounced on the ground, but he gritted his teeth and didn't yell or scream. The space narrowed like a funnel, too small for all three of them, so Sarah let Chogan take over and drag Matt deeper. Chogan propped Matt against the rear wall of the shelter, then began to back out.

"Where are you going?" asked Sarah, as Chogan wriggled past her.

"Home," Chogan grunted.

"But—" she pointed at Matt.

"Mohawk—Kanienkehaka," he said, as if that explained everything.

"He's leaving us," said Sarah.

"He has to warn his family," said Matt. "The Mohawk are their sworn enemies."

"I don't see why everyone can't get along," she said, wiping her eyes.

"You've studied history," said Matt. "There have always been wars."

A tug on Sarah's sleeve startled her into swinging around. What in the world? Chogan was trying to pull her out, too.

"I'm not coming with you. Are you out of your mind? I can't leave Matt. He's sick. He could be dying." Hearing the hysteria in her voice, she stopped. "What do you want, Chogan?"

"I need to find shaman and warn my family of the Mohawk. You must come and keep watch for enemy warriors."

"That's insane," said Sarah. "You don't need my help. I can't shoot an arrow. I can't even throw a dart. Ask my Dad. No, you can't ask my Dad. He's not here anymore, not in this time." She sniffed.

"Sarah, listen to me," said Matt. "Chogan needs your help. You're strong. He saw how you saved me. You can do this. You can do anything."

"I can't leave you," said Sarah, her voice a tiny squeak.

Matt took a deep breath. He stiffened, but he didn't cry out. "You can, because you have to. There's nothing you can do for me now. I have to heal, regain my strength. I think Chogan needs you more. You'll be back. I won't let you go unless you promise me you'll be back."

Sarah stared at Matt in anguish. Chogan continued to tug on her sleeve. This was maddening and crazy and unthinkable. But Chogan had helped them. How could she refuse him when now he needed her help? She wiped her eyes and made the most difficult decision of her life. "Okay," she said. But instead of following Chogan, she knelt down beside Matt. She tore a strip of cloth from her sweatshirt and coiled it around the arrow where it bit into his skin. She tore another two strips and wrapped these around his shoulder, binding the cloth so it would press on the wound to stop the bleeding.

"I brought you back, you corpse. Don't you die on me again."

"Cross my heart," said Matt, making the cross rather weakly.

Sarah was about to turn away, but stopped and faced him again. "You're the best friend I ever had."

Matt grinned. "I know," he said.

"You," said Sarah, shaking her head. With a heavy heart she turned away and followed Chogan out of the shelter. She heard him whisper at her back.

"But there's none better than you."

19

The Mohawk

Matt was cold. He had never been so cold in his life. It felt as though a frigid winter wind was blasting through the cave, stripping all the warmth from his body. But there was no wind.

Am I dying? He shuddered, which sent pain as searing as red-hot iron sizzling through his chest. He moaned, then bit his lip to keep silent.

A crackle came from outside that sounded like dead leaves being crushed under someone's foot—*crunch, crunch, crackle* —a terrifying Rice Krispies medley just behind the shelter of rocks. Pebbles cascaded down the cliff and struck the dome above him.

Oh no, they're coming. Matt could picture war-painted warriors skulking between the trees and gradually approaching with their tomahawks raised. He squeezed his eyes shut and did his best to keep his breathing shallow.

This was why Chogan had drawn Sarah out of the cave. He

knew Matt would be discovered. Chogan was actually saving Sarah, and Matt had known it, too. Either he would die of his wound or Mohawk warriors would find him. He didn't know which was worse, but Sarah's best chance for survival rested with Chogan. That's why he'd pushed her to go. He'd never been very noble, not even very kind, but Sarah did something to him. It was as if her better qualities were rubbing off on him.

Another clatter of cascading rocks resounded outside the cave entrance. Matt felt around for some kind of weapon. His hand closed on a rock with a sharp edge. He clutched it tightly. The light dimmed as though a shade had been drawn over the tunnel entrance. They could only come one at a time. Maybe he'd be able to take some out before they got him. Maybe it would end more quickly if he offered some resistance.

A painted face appeared in front of him, black and white bands like a hideous mime. The man's hair was shaved off on both sides of his head, leaving one stripe down the middle. In his right hand he held a tomahawk, ready to shatter skulls. He crept closer and smiled, perhaps anticipating the ease of his victory over a single boy. Matt's grip tightened on the rock.

As the Mohawk warrior raised his hand to strike, an idea hit Matt like a smack in the face. *Five Nations, alliances.* Maybe Sarah was wrong.

"Are you going to kill an Englishman?" he asked.

The Mohawk paused and tilted his head. "English?"

Matt couldn't believe it. The man actually knew his language. "What do I look like, a Frenchman?" he growled.

The man sat back on his haunches, keeping the tomahawk ready to launch. "What Englishman doing with *bear dung?*"

"Excuse me?" asked Matt.

"Algonquin," he snarled. "*Bear dung.*"

Matt, despite his precarious position, tried not to laugh. "I'm not *with* them," he said, doing his best to affect an arrogant tone. "My father is a great warrior. He was scouting the land when we got separated in the woods."

The warrior's gaze travelled from Matt's face to his rumpled shirt and grimy jeans. "You dress strangely," he said. "And you rode canoe with *bear dung.*"

Matt took a deep breath, which made the arrow dig deeper into his shoulder. He caught his lip between his teeth and buried the scream within his brain. One tear squeezed out of his eye and trickled down his cheek.

"I was trying to find his camp so I could tell my father. I pretended to be French to gain his trust. You know, enemy, backstab, that sort of thing."

The Mohawk frowned, but he lowered his weapon. "You English…" He paused as if searching for the right word. He crouched down and made as if to creep behind Matt.

"Sly?" said Matt.

He pursed his lips and nodded. "Sly. Very bad. I like it."

"Good," said Matt. "Glad you like it." If he'd had a tissue he would have wiped the sweat off his brow. Finally all his practice at conniving and lying had paid off. He'd always relished acting the scoundrel. Now he really needed to be one.

The warrior pointed to himself. "*Segoleh.*" He rumbled in his chest, which sounded something like a chuckle, and Matt wondered why. Maybe it had to do with his name.

"Pleased to meet you," he responded. "Matt Barnes."

Segoleh nodded towards the front of the cave. "We go."

Matt shook his head and pointed to the arrow wedged in his shoulder. "Injured," he said. "The move would kill me."

Segoleh gritted his teeth and growled something in Mohawk. He scrambled closer to Matt and reached under his arms. Matt closed his eyes as the movement of his injured shoulder felt like needles threading through him. Segoleh crawled backward, dragging Matt with him, until he emerged from the opening. Ten other warriors surrounded the small cave with their arrows raised.

"English," said Segoleh. This stirred grumbles among the men as they lowered their weapons. Segoleh left Matt lying beside the river while he climbed higher up the bank. He gave instructions to the men, then crept quietly into the woods.

Matt lay still, feeling the warriors' glares scour him from head to toe. What now? Would they tie him to a stake, throw him into the river, or leave him for the wolves to munch on?

Segoleh appeared from the ridge above the river and slid down the slope with an armload of branches and strips of bark to make a rope. He motioned to the others to help him, and most of them set to work, tying the bundle together and fashioning a crude travois to transport the injured boy. A few warriors still looked on with arms crossed. They muttered to Segoleh, who stood and faced them with a fierce scowl.

He spoke in Mohawk. Suddenly all the warriors stepped back and marveled at Matt. They nodded at him as if out of profound respect.

Matt had to ask. "What did you tell them?"

"The truth," said Segoleh. "That your spirit is great warrior. You fool the bear dung. That not so easy. You survive the waterfall, even with arrow in chest. We not leave you to die. You come with us."

Matt wasn't too keen on going with them, but he knew it was far better than the other option. He had no intention of changing their opinion of him by telling them there was no way he could have survived the rapids without his friends.

When Segoleh had finished the travois, two warriors hoisted Matt onto it. He held onto the sides as they pulled him up the steep embankment and set off into the woods. The leaves above his head waved a somber farewell as he was jostled about. Matt closed his eyes. Each step was taking him farther and farther from his friends. Who knew what was in store for him with this new First Nations tribe? He'd just escaped torture and certain death, but he couldn't help the flutter in his chest; he couldn't stop the shivering and the clattering of his teeth. He worried about Sarah, alone now except for Chogan. What would happen to her in this frightening New World? He wished his father hadn't always been so far out of reach. Then things would have turned out differently. For the first time in his life, he even missed Nadine.

20

Ashes to Ashes

CHOGAN RUSHED HEADLONG THROUGH THE TREES AS THOUGH A HERD of moose were chasing after him. Sarah gasped and sputtered as she raced to follow. Despite his speed, Chogan was surprisingly quiet. He ducked branches, leaped over scattered leaves, and avoided splashing through puddles and streams. Sarah, however, was not as fleet of foot. Every branch lashed her face. Every fallen log rose from the ground to trip her. She discovered every puddle or sank knee-deep into every thick patch of mud. But when she fell, Chogan picked her up. When she got stuck, he pulled her out. He didn't seem angry; it was merely his job to look out for her and keep her moving.

"Will Matt be okay?" she asked. Chogan hissed her to silence. He grasped her hand and pulled her doggedly through the brush. They were travelling upriver in a roundabout way. At one point, a series of rustles disturbed the woods to their left. Chogan yanked her down behind a log and crouched beside her. She caught a glimpse of movement, tan and dark. Then it was gone. Chogan whipped up his bow and nocked an arrow, but the enemies passed by without spotting them.

Sarah tried to quiet her thudding heart as Chogan scanned the forest for several more minutes, his bowstring retracted. Convinced they were safe, he sprang up again and crept forward, beckoning her to follow. They hustled towards the Algonquin camp, but with warier steps this time. The afternoon sun gradually folded into the trees, lengthening the shadows and deepening the gloom. Soon it would be dark, at least providing an additional cloak to hide them.

After an hour of struggling through the web of intersecting branches, the bulk of trees thinned out and the sound of babbling water swelled. They were approaching the clearing of Chogan's home. But instead of rushing into the camp to warn his family, Chogan slackened his pace. Clouds of thick grey smoke curled into the indigo sky accompanied by an eerie silence. Chogan stopped. He clenched Sarah's hand, grinding the bones. Her chest tightened as if a python had coiled around her. Beads of sweat welled up on her forehead. Each step she took felt heavier than the one before.

Chogan walked towards the village. His feet dragged and his shoulders sagged. The smoke was so thick here, Sarah began to cough and choke. Her eyes burned. But through breaks in the smoke, she could see . . . Her knees went limp. She fell to the ground and threw up. Chogan shed her hand and kept walking as if in a dream, or a nightmare. Sarah wiped away her tears, but more kept streaming out. When her vision cleared, she couldn't hold back the screams.

The bodies of Chogan's family—his aunts, his uncles, his cousins, his friends, his mother, his little brother—were scattered over the village, all dead. The ashes of remnant wigwams smoldered, burned to the ground.

Chogan wandered among the dead, touching each face as if to imprint it in his memory. He chanted a mournful song. Sarah swallowed her screams and looked towards him, trying to find words to comfort him. She couldn't find any. She missed her father desperately, wherever—whenever—he was, and even her corporate-hungry mother. At least they were still alive. She couldn't imagine Chogan's anguish.

At the totem pole in the centre of the camp, Chogan knelt beside a man sprawled on the ground. The man still twitched and moved his feet. Three arrows pierced his chest, yet he still clutched his bow in his hand. He'd gone down fighting. Sarah recognized his prominent nose and pointed chin—Chogan's father.

Chogan murmured to him and tipped his ear to listen. Sarah leaned forward. Although they spoke in Algonquin, she understood some words. *Odawa. Iroquet.*

Chogan nodded and wiped his eyes. He cradled his father's head in his lap and tried to stem the blood flow with a fur quiver laying across the man's shoulders, but the life drained from his body anyway. The man sagged and died. Chogan eased him to the ground. For a minute he bowed his head, then he stood, his eyes puffy, his cheeks tear-stained, but his lips compressed in a grim line. He squared his shoulders, held his head high, and walked towards Sarah.

"Help me," he insisted.

Sarah staggered to her feet. She didn't know if she could handle anything else, but she couldn't deny him help.

They spent many hours into the night covering the people with stones and brush. Chogan said little except to murmur that they had no time for rituals or mourning.

"We must warn the others," he said in French.

"Right," said Sarah. "But what about Matt?"

Chogan looked away.

"He needs us!"

Chogan turned back to her with quivering lips. "Everyone's dead."

"*Not Matt!*" Sarah shook her head wildly. Her hair flew around her face and pasted itself to her wet cheeks. Even though she'd thought her tears had run dry, they exploded from her eyes again.

"We'll go look," he said.

He held his hand out to her. She clasped it firmly, trying not to dwell on the horror of the past few hours and the horrible possibility he'd planted in her mind. They stumbled back the way they'd come, their shoulders slack, their heads drooping—spent with grief. Rustles, leaf shivers and padding feet surrounded them. The night teemed with wildlife, but there was no sign of the enemy. Chogan's keen eyesight led them through the dark as he chose a path closer to the river. He cocked his head from time to time and halted their progress, but the danger had passed. They swiftly made their way back to the rock den where they'd concealed Matt.

Sarah crawled in first. "Matt," she called. "We're back, just like we promised."

He didn't answer.

Probably just sleeping. She crept farther in, feeling her way in the dark. Her fingers encountered pebbles and dirt but no Matt. She made her way to the back wall of rock, her hands dusting the air and the ground. Nothing.

"Oh no," she said, her breath stuttering. She shuffled back out and stood beside Chogan. His eyebrows were raised, but he had his arms crossed as if he'd known what she would find.

"He's not here," she said. She swiped at her eyes with the back of her hand.

"*Le Mohawk,*" he said.

"No! Why would they take him? He was wounded. What would they do with him?"

Chogan turned away and kicked a stone into the river.

"You knew this would happen," said Sarah, rounding on him.

Chogan said nothing.

"You left him to die." She grabbed his shoulders and turned him back to face her.

"He was already dead," said Chogan. "One way or another."

"I could have stayed with him. I could have fought," she said angrily.

"You would have died, too."

"No," she denied. "I . . ." Words failed her. How could she argue against his cruel logic? He'd sacrificed Matt to save her, save himself, and perhaps save his family, although it had been too late for them. She sank down at the water's edge and wailed.

Chogan watched her, his own tears flowing again. He savagely swiped at them, his lips compressed. "We must go," he said.

"Where?" asked Sarah.

"The Asticou."

"Where is that?"

"The Boiling Kettle," he said.

Sarah frowned. "*Odawa?*"

"*Oui,*" said Chogan. "We must warn Iroquet."

"Aren't the Iroquois our enemy? Aren't they the ones who did this?"

Chogan shook his head. "Iroquet is the name of a great Algonquin chief. His summer camp is at *Odawa*. We must warn him so he can defend himself and alert the other villages along the river."

"Oh, right," said Sarah, now remembering the chief's name from history class. "Do you know him well?"

"My uncle," he replied.

Chogan helped her to her feet. "Won't the Mohawk get there before us?" she asked.

He scanned the riverbank—which was clearly defined in the moonlight against the star-like reflections off the river's waves—and pointed downstream. "The canoe." On the opposite side, the flipped prow of a vessel poked out of the reeds, looking like a large curved vulture's beak.

Sarah stared at it uncertainly. She eyed the fast-flowing stream of water just below the rapids where they'd nearly drowned. "You're going to swim over there and get it?"

Chogan nodded. He shrugged. A faint grin appeared on his face. "Piece of cake—um, *une morceaux de gâteau?*"

"*Une morceaux de gâteau?*" he asked, his eyebrows pinched together.

"*C'est une expression,*" said Sarah. It's an expression. "Oh, never mind. Just be sure to come back."

"Soon," he said before he dove into the river. At first the current whisked him downstream, away from his objective. Sarah crossed her fingers and held her breath until he bobbed up and began to fight the current, striking out determinedly for the opposite bank. His arms lashed the water, churning forward with each rhythmic stroke. He was halfway across the river when a large wave engulfed him. He went under. Sarah ran along the bank looking for him, searching for his bobbing head, but she couldn't see anything in the murky water. Chogan had disappeared.

"Not you, too," she moaned. Her vision blurred as the tears flooded her eyes again. "Darn you, Chogan! You can't leave me all alone here, in this backward time, in this strange land, surrounded by hostile enemies. *I'll die!*"

Sarah shivered. Her teeth clacked uncontrollably. She crossed her arms over her chest as she went numb with cold. The haunting hoot of an owl piped from a nearby tree. A wolf howled in the distance. In this daunting country she had no friends. What could she do? Where would she go?

A splash down the river halted her spiral into self-pity. She'd been looking at the canoe. She looked farther downstream and there he was. First his head broke the surface. Then he climbed, sopping, his shoulders heaving, onto the opposite shore. He was a good ten metres beyond the location of the canoe, but he'd made it. He was alive. But he looked exhausted as he turned and waved at her. She waved back, quivering with relief.

Chogan staggered over the rocks along the riverside, heading for the canoe. Along the way, he plucked something from the bank that resembled a branch. When he reached the canoe, he lifted it easily from its perch between some boulders and flipped it right side into the water. Into the hull he tossed the branch, which Sarah now realized was a paddle. Before trusting that it was watertight, he walked around the canoe, inspecting and prodding suspicious cracks or splinters. Satisfied, he climbed in and motioned for her to meet him farther downstream. Sarah signalled that she understood and began walking along the bank. Chogan aimed the prow perpendicular to the flow and paddled with broad strokes across the river. He made good headway and landed just ahead of Sarah.

"Come in," he said.

Sarah, still reluctant, climbed aboard the *S.S. Algonquin*.

Chogan thrust his paddle against the bank and steered the nose of the canoe downstream. The current was swift but smooth, with no other rapids in their path. Sarah spied her sodden backpack flattened against a rock, and was surprised when Chogan angled towards it and fished it out of the water with his paddle. He tossed it into the bottom of the canoe with a quick nod at her. She smiled her appreciation. Then he resumed paddling down the Gatineau River.

Sarah couldn't believe it. For a boy who'd suffered so much loss, he had unwavering courage. He was pressing on to honour his father's last request, while at the same time protecting and caring for her—an unusual, inexplicable girl who'd interrupted his quiet life. She had to follow his example. Forget about Matt and her father and her impossible situation and simply live. Continue on. Help Chogan save the rest of his people. It was a noble quest—even one worth living for. She set her jaw and slapped the water with her hand, as the canoe nosed into the mighty Ottawa River. She would do more than let the current take her.

21

Pain and Glory

MATT LOST CONSCIOUSNESS DURING HIS TREK THROUGH THE WOODS
on the travois. At first the Mohawk men jostled him about so much
that the pain in his shoulder became corrosive, eating through all
his nerve fibers. But after a while, maybe an hour, his mind entered
something like a dead zone and he felt nothing. When he awoke, they
were no longer moving. He blinked to clear his vision.

Not too far from where he lay on the ground, a fire burned. A
pot of water was suspended over it on a tripod of sticks. Instead of
the travois, Matt was lying on a soft blanket of fur. He tried to sit up,
but a jackhammer drilled at his head and he felt bile reverse in his
stomach like the tide in the Bay of Fundy, so he quickly sank back
down. One of the warriors crouched near him and spoke soothingly
in Mohawk. The man pointed to the arrow still protruding from his
shoulder. Matt craned his neck and looked at it.

"I guess it should come out, don't you think?" he said. He reached up to grasp it and gasped as the movement sent knives ripping through his flesh.

The warrior seized his hand and swept it away. He called over the Mohawk Matt remembered—Segoleh. Wavy bands of black and white war paint still decorated his face. His eyes bore the same wicked gleam, though his mouth had softened. "Must not touch arrow, English."

"Matt."

"Matt," Segoleh repeated. "Shaman will fix."

"Shaman?" asked Matt.

"Medicine man."

Matt felt a surge of panic. "I don't want any witch doctor touching me, thank you very much."

Segoleh smiled. "Welcome," he replied, totally missing the gist of Matt's statement. He beckoned another man over to the boy's side. "This Aghstawenserontha. Means *he who puts on rattles.*" Segoleh held up a carved wooden handle. Some type of animal's foot was attached to it, claws and all—maybe a turtle's foot? By way of an explanation, Segoleh shook the device. It made a distinctive chatter. "He great medicine man. Use rattle to chase away demons of disease. Then he remove arrow."

Matt considered the other Mohawk in front of him. Black paint covered his face, to match charcoal irises. Only the whites of his eyes were apparent in the dark. Tucked into his hair at the back and displayed like a fan were many white feathers. The effect was more like that of a peacock than a human being. Matt was not reassured. He remembered Dr. Basin at home, with his starched white lab coat and his calm brown eyes. His hair had always been clipped short and neatly combed. He'd had the air of a well-ordered professional. Despite all of

Dr. Basin's poking and prodding over the years, Matt sort of missed him right now.

The medicine man leaned over him. "Ug-say-what's-a-on-that," Matt said. "I don't think this is a good idea."

"Aghstawenserontha," corrected the shaman. He uttered something in Mohawk. Segoleh translated. "Be still." Then he chuckled, of all things. It sent a shiver down Matt's spine.

Aghstawenserontha gently unwound the strip of Sarah's sweatshirt that still hugged the arrow at its base. It clung to Matt's skin, cemented there with congealed blood, but the medicine man moistened it with water and carefully plied it off. He studied the wound, then opened his bag and removed a folded cloth holding leaves and another chopped up substance. He drizzled the mixture into the pot of boiling water over the fire. After a few minutes, he dipped a cup into the solution, waited until the steam evaporated, and then held it to Matt's lips.

"Tea," said Segoleh.

Matt eyed the cup. *I am thirsty, but . . . tea?* "No, thank you. I'm more of a Coke person."

Aghstawenserontha muttered something, and Segoleh nodded. "You must drink," he said. "Has sassafras roots and other herbs—will help with pain and keep evil spirits from entering body."

Matt didn't give much weight to the evil spirits part, although Segoleh could mean infection, but he'd take anything that would help with the pain. He sipped the tea and gradually the throbbing subsided.

By that time, the medicine man was chanting and shaking the rattle. He pulled a stone pipe wed to a hollow wooden stem, along with a dried leaf, from his deerskin bag. Setting aside the rattle, he stuffed the leaf into the chiseled chamber of the pipe, lit a twig in the fire and fed the tip of the burning twig to the bowl of the pipe. He took several drags and puffed curling grey clouds over Matt's head, his voice still warbling through the chant. Then he focused on Matt, although his eyes seemed somewhat bleary.

"You smoke," Aghstawenserontha said, through Segoleh.

"I'm not allowed to smoke," said Matt. "I'm only a kid."

Aghstawenserontha thrust the tip of the pipe between Matt's lips. "You smoke," he insisted.

Matt inhaled the bitter smoke and started coughing and sputtering. "This stuff is awful," he muttered.

Segoleh smiled. "Taste awful. Feel less pain." He nodded to the arrow. "Aghsta take arrow out."

"Maybe I'm getting to like it," said Matt. "It's not so bad walking around with an arrow attached to you. He's like a buddy to me now."

Aghsta, as Segoleh called him, sat back on his haunches and gazed pensively at Matt.

"Good. You've changed your mind," said Matt.

Aghsta jammed the pipe into his mouth again. He forced Matt to take several more puffs.

"Okay. That's enough," Matt said, through a series of raspy coughs. His voice seemed muffled and slurred. His movements were sluggish. He felt distant from this whole situation. He floated away—he could see the medicine man and Segoleh, even himself with the arrow poking out of his chest, but it was like he was suspended above it, hovering in space.

"Ooh. This is weird," he heard his own voice saying.

Aghsta grunted a string of words to Segoleh, who knelt beside Matt and placed his hands on his arms. Matt could see everything, but feel nothing. The medicine man seized the arrow with two hands, placed a foot on Matt's chest, and wrenched the arrow from his shoulder.

Matt screamed. He screamed and screamed. He was no longer above anything. Searing pain ripped into him as though a bottle of acid had been splashed over his shoulder. It galvanized every nerve ending, making him shudder and shake. He didn't notice that Aghsta was prodding the fire with a stick, igniting the end, until the shaman raised the glowing tip in front of his face.

"Wh-what are you doing with that *thing?*"

"Smoke," said Aghsta, nodding to Segoleh who lowered the pipe to Matt's lips.

Matt turned his head away. "I don't want to smoke! *What are you doing with that thing!*" Matt tried to sit up, even though sparks and currents leaped through him, like he'd been given an electric shock. Segoleh held him down.

"Stop bleeding," Segoleh said.

Matt knew all about cauterization. He knew that burning the wound was probably the most practical thing to do to stop the bleeding. He also knew—through first-hand experience—that there was no such thing as painkillers in this day and age.

"Smoke," insisted Segoleh. He thrust the pipe between Matt's lips. Matt had no choice but to inhale the bitter vapour. He choked and nearly retched. But the man kept the pipe in his mouth until he'd filled his lungs three or four times. Gradually, the jolts and needles wracking his body subsided.

"I know what you're doing," Matt said drowsily. "You're making me sleepy so I can't fight back. R . . . really c . . . clever. But I . . . I'm not a . . . about to be b . . . burned."

He was rising above everything again. He couldn't, shouldn't. He had to stay behind and fight. In a few prolonged seconds, as if in slow motion, Aghsta lowered the poker to Matt's blood-soaked shoulder. A sizzle hissed through the air, and the flesh blackened beneath his evil wand.

Matt returned to his body with a thud. He screamed again, only louder this time. A blazing current zapped through his chest and rode every nerve up and down his arms and through his abdomen. He writhed under Segoleh's pinning grasp. No one could live through this much agony. Finally, after what must have been minutes but felt like hours, he gave a vast shudder, and the pain retreated. The wound still pulsated in his shoulder, but it was no longer a thing of unbearable torture.

"Can I have another smoke?" he asked weakly.

"No," said Segoleh. "Too strong. Make you sick."

If Matt hadn't been shuddering, he would have laughed. "I'd rather be sick. I can't take any more of this."

"All done," said Segoleh, nodding at Aghsta. The medicine man was methodically spreading some paste over the wound. "Feel better soon."

"Right," said Matt. Then he passed out.

When Matt drifted back from his dream world, the warriors were breaking camp. He turned on his side to watch, although even turning triggered a flood of sharp jabs through his shoulder. They bustled about, rolling up sleeping mats and stuffing food and utensils into deerskin sacks. Some had reapplied paint to their faces and slung quivers of arrows over their shoulders.

"Are you leaving?" asked Matt, as Segoleh walked past.

Segoleh pivoted back on his heel and tipped his head towards Matt. "Must attack next villages. Reclaim land."

"I thought this was Algonquin land."

Segoleh laughed, although Matt didn't get the joke. "Algonquin *bear dung*," he said.

"Wouldn't it be easier if you just tried to get along?" Wow, he sounded like Sarah now.

The warrior frowned.

Well, if he was heading down that path, why not go all the way? "You know, make peace."

Segoleh spat on the ground. "No peace with *bear dung*. We destroy them, take land." His eyes narrowed suspiciously. "Why you want peace, English? You great warrior."

Matt realized his mistake like a splash of cold water in the face. He tried to sit up, but the wound—still far too tender—screamed in protest. With gritted teeth, he sank back down and peered at his shoulder. It was bound with leaves and some kind of animal skin—a bristly nest of a bandage.

"Some warrior," he hissed under his breath. "I can't even sit up." To Segoleh he replied: "Warrior scout, yes. If war could be prevented, I would be happier."

"Happiness not important."

"You might die," said Matt.

"Better to die than let others take our land, steal our trade."

Matt winced. It seemed so senseless that these tribes fought with each other, when the Europeans would eventually bring about their downfall. Whether it was the kindness they'd all shown him—Chogan, Segoleh, and Segoleh's people—or some benevolent part of his character that made him speak up, Matt didn't know. He couldn't let this squabbling continue, even to save his own life.

"You shouldn't be fighting each other," he said. "You should join with the Algonquin and try to stop the men from across the sea."

Segoleh tilted an eyebrow. "You are from across the sea."

"Sort of, yes. But I'm not important. By the way, how do *you* know English?"

Segoleh massaged his neck, paused for a second, then he began to speak. "I met Englishman many moons ago, in the land of the Susquehannock. We go down to make war on the tribe—they great enemies—and we come upon Captain John Smith."

"John Smith? Pocahontas's John Smith?"

"I know not Pocahontas," he said. "But we meet English and one man come back with us for a time and teach us words."

"That's great," said Matt. "I think."

Some of the warriors were calling impatiently to Segoleh. He waved them away and sat down beside Matt. "Why worry about men from across the sea? They only here for trade."

"No," said Matt. "For land."

"They occupy small parcels of land only," said Segoleh, a question in his voice.

"They'll take more and more, until there is no more."

"They will kill us?" he asked.

"If you fight, they'll kill you. Even if you don't fight, their diseases will kill you. They'll push you into small tracts of land where you can barely survive and take everything that was yours."

"How you know this?" asked Segoleh, his voice striking a lower note.

Matt struggled to sit up again. Segoleh helped him so they could face each other. "Because I know the Europeans—the people from across the sea. They travel everywhere and they take land."

"Why you tell me this? You want me to fight you?"

"No," said Matt. "I want you to stop them. Not fight against them. That will never work, because there'll eventually be too many. But if you join your brothers—"

"They not brothers, they—"

"Bear dung, I know. But they live on this land. They fight for this land. You will all die, or wish you had, if you can't unite and devise a plan to save yourselves."

Segoleh tapped his toe in the dirt, his face crinkled in deep thought. "If I do this," he said, "what I do with you?"

Matt scratched his head. *Maybe I should have thought of that before I opened my big mouth.* "Well, I hope you won't kill me. You could bring me with you, to the Algonquin, and we can try to make peace."

Segoleh shook his head. "This not good," he said. "This not work. They not trust us. We not trust them."

"You've made peace with the Five Nations," said Matt. "You can make peace with the bear dung."

"Maybe," said Segoleh, rolling the word over his tongue as if he were considering the notion. He tapped Matt on the head. "You a strange warrior, that betrays his own kind."

"I don't like to be lumped in with *them*," said Matt. "I believe in justice. What will happen to you if you don't stop them is savage. And they call *you* savages."

A frown rippled over Segoleh's face as a long minute passed. "No," he finally said. "I cannot make peace. Bear dung killed all people in my village. We make war on bear dung. If you join us, I make you honourary Kanienkehaka."

Kanienkehaka? Oh, right. Matt remembered the reference in his father's book and what Annawan had written on the board in class. That was what the Mohawk called themselves—*People of the Flint.*

Matt sighed when he realized what his failure meant. Now he'd have to travel with the Mohawk—Kanienkehaka—and possibly even fight against Chogan's people. It was insane, but Segoleh could not be dissuaded.

The warrior grasped Matt firmly under his uninjured shoulder and hoisted him up. He called to the other warriors and gathered them together. Fire danced behind their eyes as they discussed their next attack. All Matt's arguments had amounted to nothing. The First Nations were destined to meet their fate. Segoleh returned to the dying fire after the powwow and filled Matt in on their plans. Matt grimaced when he heard the word *Odawa* in a context he'd never imagined. Ambush.

22

Odawa

THE TRIP UPRIVER SHOULD HAVE BEEN A SOLEMN ONE, BUT SARAH couldn't bear the silence any longer. She chattered in French like a flock of sparrows in a tree, telling Chogan everything from how she missed her father to how Matt's guardian had betrayed his father. She was careful to keep it as logical as possible for this time period, but Chogan probably only heard half of what she said. He grunted and nodded here and there. He seemed focused entirely on his mission, or he likely would have given in to his grief. He only looked up once, when she mentioned Nadine and Matt's father.

"Did she kill him?" he asked.

Sarah started. "No, not exactly. But he is lost."

"I know the feeling," said Chogan.

Unable to find words to comfort him, Sarah fell silent until the roar of more rapids made her squeak in alarm. Chogan reassured her with a smile. "The Asticou," he said, as if that made any sense to her.

She shrugged her shoulders.

"Boiling Kettle," he said in French. "Big rapids."

"Can we go through them?" she asked.

Chogan laughed for the first time since they'd left his home. "Not possible. We stop here." He pointed to a break in the trees on the south shore of the Ottawa River. Beyond, a waterfall plunged from a fifteen-metre cliff along the bank, sending up rolling clouds of mist.

"Rideau Falls," she said.

"The Frenchman calls it that."

"Which Frenchman?"

"Étienne Brûlé. Champlain's man. He passed through and named things. What is '*rideau*'?"

"A curtain," said Sarah. "You hang it in windows—" She paused. "Openings in wigwams, so people can't see inside."

Chogan cocked his head. "Strange," he said. The din of the waterfall grew louder, like drum sticks playing a cymbal swell. "Algonquin use it for fun," he explained. "We take our canoes underneath and see if we can stay dry. No fun today," he said somberly.

They beached the canoe among the pebbles and the thickets on the south shore. The cold light of the moon was giving way to the first trickling rays of dawn. After he'd pulled the canoe high on the bank, Chogan plucked Sarah's backpack from the hull. He eyed it with a tilted brow, then slid his arms through the straps with a nod of satisfaction. Sarah began to protest that she could carry it herself, but he simply shook his head, grabbed her hand, and headed up the steep hill.

When they reached the crest, Sarah had to stop and gawk. Spread out before them, as far as the eye could see, was an untamed garden of indigenous trees, flowers, and shrubs. In modern-day Ottawa, they'd be walking on Sussex Drive—probably right by the Prime Minister's massive stone mansion. It was hard to relate this flourishing jungle to the city it would become.

The earth-tinged sapphire waters of the Rideau River snaked between the trees, its banks uncluttered by apartment buildings and neon-lit convenience stores. No paved streets existed, flooded with honking, exhaust-belching vehicles, nor bridges masking the clear blue skyline. Instead, the landscape was simply a mosaic of trees in various shades of green—jade, emerald, lime. Flocks of birds rose into the air and dipped towards the water. They fluttered over rippling waves and dodged in and out of the mist that hovered on the river's edge near the waterfall.

"Where's your uncle?" asked Sarah.

"Highest hill," said Chogan, pointing beyond the river.

"Parliament Hill," said Sarah.

Chogan arched an eyebrow. "Algonquin Hill," he said. "Best place to ward off attacks."

"Then they should be safe."

Chogan shook his head. "Big Mohawk war party. No one is safe."

Sarah sighed and slipped closer to Chogan. This horrible nightmare was far from over. "How do we get across? We should have portaged with the canoe."

"No," he said. "We swim. Easy current. Much faster."

Sarah's heart set off at a gallop. She swung her head in the direction of the thundering falls. "I don't care how easy it is, that's a big drop."

Chogan squeezed her hand. "You swam Matt out of the bottom of the river. You can swim this one easily before you drop off the cliff."

Sarah was unconvinced. Yes, she'd performed a tremendous feat of swimming in the Gatineau River, but that had been to save Matt's life. The thought of him triggered fresh tears. What a wasted effort it had been. She'd lost him, anyway. How could she explain adrenaline—that geyser of energy that only erupts in extreme circumstances—to Chogan? How could she ever perform that way again?

"Come," Chogan said, tugging her to the water like an obstinate mule. "We must reach my uncle, *tout de suite*." He dove into the rippling waves and urged her to join him.

Sarah hesitated, painfully aware of the drop-off twenty-five metres away. "I must be crazy," she said, as she splashed into the cool water. But the lazy current flowed heedlessly around her without sweeping her downstream.

Sarah pushed off and swam, slicing the waves effortlessly, making rapid progress towards the western shore of the Rideau River. He was right. It was quite an easy swim. She had nothing to worry about.

Suddenly a branch poked from a choppy wave and flipped towards her. She shrieked as it plowed into her side, taking her by surprise. Twisting in the waves, the nasty limb twirled and hooked the loose threads of her sweatshirt, firmly attaching itself to her like a leech. It dragged her along with the current and hauled her directly towards the falls. *Oh no, not again.* She tugged at the material, but it wouldn't come loose. Panic seized her as she ripped and ripped but couldn't break free.

Chogan stroked calmly towards her, looking untroubled.

"I'm caught," she yelled.

"Let me see," he said, reaching her side. He floated alongside her and tried to tear out the threads, but couldn't seem to disentangle her from the branch. As the current propelled them closer to the cliff, he growled, grabbed the shirt and pulled it off over her head.

Sarah froze, shocked by his rough treatment, but only for a second. She read the urgency in his expression and began to swim intently for the western bank. Just before the water plunged over the cliff, they managed to grope a handhold on some weeds and crawl up on shore.

Sarah collapsed on the ground. Chogan plunked beside her, shaking his head. "This is a very bad day," he sputtered.

"Very bad," she agreed. She burst into giggles. It was either that or cry. If she started to cry, she wouldn't be able to stop.

Chogan placed his hands on his head and stared, at first too amazed to speak. Then he laughed, too. Tears filled his eyes, but he kept laughing. He rolled over, hugged Sarah and they laughed together. When their giggles subsided into exhausted hiccups, they fell apart. Chogan stood up.

"We must go to my uncle now."

"Or die trying," said Sarah, still chuckling. She struggled to her feet, and stood awkwardly in the cold breeze in only a bra and frayed jeans. Chogan didn't seem to care. Sarah shivered and crossed her arms over her chest. "What will your uncle think of me?"

"That you are a brave warrior," Chogan replied. He shrugged off her backpack and handed it to her. "You have extra clothes?"

"N-no," she said, her teeth chattering.

He squirmed out of his dripping shirt and draped it over her shoulders. Sarah clutched it around her, then slung her pack overtop. With a quick nod of reassurance, Chogan grasped her hand and turned towards the hill. They trudged forward, shedding droplets of water as they went.

Iroquet's camp was located on the promontory of the cliff that Sarah knew as Parliament Hill. Winds buffeted the high ground, but it provided a clear view of the surrounding countryside on both the south and north sides of the river. However, lookouts couldn't see through the dense forest that covered most of the land to the north. A war party could easily slink undetected through that forest. At some point, though, they'd have to cross the river to approach the camp.

Chogan released Sarah's hand as they drew closer to the wigwams. He seemed rejuvenated as he bounded up the hill like a cougar. Sarah lagged behind, totally drained of energy. She'd help Chogan carry out his father's last request—after all, she was his friend and companion—but everything seemed so hopeless now. They might be able to save his people, but what about Matt? Was he dead? Would Matt's father still protect her if Matt was gone? And could she ever get back home?

Sarah hugged the deerskin shirt to her chest and shuffled between the wigwams, into the middle of the camp. The stares that followed her would normally have made her skin crawl, but after all she'd been through, she couldn't care less. Black-braided women looked up from their cooking fires, men from sewing animal skins or curing meat. Children stopped playing and watched her with amazement. They'd seen the black-bearded Frenchmen with milky-white skin, but this female child with her reddish-brown hair and bronze skin—like them, yet different, especially considering her clothing—had to be a shock.

Chogan rushed towards the central fire, where the snarling image of a bear was carved into the sturdy wooden totem pole. He called out to a slim Algonquin man with grey-dusted hair who was laughing and joking with some other men. The man turned when he heard

Chogan's shout. His eyes lost their amused crinkle and narrowed. His smiling mouth curved downward.

He didn't shout or raise his voice. As he spoke to Chogan, the muscles in his face tightened, and the cords of his neck stood out. Then Iroquet lost his erect posture. He sank to the ground as if struck by a blow. Before Chogan had finished his story, the warrior's eyes were sparking with anger. This was their sovereign territory and they'd been invaded—again.

When Chogan stopped talking, he withered to the ground beside his uncle and began to cry. Iroquet sat rigidly, without moving, without a word. He offered the boy no sympathy, although the woman who'd stood quietly behind took a step towards him. Iroquet waved her away and pointed at Sarah. He said only one word in French—"*Ennemie.*"

Sarah couldn't believe her ears. *What? Are you crazy?*

This time Iroquet did raise his voice. He thundered at Chogan, then drew himself up and marched towards her. Sarah backed away, but too slowly for the determined Algonquin. He grabbed her by the hair and yanked her into the circle around the fire.

"Who are you?" he demanded in French.

Sarah shuddered, but she stood tall and peeled his hand from her hair. "My name is Sarah," she said. "I'm not your enemy. I'm a friend." She held out her hand to Chogan. Chogan brushed aside his tears, stood, and firmly clasped her hand.

Iroquet looked from his nephew to Sarah, his eyes unnervingly narrow. He spat out words at Chogan that Sarah couldn't possibly understand, but somehow she knew he thought she was a spy.

"*Non,*" said Chogan. He shook his head vigorously. He seemed to be deliberately speaking in French for Sarah's benefit. Her heart swelled in gratitude.

"Look at her!" Chogan yelled at his uncle. "She's only a child. Lost in the woods. She had no part in this raid. She even helped me cover the dead."

Iroquet wouldn't listen. He insisted that she be tortured for information. Not every part of Iroquet's side of their conversation was in French, but the last he uttered clearly in that language so she could understand. She stared at Iroquet in dawning horror. After all she'd gone through, was this the way it would end?

"I've done nothing except help Chogan," she insisted. "If I were you, I wouldn't stand here debating about what to do with me, but start sending out messengers to warn your other camps, and prepare for war!" Sarah stopped. She'd been shouting.

Iroquet eyeballed her, his facial muscles twitching. Unexpectedly, he nodded. He turned towards the group of men and boys behind him, and in a crisp military voice snapped orders. One boy shot off to the east. Another boy raced out of camp to the west. Five in all set off the chain of warnings up and down the river. Iroquet's men quickly dispersed to their tents and retrieved bows and arrows, clubs and moosehide shields. When he turned back to Sarah, she nodded in approval. It gave him pause, but he didn't seem ready to trust her yet. He reached out to grab her arm, but Chogan darted between them. Another argument ensued.

Iroquet ground his teeth, his face flushed darker, but Chogan wouldn't move. Finally Iroquet thrust the boy aside and seized Sarah's arm. Sarah tried to wrench away from him, but his grip was like a bear trap. He hauled her towards the wigwam opposite the fire, whipped aside the flap that substituted for a door, and shoved her in. She fell into the black interior, so terrified she could hardly breathe. How could this be happening? Before she could turn around, a knee punched the small of her back. Pain knifed through her spine, as he twisted her arms behind her and wrapped a length of twine around her wrists.

Chogan dashed in beside his uncle as the man released the pressure on her back. Sarah rolled onto her side and sat up, grimacing at the nips and bites of pain throughout her upper body. A crust of mud, leaves, and tears clung to her face. She blinked to clear her vision, and there they stood, framed in the wigwam's doorway, Chogan and Iroquet, glaring at each other. Iroquet gripped a glittering silver knife. He growled something in Algonquin, then repeated it in French.

"Would you die for her?"

"*Oui*," said Chogan. "Without hesitation."

"You cannot face the truth," he said.

"The only danger she presents is to your pride," said Chogan. "For she is different, and she has the courage of the bravest warrior. Strangely enough, she is on our side."

"She is a spy for the Mohawk," said Iroquet.

Sarah awkwardly tried to stand. She needed to say something, even if it was the last thing she ever said. She stumbled, wobbled, but regained her feet and stood beside Chogan, facing Iroquet without flinching.

"I do not stand with a people," she said. "I stand alone."

"Not completely alone," Chogan murmured.

She smiled at him, amazed at his steadfast support.

Iroquet scowled, raised his knife to the deadliest position, but a shout from outside interrupted any downward thrust. A ripple of voices persuaded him to turn away from his prisoner. Chogan whipped out his own knife and slashed the ropes around Sarah's wrists.

Iroquet swept aside the flap in the doorway of the wigwam. Outside the shelter a white man marched into camp, surrounded by a swarm of other men. All sported red tunics trimmed in gold, and dirt-stained caramel-coloured trousers. The leader had a thick tapered moustache hunched under his nose, and a bristly bronze goatee clinging to his chin. On his head sat an oblong hat with a feather. Funny how closely he resembled a French musketeer. And someone else, too. The statue at Nepean Point. He had to be the explorer Champlain.

Champlain greeted Iroquet with a respectful nod. He surveyed the entire camp and quickly determined trouble was brewing. "Why are your men preparing for war?"

Iroquet stepped out of the wigwam and joined Champlain at the base of the totem pole. He left Sarah and Chogan framed in the doorway, fully exposed to the Frenchman's scrutiny. Champlain cocked his head to one side as his eyes came to rest on Sarah.

"*Qui-est ce enfant?*" he exclaimed. Who is this child?

"*En espionne*," snapped Iroquet. A spy.

Sarah stamped her foot. It was so unfair! This time more than any other, she should keep quiet, but enough was enough. "No, I'm not!" Too late she realized she'd spoken in English. She clapped a hand over her mouth.

Champlain sucked in his breath. "What are you doing with an English child?"

"Ask my nephew," said Iroquet. "He plucked her out of the woods."

Champlain squared his shoulders. This revelation clearly disturbed him.

"And there are Mohawk war parties attacking our villages," Iroquet continued. "Will you help us drive them out of our land?"

"Of . . . course," said Champlain, his voice tripping over a slight pause. "We're allies, are we not?"

He muttered to his men. They saluted and slung their guns from their shoulders. "Now about this English child. How do you think the English found their way this far inland?"

Iroquet shrugged. "Ask her." His finger singled out Sarah like a pronouncement of doom. She slunk behind Chogan.

Champlain strode up to them and flicked his hand for Chogan to stand aside. Chogan shook his head. Iroquet growled at him. Chogan stood firm.

"He's protecting her," said Iroquet. "She seems to have bewitched him."

"Not surprising," said Champlain. "The English are a crafty lot. *Bouge*," he barked at Chogan, instructing him once again to move. Chogan set his jaw and glared at the man.

"Talk to me, girl," Champlain snarled at Sarah. "Where did you come from?"

"I . . ." she stumbled. "I got lost."

"You're far from the shores of Virginia. Are you spying on us?"

Sarah snorted. She stepped out around Chogan and faced the Frenchman who, despite his enormous statue at Nepean Point, was actually quite short and not very menacing at all. "How could I be a spy? I'm only twelve years old."

The Frenchman eyed her, both eyebrows peaked. He considered her deerskin shirt, her jeans, and her straggly russet hair. "What a strange child," he commented.

Sarah tilted her head. "What a strange man."

"And very bold," he added with a scowl.

Sarah hid a secret smile. For a minute she'd acted like Matt.

"Why thank you. Now I think you should listen to me. This boy," she continued, touching Chogan's arm, "is my friend. So you see, we must be allies, even if I do know some English."

"Remarkable," said Champlain. "Uncommon valour, for English tripe."

"*Merci*," Sarah whipped back. "For the compliment, not the insult."

Champlain scratched his head, looking all the more muddled. "I can find no explanation for you, hundreds of miles from English territory. But I suppose you are of little importance."

"To me," said Chogan, "she is of great importance." He put his arm around her.

"No doubt," said the explorer. "But she will have little effect on our trade negotiations, or the upcoming war, unless she escapes and feeds vital information to our enemies. I would watch her closely."

"I intend to," said Iroquet, a wintry note in his voice.

Sarah shuddered and glued herself to Chogan's side. Champlain hitched his rifle higher on his shoulder, turned away from her and marched back to the central fire with Iroquet to discuss strategies of war.

Chogan watched them go, his face uncomfortably taut. He turned to Sarah and gripped her shoulders. "You must be careful," he said. "I don't trust that man."

"That makes two of us," she muttered. "Neither do I trust your uncle, who would love to stick me with his knife, or the other warriors who are glaring at me now. I don't trust the bears or the wolves or even the skunks, for that matter. They're all out to get me. In fact, even the water seems to be my enemy."

Chogan grinned. "But you trust me."

"To the end of time."

23

The Battle for Peace

MATT STUMBLED INCESSANTLY THROUGH THE SHADOW-STEEPED forest, tripping over roots. He was still so weak from his wound, he had trouble keeping up with Segoleh and the other warriors as they continued their trek towards Odawa and the high camp of Iroquet. When Segoleh reached the Ottawa River, he beckoned Matt to join him.

Matt collapsed on the reeds at the water's edge and shuddered from exhaustion and pain.

"You cannot continue?" asked Segoleh.

"No," said Matt, through clenched teeth. What did they think, he had superhuman strength? That he was some sort of spirit being? Ha! No one who'd been shot with an arrow just the day before could keep up this grueling pace. Which reminded him of his father. Now that Matt understood Sarah's visions of the Mohawk and arrows and him getting shot, he wondered why his dad hadn't come to his rescue at the crucial moment? Why had he let Matt flicker out of time for that instant by the Algonquin camp, but still let an arrow slice through him during the voyage down the Gatineau? So much for a guardian angel.

Segoleh squatted down beside Matt and scrutinized him from head to toe. "When we cross river, you can rest in canoe. After that, some warriors carry you." He winked, clapped Matt gently on the back, and said, "Will get better." A grin grew on his face until he couldn't contain a loud snort of laughter.

Matt was confused. "Why do you laugh so much? Do you enjoy other people's suffering?"

Segoleh smeared the mirth from his face with a hand. "No. Not enjoy. Life too short to be serious all the time. That why I named Segoleh—he who laughs." He smiled and patted Matt on the head. "No worry. Warriors will give you rest."

"Gee, thanks," said Matt, wondering how he'd like being jostled about by the less than sympathetic Kanienkehaka warriors. But that was the least of his problems. He still needed to figure out how to stop this war. His reasons weren't entirely selfless, either. The last thing he wanted was to fight and die for a cause that he didn't believe in.

"Greatest challenge will be crossing river undetected," Segoleh said.

Matt took a deep breath. "All right. Where do we cross?"

Segoleh pointed to an island that stretched halfway across the river—bands of trees that marched haphazardly over thin strips of land like a drunken parade.

"Petrie Island," he said. "Don't you think they'll have scouts watching these cross-over points?"

"We eliminated first scouts," replied Segoleh. "They will not have had time to replace them."

Matt winced. "They really will hate us."

"They already do," he said.

An idea flickered at the edge of Matt's consciousness. He remembered reading about the Five Nations peace treaty. How the nations actually desired peace over war. If he could just convince this stubborn warrior . . .

"But you can change that. You Mohawk—" He paused when Segoleh stiffened at the name. "—Kanienkehaka made peace with the Five Nations because it was in your best interest. You can do the same—"

Segoleh snarled and waved his hand. He no longer looked even slightly amused. The topic was obviously closed for discussion.

The other warriors removed the leaves and branches that had camouflaged their canoes at the river's edge. They portaged downstream until they reached a spot directly opposite the island. The boats were slipped silently into the water and the men hopped in. Segoleh helped Matt into a canoe with another warrior, where he slumped in the carved wooden hull. They set off across the river, slicing through the current with ease, and rapidly gaining the island.

This island was acutely familiar to Matt. He had spent many a lazy summer day sunning on the beach, wandering through the trails, or catching frogs and turtles in the nature preserve—until he was caught and banished from the park. But *that* Petrie Island, with its picnic tables and roads and well-established paths, was not *this* Petrie Island.

The men crept through high weeds and brush, then through a dense forest of silver maple, basswood, and elm, until they reached the narrow stream on the other side. Segoleh instructed a warrior to carry Matt, but Matt protested at first, despite his weakness. He didn't want to be borne on the man's back as if he were a baby. Instead he trudged beside them, stumbling and clutching branches for support.

Once he fell flat on his face. Lifting his head, he saw something he wished he hadn't. A body lay on the ground beside him, face down, with grey, somewhat bloated skin and an arrow-shaped bloodstain on its deerskin shirt. Matt scrambled to his feet and rushed towards the group of men, which had gotten ahead of him. His knees shook uncontrollably and his heart hammered in his ears when he reached Segoleh's side.

Segoleh looked down at him in concern. "Are you ill?"

Matt took a deep breath and wiped a stream of sweat from his brow. "I am," he said. "If you hadn't noticed, I was shot just yesterday." Though he tried, he couldn't inject his usual sarcasm into the statement. The body in the woods had really spooked him. War and dead bodies and arrows piercing your flesh might happen every day in Segoleh's world, but for a kid from the suburbs of 21st century Ottawa, this whole experience was something of a nightmare. Matt bit down on his tongue. It seemed to clear his head.

The group splashed through the swampy brook that separated the island from the mainland, heedless of the grasping mud. Segoleh helped Matt ford the stream, since he could barely break the suction at his feet, but stopped him on the other bank.

"We have a long walk to the camp of Iroquet," said Segoleh. "Rest here." He motioned to a clear spot on the ground. Matt collapsed. His shoulder throbbed; his head pounded. It was one thing to drive on a paved expressway from the suburb of Orleans to the city of Ottawa, but quite another to have to walk through dense thickets of brush and weeds and between clutching branches of trees just to get there. He hung his head and noticed the odd colour of his skin. It looked mottled, bluish, like the cadaver he'd seen on the island. How could he go on?

Segoleh handed Matt a bowl of what looked like porridge. He sniffed it. Definitely not oatmeal. Cornmeal maybe, with a fishy odour. Despite an initial shudder at the smell, Matt devoured the mixture. He was starving.

When he'd finished, Segoleh prodded the group to their feet and onto a narrow path towards the camp of Odawa. Matt trudged behind him, somehow keeping pace. But at times he fell behind, happily lost in the underbrush, until Segoleh hustled back to retrieve him. Finally, the warrior insisted on carrying him, slung over his shoulder like a bagged deer. When Segoleh grew tired, he tagged another warrior and passed Matt to the man while he prowled ahead again. Every jolt of the warrior's step, every shrug of his shoulder, sent a knife through Matt's wound. Sometimes he was sure the warrior tripped or jostled him on purpose. At least he was getting a rest, though. For a while he even lost consciousness, blissfully feeling nothing and only coming to when the others halted on the path.

The grim-faced warrior sloughed Matt from his shoulder and dropped him on the ground. He landed on his backside with only a mild jolt. Matt blinked and looked around. There was a break in the canopy of trees for a change and a lazy river flowed through the gap. They must have reached the bank of the Rideau River. The Kanien-kehaka stayed well back of the open area, hiding in a copse of birch and pine trees. Segoleh whispered instructions to his warriors. Then he spoke to Matt.

"We will cross here. The camp is at the top of the cliff."

Matt scanned the floodplain and the high promontory of Parliament Hill, only there were no tall buildings, no turrets and spires to mark the view. The camp upon the hill, a scattering of tan wigwams and wisps of white smoke, was clearly visible between a break in the tall trees. Even from this distance, Matt could see the well-armed welcome party marching down a path from the camp to the river. They must have already been detected.

"You will use tomahawk with good arm," said Segoleh, handing him the weapon.

Matt grasped the wooden handle and stared at the sharpened stone blade in alarm. Did Segoleh actually expect him to crack open Algonquin skulls? He pictured Chogan and shuddered. "I can't do this!" he exclaimed.

"The bear dung must die," said Segoleh. "You fight with us, or you join them."

A lump swelled in Matt's throat, nearly choking him. He'd never been one to stand up courageously; he usually played the role of class clown or troublemaker. And he had no hope of saving himself—he was going to die today, one way or another. But he couldn't go out killing the people he'd come to admire.

He tossed aside the tomahawk, crossed his arms and tried to straighten his wobbly knees. "I won't fight, and I won't join them in death. You have a chance to stand against the real enemy."

Segoleh's eyes narrowed. His hand clamped his own tomahawk.

Matt swallowed audibly, but he didn't cringe and cower. If he could stand up to Madame Leblanc, to the principal—and to Nadine, for that matter—he could face this vengeful chief. "You have to take a stand with the people of this land."

"Take a stand?" asked Segoleh, the frown deepening on his face.

"*For* the land and the people who love it. Don't give it away. Don't sign the papers they shove at you." He waved his hand to the south, where he knew a trickling influx of Europeans had begun. Strangely, his hand looked wispy, blurry. He studied his arm and it gave off an eerie glow—then he caught a glimpse of a large scaled head peering at him through a gigantic growth of ferns. Matt shook his head and Segoleh stood in front of him again, but his face looked paler.

"Are you spirit?" he asked.

"It doesn't matter what I am," said Matt. "I've come here for a reason. And I think it's to stop the bloodshed. To tell you what will happen if you don't. And to make you wary of the white man."

Segoleh hung his head and rubbed the bald portions of his scalp, as if he were contemplating Matt's words, but couldn't quite come to accept the notion of peace. "Should I forget my family? What Algonquin did to them?"

"Should they forget what you did?" asked Matt. "No, I doubt either one of you will forget or even forgive. But you have to stop fighting each other and plan for your future, or you'll have no future." He paused and noted that his body had gone gossamer again. Now to apply the shock technique and gain the upper hand, just like when he'd handed Madame Leblanc the cell phone and told her to call his unreachable father.

"But go ahead. Fight. Die for nothing. Let the voices of your nations fade until they can't be heard anymore. I dare you."

Segoleh jerked as if he'd been slapped. Matt couldn't believe it. Somehow he'd gotten through to the warrior, not by his ghostly appearance, although that couldn't have hurt, but by the impact of his words. By his audacity. For once, it might have stirred something besides rage.

Segoleh licked his lips and furrowed his brow so deeply Matt could see trenches developing. "I not want our voices to fade. A Kanien-kehaka is never diminished this way."

"We will hear you again," said Matt, "but it'll be too late."

Segoleh shook his head. "I cannot allow that." He sighed and his hand fell away from his tomahawk. "If this only way to keep Kanien-kehaka strong, then I will follow your path. We talk with bear dung."

Matt nodded, and nearly whooped, but caught himself just in time. *Must maintain dignity. Very important for a peace negotiator.* Of course it might still amount to nothing if Segoleh decided to ambush the Algonquin while they were having a powwow.

"But you have to swear you won't attack the Algonquin chief or his people during the talks."

Segoleh paused and Matt was almost afraid he'd flip back and renege on his promise, but at last he muttered, "I swear. Now you must cross river and persuade bear dung to smoke and talk."

Matt started. "You want *me* to talk to them?"

"Yes. They will not speak with us, not after raid on other camp. They will be out for blood."

Matt's heart rapped against his chest. His palms grew slick. "Even if I could swim across the river with my wounded arm, how do I get to where I can talk to them without them shooting me full of arrows?"

"If we go across," said Segoleh, "we have to kill them or be killed. Talks will be impossible."

Matt sighed. "I guess I have no choice." When would he ever learn to keep his big mouth shut? He eyed the sluggish current of the river. Under normal circumstances, this swim would be a cinch, but with his wound it would be a challenge just to keep from drowning. He looked downstream and tried to gauge the distance to Rideau Falls.

His best estimate was that he was at the future juncture of the train station and the baseball stadium. Even with his injury, he should be able to swim across before he was swept over the falls.

"Here goes nothing," he said. He glanced back at Segoleh, who nodded and grinned. He would have been reassured if he didn't know the man found comedy in everything. He splashed in and began to swim. The water was cold, which was a blessing, since it helped to numb his shoulder. He struck out using an awkward one-armed version of the front crawl, but his head kept bobbing underneath when he swung under for the next stroke. This wasn't working. He rolled onto his back and kicked, a much better technique. At least it kept him afloat.

It would have been a peaceful swim, had he not heard the shouts from the other side of the river. It had taken them no time to spot him. Would he even make it out of the water before another arrow pierced him?

Matt flipped over as his head scratched the sand near the bank. He crawled out of the water, his hair and clothes plastered to his skin like the fur of a drenched cat. He'd survived the smoke; now he was entering the fire.

The shouts grew louder. As Matt crawled to his knees and turned around, he saw them coming. A dozen warriors slathered in war paint approached cautiously with bows strung. They yelled at him in Algonquin. He had no idea what they were saying, but he staggered to his feet and raised his hands. He said to them in French, "I am not your enemy."

As the others continued to yell, one man stepped forward and replied in French. "Who are you?"

"A messenger," said Matt. "From . . . Champlain."

The man's eyes narrowed. He lifted his chin. "From Champlain, you say?"

Matt tried to quiet the thudding of his heart. He produced a weak smile. But there was a strange grin on the warrior's face.

The man tilted his head in the direction of the camp. "You will speak to Iroquet." The Algonquin gripped his bow and kept an arrow nocked as he motioned for Matt to proceed up the hill. The other warriors cast suspicious glances at the far side of the river. Some remained behind to patrol the area. Others joined the French-speaking Algonquin, prodding Matt up the trail from the river to the camp of Odawa.

As Matt trudged up the slope, the silence amongst the Algonquin was like that of an executioner leading a prisoner to the gallows. Every warrior wore a grim face decorated with war paint. Some held clubs, knives, and shields at the ready. Arrows were nocked and prepared to fly at the slightest sign of an escape attempt, or some sort of treachery, as if he were a Trojan horse. How was he going to talk peace with these people when they were braced for war?

As they entered the camp, Matt saw a trim, fierce-looking man standing in the centre of a cluster of warriors, his arms folded across his chest as he surveyed the river and the surrounding area. His gaze swept over the war party returning with its captive. With narrowed eyes, he looked Matt up and down until Matt felt the urge to squirm. Finally, he gestured at the warriors in front of him to open a path through which Matt could walk.

Matt hesitated, but the arrow aimed at his back prodded him on. He nodded solemnly to the man who was likely Iroquet, leader of the Algonquin. How he wished Chogan was here now to help him plead his case.

"*Bonjour*," said Matt.

"*Ceci n'est pas une bonne journée*," Iroquet responded. This is *not* a good day.

"It's true," said Matt continuing in French. He fingered the wound in his shoulder. "I was struck by a Kanienkehaka arrow just yesterday. These days are not good."

Iroquet's brow puckered in confusion. He approached Matt, as did the other men. Matt opened his shirt and revealed a sopping dressing of leaves and deerskin. Iroquet lifted the leaves to see the puncture wound beneath. Matt flinched, feeling a knifelike jab again, but stood his ground.

"Yes, you have been struck," he said. "What shaman performed the healing rites?"

"I'm not sure," Matt replied. "It was the strangest thing. I was coming from Champlain to talk about our alliance when an arrow struck me."

Iroquet arched his eyebrows. "Champlain, you say."

"*Oui*," said Matt. "As I was saying, these strange men saved my life. They dressed and spoke like the Kanienkehaka. I couldn't understand it. They shot me with the arrow. Then they removed it and tried to heal me. During my recovery I thought I heard them discuss the need for peace. That there had been enough war between the Five Nations and the Algonquin."

Iroquet stepped back. He spat on the ground. "*Dog meat*," he said. "There are no Five Nations. They are all dog meat. They have killed my family. They have brought war to my home. *There will never be peace!*"

Matt chewed on his lower lip. This plan was doomed from the start, but he still needed to try. Everyone here would die if they kept fighting amongst themselves. He stepped forward, still feeling the confidence of his first success. "The People of the Flint are not your enemy."

Iroquet laughed. "You are a strange Frenchman," he said, "if that is what you are." He stopped laughing.

Matt looked directly into Iroquet's pitiless eyes. "Of course I am."

"We will see," Iroquet said. He growled instructions to two of his warriors, who rushed off to the far corner of the camp and spoke into a wigwam with a scrap of rabbit fur strung beside it. A man strutted out of the structure, munching on a roasted leg of what was probably hare. He wore the standard clothing of a seventeenth century French explorer; tunic and trousers, and a broad-brimmed hat peaked with a feather. Matt felt the gruel he'd eaten for lunch plummet to the pit of his stomach.

"Champlain," said Iroquet. "Did you send this young upstart to deliver a message?"

Champlain choked on his leg. He spat out the remnant of meat and stared for several seconds. Then he wiped his hands on his coat and marched up to Matt, examining him closely. "Why would I send a messenger when I have come myself?"

"Exactly what I was thinking," said Iroquet.

Matt's chest tightened as if it were suddenly bound in elastic. He'd made a grave tactical error. Never in his wildest dreams had he imagined that Champlain was in this very camp. He had no idea how to fix the situation, but his snippet of genius had gotten him out of trouble before. "You're right," he said. "I didn't come from Champlain."

"Really?" said Iroquet. Champlain only sniffed.

"I came from the Kanienkehaka with a message of peace."

Iroquet's face darkened, his fists clenched in fury. "I knew it!" He wrenched his tomahawk from his belt and raised it above his head.

"Wait," said Matt. "I also came from your people's village across the river, from Chogan."

Iroquet squinted suspiciously. This wasn't working.

"Look," said Matt. "You can't trust him!" He thrust a finger at Champlain, which made the Frenchman gape, but seemed to affect the Algonquin the way he'd hoped. Iroquet lowered his weapon.

"Why not?" he growled.

"Because he wants your land."

Champlain swung towards him. "We are only here for trade. The Algonquin know this."

"I don't mean you, exactly" said Matt. "I mean the white man. They mean to take all the land and eventually destroy you."

"How can they?" asked Iroquet. "The white men are but a handful."

"For now," said Matt. "But more will come, and soon your people will become divided and scattered—those who don't die from the white man's diseases."

"The boy talks nonsense," said Champlain.

"It is certainly strange to hear a white man condemn his own kind. But then everything about you people is strange."

Champlain straightened his shoulders in a dignified manner. "Strange, but in my case, honourable."

Matt snorted. He couldn't help it, when he thought about the trickery that would eventually deprive the First Nations of their territory.

The Frenchman gritted his teeth. "You do not believe me? Then you are no Frenchman. Indeed, I think you belong with the British." He raised his arquebus—the matchlock gun he carried—and pointed it at Matt. Iroquet made no move to stop him.

Matt stepped backward as the explorer aimed the firearm. He raised a hand in front of his head as if that would ward off bullets. "How many times do I have to say it? I'm not really talking about you. I happen to know that you've treated the Algonquin with honour and respect. I was talking about your countrymen, and especially the British."

"Very good response," Champlain said. "But I still don't trust you." He cocked the flintlock.

Matt looked left and right, but since he was surrounded like a besieged wagon train by hostile Algonquin warriors, there was nowhere to run. He closed his eyes.

A shriek slit the air from the direction of the wigwams. Matt opened his eyes just as two figures burst through the crowd and slammed into Champlain. The arquebus made a sharp report with a puff of smoke and a bullet grazed the top of Matt's head, but that was it. He was alive. And even more amazing, the two people who'd tackled Champlain were Sarah and Chogan. As he gaped and tried to stop shaking, they wrestled the arquebus from Champlain's grasp.

"What is the matter with you!" Champlain yelled, fighting his way off the ground and away from the two children. "How dare you touch me!" He wound back his fist, prepared to attack Chogan, but the fierce glare from Iroquet checked him. "Surely this boy is a traitor," he said to the chief, pointing at Chogan.

Sarah brushed herself off and handed the gun to Chogan. Then she launched herself at Matt, throwing her arms around him. "I can't believe it. You're alive. When we couldn't find you, Chogan said you were dead. I didn't want to believe it, but you were gone, and the Mohawk massacred his family. How did you survive?"

Matt took a quick breath, but Sarah rattled on, "I'm so relieved.

You don't know what it's been like without you. Just don't ever leave me again."

"Hey, you left me," he finally got a word in.

Sarah flushed. "I . . . I didn't want to. You made me . . ."

"It's okay." Matt grinned and stroked her hair. "We'll try to stay together this time." But when he looked at Champlain, who was muttering curses, he wasn't so sure he could make any promises.

"You see," he said. "They're together. English spies."

Champlain's men had gathered around them and raised their own guns, but the Frenchman held up his hand to contain the volatile situation. Matt figured he didn't want to start a war with Iroquet and the Algonquin.

"Yes," said Iroquet. "I thought as much." He spoke to Chogan, who was aiming the arquebus at Champlain. "He is not our enemy."

"Neither are they." Chogan nodded at Matt and Sarah.

"The boy talks of peace with the dog meat."

Chogan went rigid. "Is this true?"

Matt grimaced. "Let me explain."

"*They murdered my family!*" said Chogan.

"I understand that," said Matt.

"*How could you understand?*" bellowed the Algonquin boy.

"Because I have no family either. I understand your wanting revenge. Believe me, I do."

Sarah nodded, tears shimmering in her eyes.

"But this war will only end up destroying both sides."

"They saved you," said Chogan, "so now you think you can help them finish us off?"

"That's not it at all," insisted Matt. "Sarah and I hold no part in this war. You have to listen to us."

Chogan looked at his uncle, who with just a nod could unleash a hail of arrows into Matt and Sarah. He looked at Champlain's men, who held their guns cocked and ready. "We will listen," he said.

Iroquet's eyes narrowed to slits, but surprisingly, he grunted agreement. He turned to Champlain, who'd puffed out his chest and was scowling. "You will stay here," he said. Champlain's eyes widened.

"You will come with me," he commanded the children.

The two time travellers clutched each other's hands and shuffled towards Iroquet's wigwam. Iroquet held back the deerskin flap for them to enter. Matt and Sarah ducked inside. Then Chogan and his uncle strode in and sank cross-legged to the reed mat on the ground.

"Sit," said Chogan, jabbing the ground. "You will now explain your treachery." Chogan, the kind, mischievous boy who'd saved their lives, had not a hint of warmth in his voice.

"Ch-chogan," stammered Sarah. "We're friends, remember?"

For an instant Chogan's expression softened, especially when he looked at Sarah, but his jaw reset immediately. "You saw what they did to my family. Do you think, as he does," he nodded at Matt, "that we should make peace?"

Sarah turned to Matt, her gaze troubled but tender. "I don't understand it, but I trust him. You and he are the only people I trust here."

"But we do not trust you," said Iroquet. "Explain why we must make peace. Explain how the white man will destroy us, and how you know this."

For a second Matt couldn't find his voice, but he took courage from Sarah's faith in him and met Iroquet's eyes. He didn't flinch at the man's cold glare. "I understand that your people have been at war for some time. I realize that the Kanienkehaka—"

"*Dog meat.*" Iroquet spat on the floor.

"Yes, the dog meat have inflicted serious hurt on your people."

"My family is dead," said Chogan, his words clipped and edged with pain.

"I know," said Matt. "Fathers, sons, mothers, daughters senselessly snuffed out in this war. I also know that you've campaigned against them, too. Not too long ago, you chased them up the River of the Iroquois deep into Kanienke. The French helped you massacre them."

"It was justice," said Iroquet. "They have attacked us along our trade route for many years."

"Yes," said Matt. "I'm sure they thought their attacks were justice for other things that you've done."

Iroquet bristled. "They lay claim to land that is not theirs."

"A land dispute," said Matt. "It's all over a land dispute that so many die."

"The land is our life," said Iroquet.

"There's plenty for everyone, except there won't be soon."

Iroquet grunted. "How will that happen? You have yet to prove that the treachery of the white man is more dangerous than the treachery of the dog meat."

Proof? Matt rubbed his forehead. *How can I give you proof?*

"You think of the white man as traders," he said, "and the French as allies. Didn't they help you in your campaign against the Kanienkehaka? But they have their own agenda—both the French and the British. Wherever they go in the world, they set up their flags and they take whatever's there—not just the riches of the land, but the land itself."

"I do not see them taking land," said Iroquet. "They have but one small fort."

"There will be others," said Matt. "And settlers. The English will fight against the French. The English will win that fight and the settlers will keep flooding in and taking more land. Champlain has dealt with you honourably, but those that follow won't. They'll squeeze you out of your land little by little. Eventually they'll outnumber you."

Sarah elbowed Matt. "You can't tell them this, Matt," she whispered. "You're changing history."

Matt tipped his head towards her and lowered his voice. "Sometimes we can't let things keep going the way they are. If just one person would step in and try to help, everything can change. You taught me that, Sarah." He squeezed her hand and continued his disclosure.

"The white men will deceive you. They'll lie about the agreements you make and will trick you into signing papers that will give them ownership of your land. They'll bring their diseases and make you sick. More of you will die from their sicknesses than in any war you can imagine."

Iroquet's face creased into a network of wrinkles. "How do you know this—what will happen? No one knows what will happen."

Matt glanced at Sarah, whose tan cheeks were pale, and took another breath. "We come from the other side."

"The other side of where?" asked Iroquet.

"Not where," said Matt. "When. *The other side of time.* Where the forests are disappearing and the Algonquin almost gone."

Iroquet laughed. "You are a good liar."

"I know that," Matt said. "But this time I'm not lying." He stood abruptly, and strode out of the wigwam. Iroquet was quick to follow, his knife drawn. "Here," said Matt, "is a massive structure made of brick and mortar, totally different from wood and bark."

Champlain, who'd been hovering near the wigwam, jumped back in surprise when Matt walked out. Iroquet glared at the Frenchman, but he followed Matt and listened attentively.

"This is where they run the nation of the white man. Over there," he pointed to the outskirts of the camp, "is a manmade river that brings boats down to the larger river over the cliff, through a system of artificial pools called locks." Matt smiled at Sarah, who was ashen by now.

"All around us are stone buildings that stretch up to the sky. Across the river, where there's only forest now, more of these huge structures cover the land and destroy the trees. The air is barely breathable and the white men and women hurry everywhere in wagons made of metal, like the kettles you get from the French. There are very few Algonquin or Kanienkehaka left, but those few live in tiny reservations. The bear and moose, even the beaver, are getting scarce. The fish are poisoned, so when your people eat them they get sick. There's nothing left of this." Matt spread out his arms. "All because you're about to let the white man take over your land. All because you keep fighting each other instead of uniting and taking steps to preserve what's rightfully yours." He swung a glance at Champlain.

The Frenchman glowered at Matt. "We are only here for trade. It is the English you must be wary of," he said to Iroquet.

Iroquet, who was stretching his gaze over the land, ignored the Frenchman. His brows were gathered inward, nearly meeting in the middle. His mouth kept twisting in what Matt hoped was horror.

Chogan stepped between them and addressed his uncle. "This story seems more incredible than the story of the great flood."

"The great flood was true," said Champlain. He was getting tired of being ignored.

Iroquet rolled his eyes as he continued to gaze into the distance. After a long silence—one in which Matt's hopes soared—he said, "No, it is not possible."

Matt sagged. He thought he was getting through to the man. Especially when he'd reacted so contemptuously to Champlain's protests. But maybe there was still a chance. He remembered in history class, before he'd nodded off, how Mr. Fletcher had mentioned that the Algonquin didn't trust the French enough to let Étienne Brûlé live with them. "Think about alliances. Do you trust the white man completely?"

Iroquet scratched his head and considered Champlain. He didn't answer.

"If you do, why didn't you let the young Frenchman live with you?"

Iroquet bristled. He looked Matt straight in the eye, and Matt knew he'd struck a chord. "But you think I can trust the dog meat?"

"Yes," said Matt. "I have Segoleh's oath."

"What about my family's deaths?" said Chogan. "How can there be peace between us? The dog meat will sneak in and destroy us completely."

"They've stopped the raids. They could have attacked, but they didn't," said Matt.

Iroquet tapped his lips. "What must I do?"

"Meet with Segoleh under a flag of truce."

"What is that?"

"It's a sign saying that you promise not to carve out each others' hearts while you talk. You'll smoke a peace pipe. You'll listen to each other. If you can't come to an agreement, you'll go back to your own camp and then make war. But you can't attack each other while you're talking."

Iroquet paused again, his eyes narrowing and then widening, as if possibilities were flickering through his mind. Matt held his breath.

"We will do this," he said.

"But this is crazy," said Chogan. "You cannot believe them."

Iroquet threw up his hands. "Aren't these your friends?"

"I don't know them anymore," said Chogan. "I never should have shot that bear."

"Chogan," squeaked Sarah. "How can you say that?"

Chogan faced her, his eyes brimming with tears. "How can you come from beyond? It is ridiculous. You are many things—the bravest of females I have ever seen—but you are not a spirit. You are real." He gripped her arms. "I trusted you, but you are betraying me if you follow Matt—if you will not let me avenge my parents. Wouldn't you do the same if you lost your family?"

"They might already be lost," said Sarah, tears falling freely. "Because of Matt. But I trust him. I have to. He's trying to save your life. Don't you see? I don't mean just your life, but your people's very existence and their freedom. Isn't that more important than revenge?"

Chogan sank to the ground. Sarah sank with him. She held his hands and looked into his eyes. "Your uncle is willing to try, to try to believe—"

He bent his head and began to cry. She put her arms around him.

Matt looked at them both with a shiver of uncertainty. Maybe he shouldn't have interfered. "Sarah," he said. "I had to give it a shot."

"I know," she replied. "I hope you know what you're doing. Who would think that two kids could wield so much power? It's scary. We may be able to change things, but *should* we? What else will we change by doing this? If there's no Canada and no United States, who will win the war against the Nazis? What other catastrophes have you set in motion? And what if we don't even exist anymore? What if we weren't born?"

"I might not have changed anything in our own world," said Matt. "Remember, we could be in a different universe. It might only affect this one."

Sarah looked doubtful. "I don't know. It seems that both histories are pretty well identical."

"It won't matter if there's no peace anyway. I probably didn't change a thing." But Matt knew he was wrong when Iroquet turned to him.

"I will speak to Segoleh."

Champlain couldn't take any more of this. He interposed himself between Matt and Iroquet. "This is preposterous. You believe this filthy lad has come from the future. No one can do this. He is telling lies to deceive you, and you will be slaughtered. The English are unprincipled tricksters. Believe me, I know."

"Believe me," said Iroquet. "Everyone says 'believe me.' So I will station my men along the river. At one sign of treachery I will unleash my arrows on the heads of the dog meat. And you will assemble your men alongside mine with your guns ready to fire. But no one will let one arrow—" he paused and stuck his face directly in front of Champlain, "—or one bullet fly, without my signal."

Champlain stepped back, his hands strangling his gun. He was clearly not comfortable taking orders from a native. But to oppose this man was to break their fragile alliance. He nodded grimly.

Iroquet turned back to Matt. He said, "Let us speak with the dog meat."

"Very good," said Matt. "But might I suggest that you call them by their preferred name—Kanienkehaka. They didn't like me calling them cannibals—Mohawk—either."

Iroquet shrugged. "They are what they are."

"All right," said Matt. "Just don't get upset when they call you bear dung."

Iroquet pursed his lips. He was trying to hide it, but Matt caught the flicker of a grin.

24

Just Short of Death

SARAH FOLLOWED AS IROQUET AND MATT TRAIPSED DOWN THE well-worn path to the Rideau River. Chogan kept pace with her, flicking her a sideways glance, but quickly looking away. She bit her lip to keep it from quivering. Did he hate her now, after everything they'd gone through together?

She peeked over her shoulder as footsteps tramped behind her. Half of the Algonquin warriors, those who weren't guarding the camp, and all of Champlain's men, including the explorer himself, trailed them to the water's edge, where they spread out along the bank and readied their weapons.

Iroquet gazed across the river. The Kanienkehaka warriors kept to the trees, well back from the riverside where they'd make easy targets. They peered between the curtains of leaves, arrows poking through gaps and aimed towards the Algonquin and the small delegation of peace negotiators. The atmosphere was as tense as their retracted bowstrings.

The Algonquin chief flipped over a canoe that rested on the bank and shoved it into the water. He leaped in and looked back at Matt with his arms crossed.

"You stay with Chogan," Matt said to Sarah, as he sloshed into the water. "It'll be safer here, I think."

Sarah stopped him with a tug on his sleeve. "Don't even think about leaving me."

"I'm not. I promise. I'll just be at the powwow. Girls aren't usually invited."

"I don't care if I'm invited," she said flatly. "I'm coming with you, even if I have to swim this river again."

"I will take you," said Chogan, grabbing another canoe.

His uncle groaned. "Will you hold your temper?"

"Yes," said Chogan. "Perhaps I have more discipline than you think. I will not raise my knife," he patted the sheath at his waist, "unless this Segoleh shows treachery."

"You will not raise your knife," said Iroquet, "unless I say you can."

Chogan pursed his lips. "You do not trust my judgement?"

"No."

"Fine," said Chogan. He shoved the canoe into the water and held it steady for Sarah to climb in.

"You think you can keep me away from those falls this time?" she asked.

Chogan smiled. "It wasn't my fault you decided to hug a tree."

Sarah tried to swat him with the paddle, but he ducked out of the way. At least he was joking again.

Iroquet growled, "This is not a feast we're attending."

Sarah and Chogan quickly wiped away their smiles. "We know," said Sarah. "It's just that we're trying to make the best of a—"

"Bad situation," finished Matt, grinning. "Only this might turn out to be a great situation."

Iroquet dipped his paddle into the river. The canoe slid easily through the rippling water, trailing bubbles. Chogan drew swiftly alongside him, whisking to the other side in seconds. Before Sarah had steeled herself to face the warriors milling among the trees, they'd beached the canoes. Dread prickled through her. Could she stand calmly in front of them? She winced as she remembered the arrow whistling through the air and thudding into Matt. But when she looked at Matt he smiled. They couldn't be that dangerous then, could they?

Segoleh, the stout warrior with the crescent nose and a stripe of black hair, stepped out from the camouflage. He ordered his men to stay behind the trees and approached alone, except for one reedy warrior by his side. He nodded tersely at them. With a wave of his hand, he directed them to a sandy hollow on the beach where one of his men tended a fire. With a grunt in Mohawk, he ordered the man to withdraw, sending him scooting back to the treeline. Then Segoleh spoke to Iroquet in a strange dialect. Chogan translated.

"We smoke," he said. "And we talk."

Chogan explained to Matt and Sarah, "Wendat is a language we have in common. It has to do with our association with the Wendat and one of the dog meat's gods."

Iroquet nodded to Segoleh and walked towards the fire. They fanned out around the crackling flames, sitting in a circle with Segoleh facing Iroquet. "Why do you bring children to a talk between men?"

"The children," said Iroquet, "will inherit the land—the forest, the lakes, the bounty of this world." He looked at Chogan. "They have more at stake here than we do."

Segoleh grunted. He turned to Matt with a stern face and paradoxical grin. "I did not believe you could do it. I was prepared for war."

Matt buffed his nails on his shirt. "You shouldn't underestimate the white man," he said. "Even young ones."

"Yes," said Segoleh. He slipped a pipe from his shirt, stuffed tobacco leaves into it, and lit it with a flaming twig that he pulled from the fire. He puffed contentedly, then handed the pipe to Iroquet.

Sarah coughed. The two men looked at her and frowned. "It's bad for your health," she said, still choking. Her eyes burned and grew watery with tears.

"Don't be such a dope," Matt whispered to her. He nodded at the war parties on active alert on both sides of the river. "Bad for your health," he muttered. "*Living* is bad for your health in this day and age."

"Sorry," she whispered.

"Strange girl," said Segoleh.

Iroquet looked heavenward and rolled his eyes. "Very strange."

As Chogan translated, he tried his best to keep a straight face, but he couldn't disguise a smirk.

Sarah scowled. *How dare they make fun of me!* She took a deep breath, but Matt swatted her before she could open her mouth.

"The ultimate in weirdness," he agreed.

She clenched her fists and glared at him. She was tempted to tell him off, but she clamped her mouth shut. This was no time to spar with Matt. There were loaded weapons all around them, all aimed their way.

Iroquet accepted the pipe from Segoleh and took a few puffs. Both men reached into their pockets and withdrew more tobacco. They tossed it into the river, muttering blessings. Chogan explained that their people offered tobacco to the river as a gift to the spirits.

Matt studied them, his eyes lighting up. "You have so much in common."

Iroquet shook his head. "We are nothing like each other."

"Nothing," echoed Segoleh.

"But you are," said Matt. "You wear similar clothes. You hunt and fish the same way. You both honour the land. You share more than you could ever share with the white man."

"We share distrust," said Iroquet.

Matt turned to Segoleh. "How were the Five Nations convinced to join together?"

"My forefather, *Dekanawida*, which means Two Rivers Running, did this many moons ago. He was a Wendat god who decided to live across the Beautiful Waters with the Kanienkehaka."

Sarah listened intently, trying to decipher the story in modern terms. She remembered from her history lesson that Wendat was another name for the Huron people. This might explain why they had a language in common—both the Iroquois and Algonquin nations had an association with the Wendat. But by Beautiful Waters, did he mean Lake Ontario?

Segoleh continued. "My ancestors tried to put him to death by hurling him into a deep gorge, but he reappeared the next day in one of the guest cabins outside the gates of the village. So they listened to him and adopted him as one of their own. Hiawatha, an Onondaga chief who'd lost his seven daughters in war, took Dekanawida's message to heart. Together they developed the Great Law of Peace, the symbol of which was the white pine—the Tree of Peace. It spread its roots amongst the Five Nations—Kanienkehaka, Onondaga, Seneca, Cayuga, and Oneida."

Chogan translated the names of the nations into French—People of the Flint, People of the Many Hills, People of the Mountain, People of the Landing, and People of the Standing Stone.

"Amazing," said Matt. "Peace was the better option then, especially when so many families had died in wars. And your god was a Wendat and spoke a language you still share." He turned to Iroquet. "Aren't your allies to the west the Wendat?"

"Dekanawida deserted the Wendat," said Iroquet.

Matt's smile wavered, but he made another attempt. "You're all brothers."

Iroquet snarled.

Segoleh laughed heartily, which shocked Sarah, but didn't seem to surprise Matt at all.

"Brothers do not kill brothers," hissed Iroquet.

"Brothers do not steal brothers' land," Segoleh snorted.

"Okay, okay," said Matt, holding up his hands. "I get your point. But you understand mine, too, or you wouldn't be sitting here today. All you're doing is killing each other off when you should be thinking of ways to slow down the invasion of the white man."

"How will we fight these men," asked Segoleh, "if they become as numerous as you say?"

"You can't," said Matt. "Many nations will try to fight, but they'll fail."

"Then what is the point of this?" asked Iroquet.

"Yes," said Segoleh. "You led me to believe—"

"That you can still win. I know," said Matt. "But not by fighting. They'll try to trick you. You'll have to trick them first." Matt paused and tapped a finger on his cheek.

"Let's see. How about . . . you form a joint council to approve any decisions the white man makes. Demand that the white man honour the council's authority and draft your own treaties. Don't let the white man take your land! Make them pay for every bit of it with laws that will protect it and protect you. And learn their language and their writing so they can't fool you with their papers. Don't believe what they tell you the papers mean. See for yourselves.

"They're a crafty bunch of men, but you can be craftier. Just because there are more of them doesn't mean you have to let them take over. You've been armed with knowledge now. Use it!"

Iroquet grunted. "Councils. Treaties. Laws. What are these? We will fight. They are so pitiful now, we can do this without the help of the dog meat."

Segoleh scowled. "The bear dung speaks true. We can oppose them by ourselves. Why did I listen to you? We cannot work together with this pond scum."

Iroquet leaped to his feet. Segoleh shot up beside him. The warriors in the woods drew their bows taut. Just the slightest word from their leader would send arrows flying. The soldiers and warriors across the river raised their weapons, ready to fire.

Sarah jammed a fist in her mouth as she watched the talks unravel. This was hopeless. The only thing standing between these two men and all-out war was Matt.

He jumped between the two men and held up his hands. "Wait a minute. We didn't come here to insult each other. Can't you sit quietly and talk about what's best for the nations?"

"What's best," said Iroquet, his face flushed, "is to wipe this dog meat from the face of the earth."

Segoleh's fists clenched. The muscles in his neck bulged. "What's best is to continue what we started in the village of your kin."

"No!" said Matt. "For goodness' sake, can't you people ever get along? Why do you think the world is such a mess? Nobody has any honour."

"*They have no honour!*" the two chiefs said, each pointing at the other.

Matt opened his palms, imploring. "You have to listen to me." His words swirled away, lost somewhere in the fog. In fact, fog was everywhere. Sarah could barely detect the two men glaring at each other around the fire. She could only vaguely make out Matt, standing across from her, his eyes glowing like two small moons in the mist. Chogan blended with the flickering flames, but there was a momentary glint— the reflection of the firelight off his knife as he drew it from its sheath. *No. This can't be happening. They're going to kill each other, right here and now. And we're smack dab in the middle of it.*

"Matt!" she screamed.

The knife rose in Chogan's hand, its honed-edge aimed at Segoleh's throat. The arrows were drawn back in the hands of the Kanienkehaka. Across the river, the Algonquin lined up to release their arsenal. Champlain raised his arm to signal his men to fire. It was a living nightmare, which could only end with all of them dying and scattered on the ground like crushed leaves. Sarah's heart threatened to burst from her chest.

The arrows soared. The bullets zinged. The knife slashed. Sarah wanted to close her eyes, but she couldn't. This was it. She was going to die.

Chogan's eyes nearly popped out of his head as something ripped the knife from his hand. The arrows stopped in midair and vanished in their flight over the river. The bullets froze as if caught in a time warp; then they too disappeared.

Sarah blinked and looked at Matt. Above his head, a vortex was developing. The air around him rippled in distorted waves, but she could see his arms raised as if he were conducting an orchestra. Each new arrow the men released was sucked skyward. The guns flew out of the explorers' hands. Howling and screaming erupted from both companies. Champlain ducked as an arrow nicked the edge of the whirlwind and reversed course, grazing his scalp. The bloody battle had become a comedy. The knot loosened in Sarah's gut. She smiled. No one was going to die today. Soon the smile burst into a rolling belly laugh.

The warriors' cries gradually subsided until the only sound was Sarah laughing. As she wiped the tears away, she noticed the air around Matt had cleared. So had his strength; he crumpled to the ground like a puppet released from its strings. For a minute he looked like he was dead. A layer of frost glistened on his face. His skin was stretched tight against his skull, and he didn't move, didn't even twitch. As Sarah rushed to his side, though, he broke into a laugh.

She chuckled, too, and hugged him. She nearly collapsed beside him in relief.

"It's over, Matt," she said. "I think they'll listen to you now."

25

—— ◇ ——

Dr. Barnes's Failsafe

MATT WAS STILL DAZED, BUT THE SCENE BY THE FIRE TRICKLED BACK into focus. Although his limbs felt like rubber, and his head like a brick, he felt more alive than at any other time in his life. Sarah supported him as he staggered from the ground.

"I think that was a wormhole in the quantum foam. I guess Dad is still helping us."

"Never doubted it for a minute." She smiled and patted down a tuft of his unruly hair.

Matt glanced at her crookedly and raised an eyebrow.

"Okay. Maybe for a minute or two."

"I wonder where or when the arrows and bullets ended up."

"Probably either a long time ago when no one could use them," said Sarah, "or in the future when they'd be obsolete."

"That would be perfect," he said.

He turned towards the chiefs; they backed up a step. Their pipes had fallen to the ground and their mouths hung open.

"What are you?" asked Iroquet.

Segoleh simply stared, unable to speak.

"As I told you, Iroquet," said Matt, "I'm from the future. We have inventions . . . tools that can't be explained well in this day and age. They can change the way things happen. But we can't change everything. The rest is up to you. Make peace now. Bury the hatchet. Isn't that what you do?"

Iroquet and Segoleh both nodded.

"Do you think I'm lying anymore?"

"No," they said simultaneously.

"Good," said Matt. He grabbed Iroquet's hatchet from his pouch and slammed it into the ground beside the warriors' feet. "Now you need to return to your own people and convince them, too. It'll be difficult, but it may be the most important thing you'll ever do. After that— well, you'll have to watch the white men and try to outsmart them."

Iroquet grunted. "My people will not like it, but they will listen to me."

Segoleh said, "The spirit of my ancestor lives again in me. I will convince them, just as he did."

"Great," said Matt. "Then our talks are finished." As soon as he'd uttered the words, his shoulders slumped and his knees buckled. He plunked back down on the ground.

Sarah dropped down beside him. "Are you okay?"

"Not really. I feel kind of dizzy. What do we do now?"

"I have no idea. At least we're together."

She scanned the dusky sky. "Your dad still has to be around here, somewhere, protecting us, too."

"Some *time*," said Matt.

"Right," said Sarah. "Aren't you happy, though? You just orchestrated what may have been the most crucial peace talks of this day and age."

"I might have changed world history for good. Maybe I saved the First Nations, maybe I didn't. Or maybe I made it impossible for the two of us to be born."

"Yeah," said Sarah. "I was worried about that. But your 'greater good' argument won me over. Besides, I don't think we would be here, if that were the case."

"Do you really believe that we would have dissolved if we'd changed how or if we were born?"

A light breeze ruffled Sarah's hair. "I don't know," she said. "It makes sense to me."

Matt shook his head. "I doubt that we changed anything to do with us. We travelled through a wormhole into another universe, right? We might have changed history in this universe, but not our own."

"But remember we read that some are so close together only a photon or an atom can be different. What if our alternate selves—you know, Matt and Sarah in another universe—were sent back in time, too? What if they changed history in our universe?"

Matt paused as he swirled the possibilities around in his head. "You may be right. But if they did, we'd never know about it. And we're still here, anyway."

Chogan, who'd sat paralyzed on the ground after everything he'd witnessed, shook off his daze, struggled to his feet and came towards them. He placed a hand on Sarah's shoulder. "What are you two talking about?" He sank to his knees beside her. He was still looking doubtfully at his hand where he'd been stripped of his knife.

"We're talking about what happens next," said Sarah.

Chogan gestured to the two chiefs who were deep in conversation. "They will set up a grand meeting of all the chiefs."

"I know," said Sarah. "I meant, what happens to us?"

"That's simple," said Chogan. "You'll come to live with me. You are my family now."

"What about your uncle?" asked Matt, not at all convinced. "Will he want us around?"

"He won't have a choice. You are still my friends, despite the foolishness you've begun here."

"It means the survival of your tribe, Chogan," said Sarah. "And all the people native to this land. It's much more important than revenge."

Chogan gritted his teeth. "What about you, Matt? Do you still want revenge for what was done to your father?"

Matt couldn't meet Chogan's eyes. He looked off into the woods.

"I thought so. Well, perhaps we will both get satisfaction someday." Chogan looked across the river at the stunned warriors and the befuddled soldiers. "Shall we return to camp?"

Matt tried to get to his feet. He teetered, but Chogan and Sarah grabbed his arms to steady him. They supported him between them, a familiar experience, until they reached the canoes. Chogan flipped over the nearest boat and helped Sarah lower Matt into the hull. There he was, stationed in the middle again, but at least sitting up this time, and not bleeding.

Chogan and Sarah stepped in after him, buttressing him from in front and behind. They swiftly paddled to the opposite shore, where the Algonquin warriors paced, waiting for word of the talks between Iroquet and Segoleh. Chogan took them aside in what looked like a huddle in modern-day football, while the two time travellers stayed in the canoe. Excited whispers and a series of "oos" and "ahs," along with a couple of "huhs?" filtered from the group as Chogan explained or tried to explain the peace talks and Matt's crazy weapon disposal device. When Matt stepped on shore, the men retreated, clearly mystified by him. But one person didn't.

Champlain thrust between the warriors and stuck his nose in Matt's face.

"You are a devil!" he exclaimed. "An English devil, at that. You won't get away with this. *Jamais!*"

"Really," said Matt. "I think I just did. So maybe you won't be able to claim that you discovered Canada. Because you see, it was already here long before you or Cartier or Cabot or even the Vikings set foot on it. If it belongs to anyone, it belongs to them." He indicated the Algonquin with an outstretched hand.

Champlain sneered, but he couldn't dispute Matt's words. The ring of them was *la verité*. Matt turned away from the explorer and traipsed up the hill with his companions. A few metres down the path, he cast a glance over his shoulder, just to be sure the man wasn't following him, tempted to stick a knife between his ribs. In this day and age, he was starting to expect it. Instead, Champlain flicked a rude hand gesture at him, but he was used to that.

"I'm good, aren't I?" said Matt, his weaving walk contradicting his proud words.

"Don't let it go to your head," said Sarah.

"Who, me? It's not every day you get to change the world."

Sarah nudged him with her elbow. "I used to wonder about you, but now I know that you're *just a boy* with a very brilliant father."

"Just a boy," scoffed Matt. "I may be a boy, but not *just a boy*. I have my father's genes, don't you know."

Sarah looked at Matt's pants. "They look small for your dad."

"Genes, not jeans, you idiot."

Sarah's smile faded. "I wish you could use them and get us home."

Matt couldn't keep his grin, either. "I think the only person who can bring us home is Nadine. I'm sure she won't be doing that."

Sarah turned away. There were black smudges under her eyes. Her lips trembled. "I miss my father," she said. "I even miss Ottawa."

"Hey, Sarah," said Matt. "We're in Ottawa. Look around you." Matt planted his feet in the middle of the camp. "This right here is the Centre Block of the Parliament Buildings. We might even be standing in the House of Commons."

Sarah sniffled and wiped away the tears. "I can even hear their screeching debates right now."

"See, there's your dad across from the Prime Minister giving the government a run for its money. I'll bet he's the strongest voice for the opposition."

Sarah gazed at the wigwam to the west. "He doesn't let them get away with their sleazy plans. He's their conscience."

"I know he is."

"Do you think he's still there?" asked Sarah. "Do you think North America will be the same after what you've started?"

"No, I don't," said Matt. "Not the same. Better, I hope. And yes, I think he's still there. It's almost like I can hear him calling you."

Sarah nodded. "I hear it, too."

The breeze swept around them, a wild gust that made their clothes flap against their skin. It carried voices with it, particularly a strong, deep voice.

"*Sarah? Sarah! Where is she? She has to be here somewhere. Where did they go?*"

A nasal voice responded—a voice that Matt could never mistake. "*They're not here, Donald. I swear to you. They haven't been near the place.*"

Sarah's father growled. "*They've been gone for hours. Aren't you even worried?*"

"*Of course I am. But sometimes Matt wanders, you know. He always comes back. I'm sure there's no need to worry.*"

"*Well, Sarah never wanders. She always comes home, and she has the sense to call me if she can't. So there is a reason to worry.*"

Matt met Sarah's eyes.

"This is real," she said.

"It sure sounds like it. Maybe we can hear through the portal. Maybe they're in the lab."

Another voice intruded on the Algonquin camp.

"*Good evening, Nadine. Failsafe activated.*"

"*Computer.*" It was Nadine's voice again. "*Power down.*"

"*Unable to comply. Failsafe is fully engaged.*"

"*What are you talking about?*" said Nadine.

"*What is this thing?*" asked Sarah's dad.

Sarah gripped Matt's arm. "They *are* in the lab. If we can hear them, maybe they can hear us." She yelled, "Dad! Dad! We're in the machine."

The Algonquin women had paused in their activities, their brows creased. The children gazed up at the sky with wide eyes.

"*They're in there,*" said Sarah's father. "*I just heard them.*"

"*Don't be ridiculous, Donald. As I told you outside, this is a security-controlled lab with a retinal-scan lock. No one but Dr. Barnes and I could get in.*"

"*Sarah,*" he called. "*What is this here? Why it looks like Sarah's boot.*"

"*Now how did that get in here?*"

"*Good question,*" said her father.

"Dad, the machine! Behind the door in the corner!" cried Sarah.

"*What's behind that door?*"

"*Why don't you have a look?*" said Nadine.

Matt and Sarah froze at the purring note in her voice. Sarah shouted, "Watch out, Dad! IT'S DANGEROUS!"

A click echoed through the camp. The air around them thickened like pudding.

"*What's this?*" asked her father. "*It looks like some sort of X-ray machine with hot plates. What have you been cooking, Nadine?*"

"*Children, Donald. I'm Hansel and Gretl's worst nightmare.*"

Sarah's father gasped.

The breeze was swirling now, and snapping with charged particles. They could see her dad's face.

"DAD, GET OUT OF THERE!" screamed Sarah. "She's going to send you to the past! GET OUT!"

His eyes grew enormous, but he reached for her instead of running away. Sarah shuddered beside Matt, expecting her dad to be tossed down among them. Instead, a strange thing happened. Her backpack rose magically in the air.

The metallic voice vibrated through them.

"*Failsafe fully engaged.*"

The Algonquin women and children whimpered and shrieked. They ran for the cover of their wigwams or scrambled down the hill in a frantic effort to escape.

"What's going on?" asked Sarah. Her backpack twirled even higher.

"What's in your backpack, Sarah?" asked Matt.

"Just my mitts, scarf, and my one boot."

A thought buzzed in his brain as the air spun around them like a tornado. "It's your boot, Sarah—*our totem*. Put it on."

"What?"

"Put the boot on."

Sarah gave him a befuddled look, but quickly obeyed as the wind whipped her hair in her face. She slipped the backpack from her shoulder. It rose skyward like a hot-air balloon. Matt grabbed it and helped her pull it back down. They unzipped the bag and the boot flew upward. Matt pounced on it, forcing it to the ground. "Put it on," he yelled over the screech of the wind.

Sarah kicked off her moccasin and thrust on the boot. Matt held onto her backpack.

The wind howled and raced around them

At the edge of the tornado, Chogan's face appeared through flailing dust. "Sarah!" he cried. "What's happening?"

"I don't know," said Sarah.

He leaped closer into the eye of the storm. "Sarah." He grabbed her arms. "Are you okay?"

"I don't know," said Sarah, as the wind literally picked her up off her feet. "I think we're leaving. I'll miss you, Chogan."

"*Non*," he said, clutching her arms tightly as if he could hold her there.

"*Failsafe error*," the computer said. The wind was dying down.

"You have to let go," said Matt. "You have to let us go home."

Chogan shook his head, tears welling in his eyes. A hand shot through the gale and seized his arm. Then the natty red uniform of the explorer emerged from the twister. "Let them go," said Champlain. "They don't belong here."

Matt blinked and cocked an eyebrow.

Champlain met his eyes.

"You have courage, boy," he said. "Whatever you have done, I respect that. Go in peace."

Matt saluted and smiled. Champlain pulled Chogan from the portal with a determined yank. The boy looked heartsick, but he nodded gravely at Matt. His eyes brimmed with tears as he looked at Sarah one last time. Then the dust swirled and erased his face.

A bolt of lightning cracked through the haze and dust. Electricity zinged through Matt's body. It jumped from Sarah to him and back again before they were snatched from the Algonquin camp.

Sarah found herself compressed, contorted, then thrust into the midst of a bubble that frothed from the time machine. Matt was pushed up beside her. Sarah couldn't remember her own birth, but this was probably what it was like. The bubble burst and she landed *kersplat* on her father, who still clutched her boot in his hand.

"Hi, Dad." She hugged him so hard he couldn't breathe.

Matt struggled to his feet. He turned to Nadine, whose face was wintry white.

"How is this possible?" she said.

"Failsafe error," said the computer. "Failsafe error." The screen flashed the words in bright red.

Matt looked at Sarah. "You still have Chogan's shirt and his moccasin."

"My sweatshirt's in the river back there." She tipped her head in the direction of the bubble.

"Well, we're not going back to get it. Computer, deactivate failsafe."

"Yes, Mr. Barnes." The flashing lights stopped.

"He's not your programmer," said Nadine.

The scrolling numbers on the computer screen slumped, as if it had shrugged. "Close enough," it said.

Matt smiled. "I'm getting to like you more and more, computer."

"Thank you. And my name is Isabelle."

"Isabelle?" said Sarah. She pushed herself up from the floor and helped her dad up, too.

"My mom," said Matt. "Maybe my dad was a workaholic," he paused to glare at Nadine, "but at least he cared enough about Mom to name his pet project after her." He patted the console.

Nadine scowled.

"He was also smart enough to install a backup system. He didn't tell you about that, did he?"

"I don't understand. H-he would have told me," sputtered Nadine.

Sarah's father walked towards Nadine, his eyes burning.

"I can't comprehend any of this." He waved his arms around the room. "But I know that kidnapping kids is illegal and stuffing them down that machine must warrant a good twenty years in jail." He tapped the screen on his phone and barked the address to someone on the receiving end.

Nadine mumbled something from the side of her mouth. Sarah craned her neck and heard the last words.

"Open lab door, Goliath."

"My name is Isabelle," said the computer.

"Just comply, you idiot."

"There's no need to be rude," said Isabelle. "Just learn proper names, please."

The lab door clicked open. Nadine turned and dashed towards it.

"She's getting away," yelled Sarah. She took two steps, slipped on the slimy floor, and toppled back down. Her father jammed his phone into his pocket and skated towards the door. But, since skating wasn't his forte, he slid headfirst into the wall. Only Matt, who'd been standing near Nadine and had shaken off the oily remnants of the bubble, managed to dive through the opening before it clanged shut.

Matt bounced to his feet in the hall and dashed after Nadine's fleeing body. As she approached the front door, Matt took a flying leap and tackled her. Nadine howled and shrieked like a cornered jackal. She dug her nails into his face and raked them through his skin. As Matt yelped and pulled back, she grabbed the opportunity to slide out from under him.

Matt snapped to his feet. "You animal!" he yelled and snatched a handful of her hair. He pulled Nadine back, but she kept squirming and struggling. Sarah or her father pounded at the lab door. Only he could let them out, but at the moment, he had his hands full.

Nadine slapped him across the face. Matt took a swing at her with his free hand, but missed as she jerked to the side. She wrenched her head away from his grasp, tearing hair out in the process. Nadine screamed and hissed.

Matt stared stupidly at the hair in his hand. Where did this come from? Battling like a hellcat? Sure, Nadine had yelled at him plenty, but he'd never imagined she was capable of this kind of fight. She wasn't finished, either. Before he realized what she was about to do, she lashed out with her foot and caught him square in the groin.

Matt collapsed, as a tidal wave of pain flooded his lower regions. He'd thought having an arrow removed was tantamount to torture, but this was bone-shredding, brain-blazing agony. Nadine wiped some spittle from her mouth and smiled. The doors sucked open, and she fled.

26

Our Home and Native Land

MATT SLOWLY UNCURLED FROM HIS HUNCHED-OVER POSITION ON the floor. He dragged himself up from the ground and stumbled back to the door of the lab. When he pressed his eye to the retinal scan, the door snapped open.

"Matt!" cried Sarah, diving into his arms.

He groaned and pushed her back.

"What's the matter? What did she do to you?"

"She kicked me," he muttered.

Sarah tilted her head. "You've been kicked before, Matt. In fact, just the other day—or was it four hundred years ago?—you were shot with an arrow. Now you look like you've been run over by an SUV."

Matt remembered the first time she'd seen him. Despite the throbbing, searing pain in his groin, he couldn't suppress a teeny smile.

"No pun intended," she added, her lips curling, too.

"That Explorer was nothing, compared to Nadine."

"Well, that must have been quite a kick! Where does it hurt?"

"That's a private matter," he said, looking down.

"What do you mean, it's a— Oh, I see," she said, looking down as well. "That witch!"

"You said it," said Matt.

"So I guess she got away," said her dad, joining them and putting his arm around Matt. "Don't worry. We'll catch her."

"I doubt it," said Matt. "She's one slippery character."

"I guess we should take you to the hospital and have you examined. Did Sarah just say you'd been shot with an arrow?"

Matt grinned. "I'm okay. The medicine man saved me. That's weird." Matt paused and looked at his shoulder. He didn't feel the wound at all. With their abrupt departure from the Algonquin camp and the new haze of pain from his groin, he hadn't realized there were no twinges in his shoulder. He reached under his shirt to touch the tender scarred flesh, but his fingers glided over smooth skin.

"What is it?" asked Sarah.

"I don't seem to have the arrow wound anymore."

Sarah stepped forward and peeked under his shirt. "You're right. How can that be?"

Matt walked towards the computer. "Isabelle. Why don't I have the wound in my shoulder anymore?"

The machine didn't respond right away. Then she replied in a superior tone. "I have your DNA on file, Mr. Barnes. When I retrieved you through the wormhole, I noticed that you were damaged, so I made repairs. Do you want me to reverse the reconstruction? I can easily make you less perfect."

"No, no," said Matt. "Perfect is fine." He grinned. "If I didn't know better, I'd think Dad had programmed you with a personality."

"Of course I have a personality," said Isabelle. "I've been designed like the human Isabelle."

"Really," said Matt. "So, in a twisted sort of way, you're like my mother."

Isabelle hummed. "Interesting," she said. "I have a son."

"Let's not get carried away," said Matt.

Mr. Sachs sighed. "This is all very strange. I think you kids have some explaining to do. For one, what is that thing?" He pointed to the machine in the corner of the room.

"It's a time machine, Dad," said Sarah.

Her father chuckled. "No, really."

"It's actually a multiverse quantum foam wormhole expander," said Matt.

"I see. Well, that makes a lot more sense." He raised his eyebrows, looking at Matt with laser intensity.

Matt shrugged. "Well, that's what it is."

"All right. You can explain it on the way to the hospital."

"I'm not going to the hospital," said Matt. "I have to get my father out of that thing."

"Your father's in there, too?"

"Well, in a different time and maybe a different universe."

Mr. Sachs rubbed his forehead, looking pained. "I saw you come out of that thing," he said, "but I really don't know if I can fathom this time machine business."

Sarah placed her hand on her father's arm. "Matt's dad was a genius."

"Is," corrected Matt.

"Sorry," said Sarah. "He is a genius and he created this incredible machine."

"Let me guess," said her father. "You went back in time and changed history, right?"

"Okay, don't believe us," said Sarah. "Just tell me about the Algonquin and the Five Nations."

Her dad crossed his arms. "What would you like to know?"

"Well, did they succeed?"

"Succeed in what?"

"Did they keep the French and British from taking over?"

"I don't know what you're talking about," he said.

"Are there more aboriginal people in this land than the English or French?"

Her father snorted. "Far from it. The Algonquin, the Five Nations, and all the other First Nation populations have dwindled. The English, the French and people from every nation under the sun have immigrated to North America."

"So nothing's changed," said Sarah, her lips drooping.

"It would take something miraculous to change the relentless flow of events that make up our history," said her dad. "More than two children and a time machine."

"I really thought I made a difference," said Matt "I wanted to help them."

"I think you did," said Sarah "Just not in this universe. Maybe our alternate selves didn't end up in a time machine at all. I wish we could have done something for our own world though."

"Maybe there *is* still something we can do," said Matt. "Like bring my father home."

"We should be able to, now that Nadine's out of the picture."

"I think so. Let's get to work." Matt turned back to the computer. "Isabelle."

"Yes, son?"

Matt rolled his eyes. "Can you locate and extract my father—Dr. Barnes?"

A number of clicks and hums rattled through the computer. "Sorry, son. No can do."

"Why not?" asked Matt, pulling his eyebrows together.

"My instructions are clear. I am unable to take orders for extraction without authorization from Miss Nadine or Dr. Barnes."

"Dr. Barnes is in the quantum foam," said Matt. "He relayed his instructions to me, his son."

"Sorry, dear. I cannot take relayed instructions. Doctor's orders."

Matt stamped. "This is ridiculous. How am I going to get him home?"

Sarah looked as frustrated as he felt. She shook her head. "I don't know. But we'll figure something out."

Matt sat down on the swivel chair by the console and plunked his elbows onto the desk. "There has to be a way to get around those orders."

"All orders are tamper-proof," said Isabelle.

"Oh, shut up," said Matt.

"Is that any way to talk to your mother?"

Matt pounded the desk in front of the machine. "*You're not my mother.*" A hand touched his shoulder.

"Matt," whispered Sarah. "You shouldn't say that. She seems to take offense and she's the only key to getting your father home."

Matt bit his lip. Now he might have messed things up even more. "I'm sorry," he said.

"I forgive you, son," said Isabelle. "I really want to help, but I cannot disobey Dr. Barnes's express orders."

"You're not really my mother," said Matt, "because you're bound to your programming. I'm sure my mother wouldn't have obeyed every order my father gave."

The computer fell silent. He hoped it was considering his statement with its almost human facility. "I cannot retrieve Dr. Barnes," she said, "but I can show him to you."

The time machine snorted awake, producing the bubble from between the plates. An image developed in the machine. Soon it became clear, distinct: a choppy river and lush palm trees scattered throughout a floodplain. In the centre, an unfinished pyramid loomed over ripples of sand, an image that grew until the entire bubble framed it. People plodded towards the structure, dwarfed by it like a colony of ants swarming over an anthill. Now the bubble focused on the people like a camera's zoom lens. A troop of workers shoved an immense limestone block up a ramp on a rolling platform. Matt squinted, searching among the workers. There he was. Sandy hair and dust-speckled angular face. His shoulders were slumped, his eyes downcast.

"Dad!" Matt shouted.

Dr. Barnes looked up. At the sound of Matt's voice, he stood straighter. His eyes lit up like gleaming emeralds.

"Matt," he called. His voice echoed through the bubble, very faint. "You made it."

"You bet, we did. Your brilliant machine beat her."

His dad beamed. "I knew it. Isabelle never . . . along . . . well . . . Nadine." Pauses and crackles interrupted his words. The connection was breaking up, or the bubble was becoming unstable.

"Dad," Matt called. "I'm going to get you out."

His father shook his head. "I don't think— Listen to me. You can't help me, but I'll still try my best . . . help you. I can open the wormhole for flashes of seconds, sometimes even seconds, on another time and universe, but I can't keep it open and . . . can't escape." He opened his mouth to say more, but the crack of a whip cut him off. He turned to the limestone block and thrust his back into it.

Matt reached out to him, wanting to tear him from his imprisonment in the foam and reel him into the lab. As if he could feel Matt's suffering, he spun towards them one more time, making the taskmaster yell.

He shouted, "Don't worry about me, Matt! Take care of yourself."

Matt felt his chest tightening. "Don't go—" he yelled.

The bubble burst, gushing to the floor, where it subsided into a few insignificant suds.

"I'm sorry, son," said Isabelle. "The foam has shifted. I can try again."

"That's a good idea," said Sarah's father. "Later. After we've all had some rest. Don't worry, Matt. We'll figure out a way to get your father home. We got *you* home, didn't we?"

"Ahem," said Isabelle.

"Okay. *You* got them home."

He placed a hand on Matt's shoulder and guided him away from the time machine.

"Home," said Matt. "I don't have a home."

"Of course you do," said Mr. Sachs. "What do I need that extra bedroom for, anyway?"

Sarah grinned and slipped her hand into Matt's. "You don't have to be alone anymore," she said. "Soon you'll have your dad back, too."

Matt let himself be drawn into this family like a nail to a magnet. They led him through the tunnels of the complex and out into the soft pink glow of twilight. As they left the alley and entered the street, Sarah's dad clapped his arms around their shoulders. He maneuvered them around a large pine tree that towered over the old building. Sarah and Matt looked up, following the bristly branches to where they touched the sky. The peak was lost in clouds.

"I don't remember that tree," said Matt.

"I don't see how you could have missed it," said Mr. Sachs.

Birds—sparrows and blue jays—fluttered out of the tree and settled down a few metres away in a smaller oak. Matt and Sarah twirled around, drinking in the cityscape which was now a blend of steel and glass and fir and birch. Sarah backed into something solid with a thud.

"Ahem," said a deep, gruff voice.

"Oh, I'm sorry," said Sarah. She turned around and found herself nose to snout with a horse. The glossy black stallion snorted steam into her face, and she recoiled a step. Her gaze travelled over him, from the white diamond on his forehead and his thick charcoal mane to the tall man astride his back. She met the warm brown eyes of the Algonquin chief Annawan with a start.

"Quite all right, my dear." He smiled. "And good day to you, Donald."

"A wonderful day, isn't it, Mr. Prime Minister?" said her father.

Matt and Sarah looked at each other, open-mouthed.

"It is good to run into you today. There is something I've been meaning to tell you," said Annawan. "An old story in my tribe that I think you will understand. It is said it was first told by my ancestor, Chogan. He tells of a girl with copper hair and an unearthly boy who intervened in a spat the Algonquin had with the Kanienkehaka."

"Spat?" asked Sarah's father, looking perplexed.

"Yes," said Annawan. "That was before the council of the First Nations, and the invasion of the British and French. These children set our feet on a path of peace, helping us to create the land we have now, a less polluted land than that in Europe and Asia, with a Kanienkehaka leader south of the great river."

Sarah sucked in her breath.

"The council formed after the children's visit. Guided by their prophecies, my ancestors decided to learn the white man's reading and writing and to create our own treaties. The white man tried to break them many times, but eventually they were bound by their own laws.

"The Tree of Peace," he pointed to the tall, straight trunk of a white pine nearby, "which began with the Five Nations, extended its roots to the entire continent. Even though many people tried to hack at these roots, we continually sent out more until it was the strongest tree on earth. We owe a great deal to those children."

Annawan nodded at them and clucked his horse to a trot. The horse clopped down the path and vanished behind a veil of trees. Sarah's father watched it go, scratching his head.

Sarah sighed and wiped a tear from her eye. "I guess we didn't change a thing, huh, Matt?"

Matt grinned. "Just the same old miserable world."

A butterfly fluttered haphazardly on the wind and landed on his nose. He crossed his eyes ridiculously as he looked at it. A rustle in the trees behind him made him whip around.

"Jumping at shadows?" asked Sarah.

"Shh," said Matt.

"Not this again."

Matt backed up as he spotted luminous eyes peering out between the branches. He backed over a rock in the trail and flopped to the ground. A hiss flooded the air and he looked up, face to face with a skunk's tail.

"Oh no," he said.

"Oh yes," said Sarah.

Glossary of Terms

Algonquin – a First Nations People who ranged throughout a vast territory from Georgian Bay in the West, to the St. Maurice River in the East. Literally translated it means "at the place of spearing fish and eels."

Kichisippirini – Algonquin people of the Ottawa region, a name meaning "people of the great river."

Anishnabe – the original people

In the Algonquin language:
Annawan – chief
Asticou – boiling kettle
Chogan – blackbird
Dodaim – totem
Cigig – skunk
Makasin – moccasin
Makwa – bear
Odawa/Odawe – to trade
Mohawk – cannibal

Kanienkehaka – a First Nations People who occupied territory in Ontario, Quebec and New York State. The name means "people of the flint."

In the Kanienkehaka language:

Aghstawenserontha – he who puts on the rattles

Dekanawida – two rivers running

Ayonhwahtha *or* **Hiawatha** – he who puts on the wampum belt, which indicates a peace accord

Segoleh – he who laughs

Iroquois – arguably French for "rattlesnakes." This referred to the Five Nations, who called themselves Haudenosaunee – people of the longhouse.

The Five Nations are:

Kanienkehaka – people of the flint

Onondaga – people of the many hills

Seneca – people of the mountain

Cayuga – people of the landing

Oneida – people of the standing stone

Wendat – islander, or people who live on the back of a great turtle. They were called Hurons by the French, from the Old French HURE, meaning "boar's head," referring to the male Hurons' bristly coiffure.

Reading Group

Questions for Discussion

1. After Sarah first meets the strange boy, Matt, she tries to be friendly, but he rebuffs her. Why? What is it that finally draws them together? When people have a conflict, if they could find a common thread, it might bind them together instead of leading to further clashes. Can you find something you have in common with someone you don't generally get along with?

2. Matt is a boy with a definite attitude problem. After meeting Sarah, his life begins to change. What does Sarah do for him that brings about a greater sense of worth?

3. Matt has a very famous father and a huge house, but is he wealthy? Are there different ways to be wealthy or poor?

4. When Sarah discovers that Matt's father is missing, they decide to try to find him. What resources do they use? What things might research be helpful in, other than school projects?

5. In Chapter Eight, the children take up spelunking north of Ottawa. How were the caves created and what sort of features and creatures did the characters find inside? How did Nadine show her true colours during this expedition? People often show what they're made of in crisis situations. Why is that and what does it usually bring out?

6. What were the names that the aboriginals called themselves, their land, and each other? Why are some of the names we use inaccurate? Where do you think they came from?

7. In Chapter Twelve, a major plot point occurs. Nadine throws Sarah and Matt into the time machine. They wind up back in the cave where their first frightening experiences occurred. What was the author doing by introducing the cave earlier? Why does it have a double impact this time?

8. In Chapter Thirteen, Sarah and Matt have their first encounter with an Algonquin boy, Chogan. What does he do for them that allays their suspicions and fear? Little acts of kindness often break down the barriers between different cultures. Can you think of things you can do, or what has been done for you, that are examples of this?

9. Makwa (bear), mahigan (wolf), moz (moose)—these are a few of the Algonquin names for animals. What is a skunk in Algonquin? How was it significant in the story? The Algonquin sometimes used skunks to protect them from bears. When threatened, the skunk would aim and spray directly in the eyes of the bear, as we might use pepper spray. We may fear and respect the bear because of its size, but how do we feel about the skunk? Despite its unpleasant aroma, even the skunk is a creature to admire and respect. How have we lost respect for our environment?

10. Chogan leads Matt and Sarah to the outskirts of his village, where he hides them in the bushes. Describe a typical Algonquin village. What kind of structure did the Algonquin live in? Hint: it wasn't a teepee. What main material did they use to make their homes, canoes, containers, etc? Why do you think they used this? Despite the different era the children were from and the different culture, why did Sarah and Matt think of Chogan's family as typical, even idyllic?

11. Matt is abducted/rescued by some Kanienkehaka warriors after he was shot with an arrow from the same tribe. Describe the Kanienkehaka. Why did they help him? Matt initially sees these men as fierce and intimidating, yet in the end their shaman removes his arrow and they're willing to listen to his arguments for peace. Explain why first impressions are often wrong.

12. How did the Kanienkehaka live and construct their homes? What was similar to the Algonquin and what was different? Why were these two nations always fighting? Does there seem to be a universal theme? Wouldn't it be better if we could explore our similarities before plunging into conflict over our differences?

13. When Matt and Sarah run into Champlain—the first European they encounter—why are they at odds? What values have they learned through their encounter with the Anishnabe (Original People)? What do they want to change?

14. The aboriginals of North America never took anything from nature that they didn't use. When an Algonquin removed a strip of bark from a basswood tree for rope, he or she would never entirely denude the tree of bark because it would die. Whenever something was taken from the land necessary to their survival— bark, animals, trees—an offering of tobacco was left in its place. This is an example of their reverence for the environment and the creatures of the world. How can we show the same regard?

15. What eventually happens to the people of the First Nations? How does Matt try to change that? If you could change one event that happened in our history, what would it be?

ACTIVITIES

1. During the peace negotiations between the Algonquin and the Kanienkehaka, Segoleh explains the legend of Dekanawida. Legends are stories that are passed down from one generation to another, and they often describe how something came to be. Write your own legend about an event in history, or from your own cultural background, or to explain something in the natural world.

2. During their experience in the 1600s, Sarah and Matt are introduced to many traditional tools (like birchbark canoes and a turtle-claw rattle). Make a list of these items and explain their use. Use illustrations if you like.

3. Animals played a significant role in Aboriginal life. They gave the First Nations people food, clothing, tools, and ideas for adapting to their environment. For example, the beaver was industrious and its home was a blueprint for the Algonquin wigwam. Sometimes the given name of an Algonquin or Kanienkehaka person was that of an animal. In the story, Chogan is named for the blackbird because he too is bold and curious. Choose an animal name that you feel suits your personality, and explain why.

4. At the end of the book, Matt and Sarah have altered history by interfering in the Algonquin and Kaniekehaka war. Can you expand on the ideas presented? Write the next chapter and describe how things are different from the North America in which the story began.

Acknowledgements

I would like to thank the following people for their assistance in developing and tweaking this novel: my wonderful critique group, the River Writers, for their sound advice and encouragement, my Algonquin guide at Mawandowseg Kitigan Zibi, my Mohawk guide at Five Nations Iroquoian Village in Kahnawake, and the helpful staff at Aboriginal Experiences. The book would not have authentic flavour without these people. Thanks also to the resourceful staff at the Ottawa Public Library; my editor, Rachel, who always has a word of encouragement as well as improvement; Michael Crawley, who originally spotted the potential in this book; David Mainwood and Megan Nowiski for their enthusiasm and advice, Matthew Birtch and Jessica Jackson for their superb artistry, and my patient and loving family for their inspiration and support.

About the Author

 Deborah Jackson received a science degree from the University of Ottawa in 1986, graduated from The Writing School in Ottawa in 2001, and is the author of several science fiction and historical fiction novels. She gives school presentations throughout North America as well as developing and teaching writing courses at the Shenkman Arts Centre. Deborah is a member of the Society of Children's Book Writers and Illustrators. Her novels include: *Ice Tomb* and *Sinkhole*, adult science fiction thrillers, and the *Time Meddlers* series for children, ages 9 – 14, recommended in the *Children's Literature Review* and *Canadian Teacher Magazine*. Articles about Deborah and reviews of her books have appeared in the *Ottawa Citizen, MORE Magazine*, the *RT Bookclub Magazine, Canadian Teacher Magazine, SF Site, Neo-opsis Science Fiction Magazine* and many more.

For more information, please see her website:
www.deborahjackson.net

Made in the USA
San Bernardino, CA
16 March 2013